To Laura!

IF I CAN'T HAVE YOU

Trickle Creek

Book 2

ELENA AITKEN

Happy Reading!

Elena Aitken

Also by Elena Aitken

Finally Mine

Finally Fell

Finally Forever

Finally Free

Vegas

Nothing Stays in Vegas

Return to Vegas

Timber Creek

When We Left

When We Were Us

When We Began

When We Fell

Timber Creek: The Complete Series

Castle Mountain Lodge

Unexpected Gifts

Hidden Gifts

Unexpected Endings - Short Story

Mistaken Gifts

Secret Gifts

Goodbye Gifts

Tempting Gifts

Holiday Gifts

Promised Gifts

Accidental Gifts

Chapter One

THE RED CHRISTMAS balls tucked into the pine boughs with sprigs of holly berries were super cute and perfectly festive for the holiday season. Which was exactly why Charli Carlson yanked them ruthlessly from the window boxes that sat out front of the Bean Bag, Trickle Creek's popular cafe located in the bustling plaza. She dropped the decorations into the basket at her feet until she once more had a blank slate.

"Oh, no!"

Charli looked up to see Annie Darling, her friend and sister-in-law-to-be, open the door to the cafe. "I really liked those," she groaned when she saw what Charli had done. "The boxes looked so beautiful. I swear, I smiled every time I came in to work my shift."

"You would smile even if there was nothing but rocks in here." Charli crouched and started to sift through the basket of supplies she'd brought with her. "I don't think I've ever seen you without a smile on your face." She looked up at Annie, who genuinely was one of the happiest and kindest people she knew. "Besides, you're going to love what I do next. Christmas is over." Charli rose, a different selection of evergreen branches

1

in her hand. "It's a new year, which means a new display." She started to arrange the boughs, adjusting and readjusting until they were just right.

"I know I will." Annie wrapped her arms around herself and shivered. "Come and grab a coffee when you're done. It's freezing out here."

"Only if you make me one of those vanilla lattes that are so yummy."

"Deal."

Her friend retreated inside to the warmth of the café, and Charli focused on her task. When the evergreen was perfect, she began to place the oversized pine cones and little silver stars that she'd found on her last trip to the city. As soon as she'd seen them, she knew they'd look perfect in a January display. Just the right amount of pop and shine to brighten up a snowy winter day and draw attention to the cafe doors. Outdoor arrangements were still pretty new to her, but when Annie asked Charli if she'd be willing to do something for the Christmas season, she jumped at the opportunity. The winter season, when the tourists flocked to the ski hill, brought a lot of traffic to the town of Trickle Creek and every business in town. *Almost* every business.

Charli's flower business became virtually nonexistent as soon as the temperatures dropped and the flowers froze. Then again, you couldn't really call a stand at the seasonal farmers' markets a *business*. At least, she didn't. Her little hobby was nothing compared to what her siblings did—each of them with successful businesses, or running the family business empire, Carlson Corp.

Maybe it wasn't as *important* as what the rest of them did, but it made her happy, as did creating the displays for the Bean Bag.

A few minutes later, when Charli pulled the door to the

cafe open, she was hit with a blast of warm air. A sharp contrast to the cold January day.

She pulled her parka off, found an empty table, and draped it over a chair. She tucked her basket out of the way and made her way to the counter, where Annie was finishing up her latte.

"I wish you'd let Dale pay you in money rather than coffee." Annie handed over the drink. "Your work is gorgeous. We get so many comments on it from our customers."

Annie's compliment glowed deep in Charli's chest.

"I'm just so glad I can make people happy," she said genuinely. "And these lattes are delicious." She lifted the coffee to her mouth and laughed at the image of the flower Annie had created with the foam on top. "Super cute."

"Just for you." Annie winked but immediately turned serious again. "But seriously, if you charged for what you—"

She stopped her with an outstretched hand. "No one is going to pay for it." She shook her head and once more wrapped both hands around her mug. "And besides, I love doing it. Honestly. It's fine."

Annie looked as if she wanted to say more, but she was distracted by the ringing of a bell from the kitchen, alerting her that an order was ready.

Charli waved her away, thanked her once more, and retreated to the table by the window where she could enjoy her coffee and look through the new stack of seed and bulb catalogs that had come in the mail the other day.

Flipping through the pages, looking at all the glossy images of beautiful bright blooms, daydreaming about what they'd look like in her arrangements, was one of her favorite pastimes in the colder winter months when she couldn't be in her gardens. Which was where she preferred to be whenever she wasn't working for Carlson Corp, the family business her father had started that had singlehandedly saved the town of Trickle

ELENA AITKEN

Creek by bringing in tourism in a big way when the zinc mine closed years earlier.

Without a college education like the rest of her siblings, Charli didn't have any real marketable skills besides exceptional customer service, which was why she'd been given the role of community outreach manager. Her brothers and sisters had never said anything, but Charli knew her father had created the position just for her. Truthfully, it wasn't very hard, and she spent most of her time interacting with guests of the ski resort in the winter and the world-class golf course in the summer months, trying to feel useful.

Charli sighed heavily, her gaze lifting away from the pages of the catalog she realized she hadn't been paying much attention to, and spent a few moments watching the bustle of the people outside. Annie was right; more than one person walking by stopped to admire her window box arrangement before entering the cafe. It was a simple thing, but it warmed her with pride. She might not be very good at much, but she was damned good at flower arrangement. For whatever that was worth.

She took another sip of her coffee, which was quickly growing cold in front of her, and focused out the window once more. This time, her eyes traveled across the bustling plaza, the pedestrian-only shopping area that was the heart of Trickle Creek, and landed on a large red sign in a storefront. *Closing-out sale. Everything must go.*

"Annie?" She reached for her friend as she walked by, a coffeepot in her hand. "Did you see that Muddy Mugs is closing down?"

The local pottery shop had been operating in town for only two or three years, but it had become a favorite of tourists and locals alike with unique mugs, bowls, and more, all with an authentic mountain theme that had proved quite popular.

Maybe not popular enough?

"It's really too bad, isn't it?" Annie followed Charli's gaze. "I love her stuff."

"But why? I thought Marta was doing well?"

"She is. She's doing great."

Charli tipped her head and looked at her friend quizzically.

"I think that's the problem," Annie explained. "She's spending too much time minding the store and doing the *business* things." She used air quotes. "And she wants to spend more time in her pottery studio." Annie shrugged. "Besides, she has what...eight grandchildren now? I think the real reason is she'd rather spend time with them."

Charli smiled and nodded. "That makes sense, and it makes me feel a lot better. I would hate it if she was in financial trouble and forced to sell."

"From what I understand, that's not it at all." Annie shook her head. "But it will be interesting to see what goes in there next. Any guesses?"

"No clue." She couldn't even begin to imagine what would fit the space. "But I hope it's something great."

"I'll miss Marta," Annie said. "But I'm sure whatever business takes over, they'll do great. Can I get you more coffee?"

Charli shook her head and pulled her gaze away from the window. "No," she said. "I should get going. I need to go home for a bit, and I wanted to make a stop before heading up to the big house for the family dinner. I'll see you then?"

"I wouldn't miss it." Annie beamed. "Chase insisted on making a huge batch of beef stew." Her smile slipped a bit. "He thought maybe it was a good idea for some comfort food before, well..."

"The will reading," Charli finished for her. "It's not a bad idea." She worked hard to keep the smile on her face, but on the inside, Charli was definitely not smiling.

Weekly family dinners were a normal part of Carlson family life, the will readings...not so much. Although, that seemed to be changing, too.

Six months ago, their father, the patriarch of the family, Michael Carlson, died and left a less than orthodox request in the initial reading of the will. He'd shocked everyone when he'd left a very specific caveat in his will that forced Chase, the eldest of the siblings, to live in Trickle Creek for six months before the second part of the reading could take place. Obviously, that had worked out for everyone, including Annie, who was now very happily engaged to Chase. But to say that they weren't all nervous about what else their father might have in store for them would be a huge understatement.

They wouldn't have to wait much longer, though, because part two of the will was set to be read after dinner.

Annie pulled her in for a quick hug. "It's going to be okay. Your father was a kind and generous man. He only wanted the best for all of you."

Charli knew that to be true. Still, as she made her way through the plaza back to her car, she knew in her heart that whatever was going to be in the will tonight, there would be nothing straightforward about it.

The hill was steep, a fluffy layer of fresh powdery snow over what Symon Scott knew was a solid, deep base of snow. He knew every single detail, every tree, every turn, every obstacle, every jump, of every single run at the Trickle Creek ski resort by memory. He'd spent some of the best years of his life on the hill and couldn't even begin to count how many hours were spent racing down the hill, honing his skills, learning how to *fly*.

It was home. *He* was home.

So why did he feel so empty as he stood at the base of the hill next to the high-speed quad chairlift that would take him to the top of the mountain, where he knew he would feel like he was on top of the world?

Symon closed his eyes against the lightly falling snow, lifted his face, and inhaled deeply.

Home.

When he opened his eyes, he still felt nothing. A chasm of blankness in place of the fire that used to fill him at the prospect of clicking his ski boots into his bindings. Maybe if he just forced himself to do it, it would feel differently. There was no pressure here. Not yet.

There wouldn't be any questions about the injury that side-lined him from Team Canada and his dream of skiing. There wouldn't be anyone watching him carefully to see whether his knee would hold up. No expectations. It was just him and his home hill. The perfect place to get back on the proverbial horse after nine long months of rehabbing his injury after surgery.

It wasn't his first time back on skis, not by a long shot. Symon had clicked into his bindings more times than he could count since he was cleared by the physiotherapist and released from the months long rehab since the accident. But just because he got his skis on, didn't mean he'd actually skied.

That was the problem.

But all that would be fixed now that he was on his home hill. Surely, whatever fear was holding him back would vanish with the familiarity.

At least, he hoped like hell it would.

With no more excuses, Symon dropped his skis to the ground and, with movements that were as natural as breathing, he planted his poles on either side of him and one by one, clicked his boots into the bindings, securing him into his skis.

He pulled his goggles down over the top of his helmet to cover his eyes and pushed off on his good leg toward the chairlift.

He hadn't expected so many people to be there in the middle of the week, but he'd also vastly underestimated the increasing level of tourism that Trickle Creek had experienced over the last few years. The condos and vacation properties scattered around the base of the ski hill had grown from only a handful to dozens since the last time he'd been home.

When had that been?

Too long, if he asked his grandmother. A flash of guilt shot through him. But there was only room for one personal challenge at a time. And right now, he was determined to focus on the one in front of him.

Skiing.

Not long ago, it had been as natural as walking. Symon had quite literally dedicated his entire life to the freestyle moguls ski team, and he didn't regret a thing. At least, he *hadn't* regretted anything. Now, he absolutely regretted the split-second decision to attempt a D-Spin instead of the easier—and safer—daffy that he'd executed flawlessly more times than he could count. That decision had cost him a lot more than the championship. Symon glanced down at his left leg. *A lot more.*

The truth was, he knew he couldn't win with the safer jump. The newer, younger skiers were faster, stronger, and more daring. They took risks, and that's what he'd needed to do if he wanted to win. It just hadn't worked out the way he wanted it to.

Symon's skis slid easily on the snow as he maneuvered his way into the line behind a family. Happy chatter surrounded him, and two young boys, probably around fifteen or sixteen, took the spot in line behind him.

"Did you see that jump?" one asked the other. "It was killer."

"Dude, I caught *so* much air!"

Symon smiled a little to himself, memories of him and his buddies at that age flooding through him. It felt like a lifetime ago.

"Hey," one of the boys said.

It took Symon a moment to realize he was talking to him. Slowly, Symon turned to face the kid.

"Are you with Team Canada?"

Symon froze. His helmet and goggles would hide his identity, but...*shit*. His ski jacket had the recognizable maple leaf with two lines to represent skis on one side on his left arm. Most people wouldn't recognize the significance. He glanced down at his arm before looking up at the boy and grinning. "Nah, I found this jacket at the thrift shop."

"Really?" the boy said.

"So cool," his friend added. "Maybe it was Symon Scott's. Did you know he's from here?"

Symon shrugged. "I might have heard that."

"He has two gold medals!"

"He's awesome!"

"He *was* awesome," the other boy corrected his friend.

Symon couldn't help himself. "What do you mean, was?"

"He bailed hard last year."

"It was epic."

"Epic?" Symon could think of a lot of ways to describe his wipeout, but *epic* had never crossed his mind.

"So gnarly, man," the first boy said. "He would have won, too, if he'd landed it." His friend nodded in agreement.

"You guys follow freestyle racing?" Symon knew the answer before they nodded vehemently, because he and his friends followed the racing circuit when he was their age, imagining themselves on the screen, numbers on their chests, bouncing through the moguls and racing toward victory one day themselves. He'd had that. Until…his *epic bail.*

"You guys want to race one day?"

The first boy nodded. "Totally. I'm going to be just like Symon Scott."

Sy felt a flare of pride in his chest, until he noticed the other boy shaking his head.

"Not me."

"No?"

"No way. He bailed and never got up."

Again, Symon thought he should just turn around and let it go. But he couldn't.

"What do you mean?"

"He's not racing anymore." The boy still shook his head, clearly disappointed in the hometown racer he didn't realize he was speaking directly to. "Never went back to the circuit. Just quit."

With nothing else to contribute, Symon turned around again as the line moved forward. He hadn't quit. Not really. He just hadn't skied again yet.

Yet.

He would. At least he hoped he would.

It was almost his turn to take a spot on the chair that would deliver him to the top of the mountain. He hadn't so much as been on a chairlift since the accident. Because what went up a mountain, had to come down. His physiotherapist had cleared him physically. There was no reason he shouldn't be able to do this. Yet, there was something in his brain blocking him from doing the one thing he loved more than anything else.

Behind him, the kids resumed their chatter. Symon tried to swallow back the guilt of lying to the boys. But it was only temporary. *Once he got this run out of the way, it would all be different, and he could—*

"Let's do that run again," one kid said to his friend. "That time didn't count. I caught an edge."

"You bailed *so* hard, man."

Symon's chest tightened. He forced himself to breathe deeply. Despite the snow and cold, he was too hot. He unzipped his jacket halfway, letting the frosty air hit him. It wasn't enough. His heart raced, a trail of icy sweat dripped down his spine, and his vision blurred as he worked hard to regain what little control he had. These kids were too much.

"Dude."

The sharp poke of a ski pole in his back brought Symon to attention. He turned to see the kids staring at him.

"Dude," the boy said again. "It's your turn." He gestured with his pole.

Symon turned around to see that the line in front of him had moved up, and it was in fact his turn to get on the chairlift.

"Sorry," he mumbled. Symon took it all in: The chairs that were spinning around empty on their track, waiting for him to move forward. The skiers moved gracefully from side to side on the hill as they finished the run and returned to their spots in the chairlift line. The kids behind him.

He shook his head, muttered another apology, and with a wide step sideways, pulled himself out of line. Symon immediately used his poles to click out of his bindings. He grabbed his skis, lifted them over his shoulders, and as fast as he could, made his way back to his truck at the back of the parking lot. Unceremoniously, he tossed his equipment in the truck bed and leaned against the driver's side door.

Symon pulled his goggles and helmet from his head and dropped them both to his feet, all his focus on pulling in one deep breath after another.

"Fuck." He kicked at an ice ball with his ski boot. "What's wrong with you? It's just skiing. You've done it a million times."

It didn't make sense. There was nothing logical about it. Skiing had always been his escape. His greatest joy. His *passion*. It was the only thing he'd ever wanted to do with his life. And he'd done it. He'd made his dreams come true. He'd made the Canadian freestyle ski team. He was winning. And then...he'd crashed.

Just like that, it was all over.

Everything he'd worked so hard for was ripped away from him because of one bad decision. There was no going back. Not for him. The kid was right. He wasn't worthy of being anyone's hero.

Sure, Symon knew plenty of skiers who'd come back from injury and gone back to compete and win. And at first, he was sure that would be his story as well. The accident happened in Austria, during a summer ski circuit high in the alps. By the time he got home and saw the team surgeon, weeks later, they'd determined that surgery was the only way to get him back on the hill.

After he was healed enough, no one went after physiotherapy the way Symon did. For months, rehabbing his knee and building muscle and strength had been his only job, which was why Symon had been so sure that as soon as the snow fell, and he got back on his skis, he'd be stronger than ever.

What he hadn't counted on was the overwhelming, paralyzing fear that had consumed him that first time he put his skis on. And then the second.

He couldn't even make himself get on the chairlift, let alone ski.

Alan, his coach, told him it was temporary, and he tried to be patient with him. But the season had already started, and Symon was already behind. So, Alan sent him home.

"Get your head straight," Alan said. "Take some time and sort it out."

"There's nothing to sort out, Alan. I think it's over."

"That's bullshit, Sy, and you know it. You got hurt. So what? Skiers get hurt every day. You're better now. Your knee is stronger than ever. *You* are stronger than ever. You have too much to offer, Symon. Your team needs you."

He couldn't bear to look his coach and friend in the eyes. The truth was, as the oldest, he had taken on a big brother role to a lot of the guys on the team. More than once, he'd counseled them on both personal matters and those involving skiing. His experience was called on frequently, and the other team members did look up to him.

Which made the whole situation even harder.

"How can I be a role model when I can't even get out of my own head, Alan?" Symon shook his head. "They don't need me. They don't need that. What they need is a new team member who will lead them to victory. Someone younger, faster, and…well, not broken."

He didn't want to leave the team, but Alan was right. He needed to get his head straight. Either that or he should just quit altogether. It was an idea that was creeping into his thoughts more and more lately.

"That's a load of crap, Sy, and you know it. You're scared. Not *done.*" Alan shook his head. "And that's a bullshit reason to throw it all away. Which is why you're going home for a rest. That's it. You'll be back."

Alan had sounded so sure. But now that Symon *was* home and things still weren't different…well, it was getting harder and harder to stay positive.

He took another deep breath and looked back toward the ski hill, dotted with skiers moving down the mountain.

He'd been so sure that the moment he got here, everything would be fine. That his body and his brain would remember how good it felt to be on his skis, flying down the slopes, and it would all click together.

"Fuck." He cursed at himself again.

Obviously, it wasn't going to be quite as easy as he'd assumed it would be.

Symon ran a hand through his dark hair, inhaled deeply, and looked away.

Maybe he could figure it out. Maybe he couldn't.

Either way, he was out of options. Trickle Creek was his best hope and his last chance.

Like it or not, he was home.

Chapter Two

CHARLI MANAGED to take her mind off the impending evening by spending a few hours in her greenhouse, tending to the calendula seeds she was germinating and checking on the moisture level in the soil for the ranunculus bulbs she'd planted a few weeks earlier. She could have spent even longer puttering around and busying herself with the never-ending tasks that her plants and flowers required, but the alarm she'd set on her phone warned her that if she wanted to have time for one last stop before heading up to the big house for dinner, she'd need to leave soon.

Reluctantly, she closed up the greenhouse, making sure the temperature was set just right before she left, knowing as she did so that she'd check it as soon as she got home, too. Her family saw her flowers as an extravagant hobby, but to Charli, they were so much more. Not that she could explain to her brothers and sisters how it felt to dig her hands in the earth and feel connected to something greater than herself.

How when she nurtured a seed into a strong, healthy plant, she felt deep, personal satisfaction and pride knowing it was because of her and the attention and care she'd taken. And when her plants bloomed in turn, almost like a well-orchestrated symphony from early spring all the way until the first frost, in waves of glorious color and texture that she'd carefully planned for, it was a personal triumph. And then later, when she gave away her bouquets or sold them for just enough to cover the cost of the table rental at the local farmers' market, seeing the happiness her flowers brought to people, the smiles they put on the faces of strangers, filled her with a sense of joy nothing else could come close to.

Charli stopped at the barn, her heated workshop, which was her second favorite place to spend time, to grab a centerpiece arrangement she'd put together for the big house. It was always a fine line after the Christmas season to create a beautiful piece that wasn't too festive. She was pretty sure she nailed it with the addition of little wooden snowflakes that she'd painted white and tucked into the evergreen boughs and pine cones. She'd even added a few of the white carnations she'd recently started growing in her greenhouse. The result was beautiful, and it would be perfect on their family dinner table.

"What do you think, Lilly?" She stopped to scratch her orange tabby cat behind the ears. Lilly purred in response and arched her neck into Charli's attention. "I agree," she said with a laugh. "I *did* do a pretty good job."

She gave the cat one last pet before scooping up the centerpiece and heading out. She still had one more stop she wanted to make, and she didn't want to be late for the family dinner, tonight of all nights.

Charli only lived a short five-minute drive up the mountain from the big house where she was raised. She hadn't planned it that way but when the property came up for sale, it was absolutely perfect, with its old farmhouse and two acres to dig in as many flower beds as she could handle. Plus, the old barn had been just right for her workshop. Besides, she loved her family and although living so close by wouldn't be an ideal choice for many, it was the ideal scenario as far as Charli was concerned.

Instead of continuing up the main road that would take her to her childhood home, Charli took a small detour onto a logging road and pulled off as far as she could to the side in case anyone else happened to come by.

Even with the heavy snowfall, she had no trouble finding the trailhead. She strapped on the snowshoes she kept in the back of her car and moved quickly into the trees.

She could have walked the trail by memory in any season, despite the fact that it had been years since she'd taken it. There'd been a time she'd walked this trail almost daily, but now, she couldn't remember the last time she'd been out there. Nor could she explain why she'd woken up that morning with the deep feeling in her heart that it was exactly where she needed to be today.

Even without a packed trail to follow, Charli took the turns and navigated the snowy path with relative ease until she came out in the clearing next to the creek and the small waterfall. In January, it was frozen solid, creating a dramatic and stunning art piece.

"Wow."

She'd seen it many times, but even so, the waterfall never failed to impress her.

Charli closed her eyes and inhaled deeply, letting the peace and calm wash over her the way she knew it would. She'd only been about eight years old when she discovered the small waterfall along with her best friend Symon. The two of them were inseparable back then, choosing to spend all of their free time running through the woods and exploring. When they'd stumbled upon the pretty spot, too small to be a tourist attraction like the bigger waterfalls on the other side of town, but even more special than any of those others, Charli and Symon had declared it their own. It was a magical place and their young imaginations, still so innocent, insisted there must be fairies that lived there that would grant their wishes. They'd dubbed it Fairy Creek Falls, and it had been their special place ever since.

Charli unstrapped her snowshoes and picked her way across the rocks toward the frozen ice. Maybe that's why she'd been called to the falls today. She was going to need the magic of the fairies to get her through the upcoming will reading.

Charli and Symon's visits to Fairy Creek Falls slowed when they became teenagers. Symon spent more and more time on the mountain with the ski club, and when he wasn't skiing or training, more and more frequently he chose to spend his free time with his teammates.

The last time they'd been there together was the day of their high school graduation. Charli could still picture exactly where they stood, the wish she'd made to the fairies, and then the way it had come true when she shared her first kiss with her best friend, who she'd been so secretly and desperately in love with.

She squeezed her eyes shut at the rest of that memory. So young and naive, Charli had been so sure that kiss meant that everything would change. And it did…only not in the way she'd expected it to.

When the kiss was over, Symon had taken off without a word and left her there by herself.

The next day, he was gone. He'd accepted a spot on Canada's junior ski team and moved to Vancouver without even telling her.

What should have been one of the happiest and most exciting days of their young lives became one of Charli's worst. Not only had Symon rejected her, but the diploma she'd held in her hand had been fake. The shame and disappointment she'd felt in failing to successfully pass her math course and get the credits she needed, despite all her best efforts, was only eclipsed by the heartache of losing her best friend, the one person she would have confided in, if he'd stayed.

She'd only been back to the falls sporadically after that. It was hard to believe in fairies and wishes when your heart was broken.

But that was a long time ago. Sure, she didn't believe in fairies anymore, but in a time like this, she'd take all the help she could get. "Maybe there's a fairy hiding in there after all," she muttered. "Come on, fairy. You owe me one."

She tilted her head back, inhaled deeply, and attempted to make a wish, just the way they used to. "I wish that whatever happens tonight, it will—"

"That's not how it works."

The voice startled her. Charli jumped, her eyes flying open as she took a step forward and spun around.

"Symon?"

"Hi, Charli."

The last person Symon expected to see at Fairy Creek Falls was Charli. Of course, it was fitting that she *was* there. And definitely a happy surprise. How long had it been since he'd seen her? A few years, at least, since the last time he'd come back to visit Gran. He'd bumped into her at the grocery store when he'd run out to do a few errands for Gran and they'd grabbed a coffee. She'd looked good then in her jeans and sweater. Hell, Charli always looked good. But now...with her knit cap pulled low on her head, her blonde hair sticking out over her shoulders, her cheeks pinked from the cold, and the smile on her face that told him how glad she was to see him, she was downright gorgeous.

Symon felt that familiar tightening in his gut every time he saw Charli Carlson. *Hell, that hadn't changed.*

"What are you..." Charli shook her head. "You're…" She laughed at herself, and her eyes sparkled. "Symon? Why are you here?"

"I texted you." He took a few steps toward her and grinned. "I told you I was coming this time." It was true. Mostly. He *had* texted her around Christmas to let her know he'd be moving back to town for awhile. He'd been a bit sparse on the details, but he *had* told her.

"You know full well you could have let me know when you got here?"

He shrugged and flashed her another bright smile. "To be fair, I just got here." It was mostly true.

"Men are so ridiculous." She shook her head and rolled her eyes a little, but she was still smiling. It was the same bright smile she'd had since they were kids, that, when it was focused on you, made you feel like the most important person in the world.

"Well?" He held out his arms. "Are you going to give me a hug, or what?"

That was all it took before she was in his arms. She felt good. Even through their thick parkas, he swore he could feel the heat from her body, warming him thoroughly. The empty, cold loneliness he'd been shrouded in for the last few months began to thaw almost at once. Symon inhaled and pulled her closer. She smelled so good. A mixture of cinnamon and pine and something else that was both sweet and floral and earthy at the same time. "It's good to see you, Charli."

He didn't want to let her go. Quite the opposite. He wanted to pull her close and tell her all his deepest, darkest secrets, just like when they were kids. It would feel so good to confide in her about his fear of skiing again, and he knew she wouldn't laugh or make him feel small. But it wasn't the right time. He couldn't just lead with, "I know it's been awhile, but I'm an emotional wreck…can you help me out?"

Aware he was probably holding on a little too tight, Symon released her and instantly missed the feel of her in his arms.

At once, she smacked him in the chest with her mittened hand. "I still can't believe you didn't tell me you were coming."

"We just went through this, Char. I did tell you." He tried not to laugh. "I texted you."

"You know what I mean."

"Does it matter?" He shrugged. "I'm here now."

"True." She laughed; the familiar sound traveled through him. "Here you are." She waved her hands around. "I can't believe how random this is. I didn't even plan on coming here today, but I just had a feeling that I needed to stop by."

"And make a wish?" He'd heard her. And he'd felt a little guilty that he'd interrupted her before she finished her wish. But it was either that, or he would have to eavesdrop on it, and as curious as he was to know what had brought Charli out here to make a wish, that didn't feel right. "I wasn't trying to listen in, Char. I'm—"

"It's fine." She shook her head and glanced at the waterfall. "I wasn't really… It's nothing."

It seemed like something, but Symon wasn't going to push.

They stood in silence for a few moments, a million memories about all the times they'd been at the falls together over the years cascading over him. Including the last time.

"Do you come here—"

"It's sure been awhile—"

They spoke at the same time, their words coming out in a rush.

"You go first," Charli said.

He didn't bother to argue. "I was just going to ask you if you still came here a lot?"

Her smile dipped a little and a shadow passed over her features, but only for a moment. "Not really," she said. "Only a few times since that last time."

That last time.

He knew exactly what time she was talking about. It was the day they graduated from high school and they'd snuck away from the party Michael Carlson had thrown them at the big house. They hadn't planned to go to Fairy Creek Falls, but neither of them was surprised when they ended up there.

They'd made wishes and taken sips from the bottles of beer they'd snuck from the house as they sat side by side, laughing with their feet in the creek. When Charli looked at him, the laughter dying on her lips, Symon knew exactly what was going to happen. And more than anything else, he wanted it to happen, because as long as he could remember, he'd been in love with Charli.

When they were kids, that love took the form of a deep friendship. They were completely inseparable from the moment they met, and it wasn't long before Symon couldn't imagine a life without Charli.

Things had changed a little as they grew up, as they always do. Charli grew into a gorgeous young woman who got more than her share of attention from the opposite sex. Even if she didn't realize it. Symon had done his best to threaten his friends from the ski team away from her. The few times that she *had* gone out with a boy who had somehow snuck past his threats, Symon was not shy to tell her exactly why he wasn't good enough for her. At first, it had been out of a protective nature because her big brother Chase wasn't around to do it. But then things changed. And it became more personal.

Even at eighteen, Symon was sure of his feelings when one day he looked across the table where they were doing English homework and watched her push her long hair away from her face before looking up to see him watching her. It was in that completely ordinary moment that he knew for sure that what he felt for Charli was far more than friendship or brotherly concern. He was in love with her. It was shortly after that that he realized that he could never be with her. Kissing her, as amazing as it had been, had been a mistake.

"So, what's so special about today?" He ignored the reference to their history, the way he always had. In fact, they'd never discussed the kiss or his subsequent disappearance. Years later, when Symon finally got brave enough to reach out again, he took the approach of pretending it had never happened. It seemed to be a strategy that worked for both of them, so there wouldn't be any point in changing it.

"Well, you're here." She winked. "It's not every day that a Canadian ski team member shows up at Fairy Creek Falls. That's pretty special."

He winced at her mention of the ski team but did his best to cover it. "It sure is."

"So, are you going to tell me why you're here?" She turned the question on him. "I mean, you can't tell me that after all these years, you had a burning urge to make a wish at Fairy Creek Falls?"

He shrugged.

"You did?"

"Don't look so surprised." He laughed. "I can still make a wish."

She tipped her head and eyed him. "I mean…I guess technically, but…"

"You don't believe me?"

"No."

23

"I'll show you."

He regretted the words the moment they were out of his mouth. He hadn't been lying when he told her that he could still make a wish, and yes, there was a part of him that thought maybe it wouldn't hurt to wish to the fairies for him to get over his stupid phobia and just let him ski again. But he was just grasping at straws with that thought, and there was *no* way he was going to make the wish in front of her.

Still. He couldn't back down. Not without telling her why he was really back in town. And he wasn't ready to do that.

With confidence he didn't totally feel, Symon took a step away from her and toward the frozen waterfall.

"Do you remember how?"

"How could I forget?" He glanced over his shoulder and took a few more careful steps until he was in position.

He closed his eyes, tipped his head up to the sky, and began.

"Powerful and magical fairies of Fairy Creek Falls," he began, reciting the script they'd created when they were children. "Please hear my wish." Behind him, Symon was sure he heard Charli giggle, but he didn't turn around. He squeezed his eyes even tighter and decided to take a chance, because why not? What did he have to lose if the fairies ignored his request now? "I wish for a beautiful woman to keep me company and spend time with me while I'm visiting Trickle Creek. Please, powerful and magical fairies, grant me my wish," he finished before stamping twice with his left foot and clapping his hands together three times.

Wish completed, Symon turned and slowly opened his eyes to see how it was received. "See?" He spoke. "I didn't forget how."

Charli stood perfectly still. Her mouth was hung open slightly. Her eyes were unfocused, and Symon instantly regretted his wish. He knew she wasn't married; he would have heard that news. But for all he knew, she could be dating someone who he hadn't heard about yet.

Shit.

Before he could attempt to dig himself out of the hole he'd just dug for himself, she seemed to recover from whatever shock she was feeling.

"Well, holy shit, Sy! I'm impressed." She clapped her mittened hands and laughed. "You really did remember."

Symon blinked. "I did."

"I think I know exactly how the fairies are going to make your wish come true." She reached for his hand as he made his way back through the deep snow. "But first, I'm going to be late for the family dinner at the big house, and you *have* to come."

Chapter Three

ANY OTHER FAMILY dinner on any other night, and it wouldn't have been an issue. But with the excitement of seeing Symon again, and all the feelings he still brought up in her after so long, she'd completely forgotten about what was supposed to happen *after* the family dinner.

By the time she'd remembered about the will reading that she was certain would not go smoothly, they were pulling up to the big house and it was too late.

Not that there had been any other choice, anyway. Not when she hadn't seen Symon for so long. No. The only choice was to invite him for dinner.

"Are you sure it's okay to crash your family dinner?" he asked the moment she'd put the car in park and pulled the keys from the ignition.

There was no way she could let him walk into the house without any warning of what was about to happen. It wasn't fair. She turned to face him. "Truth?"

"Always." He pressed his lips together, and Charli had to swallow hard.

Why was he so damn good-looking?

And more to the point, why did he still make her stomach flip after all these years?

So many questions that she wasn't likely to get answers to any time soon. Never mind that wish he made. A beautiful woman to keep him company while he was in Trickle Creek? *Seriously?* She'd come to terms with the fact that Symon didn't feel the same way about her when they were eighteen, and time did soften the blow of that moment. But having him wish for a woman in *their* spot? That stung a little.

"Everyone is going to be thrilled to see you," she answered honestly. "But I do need to warn you—"

A sharp rap on the car window startled them both. "Charli, you're late!"

She turned to see her brother Craig staring into her car window.

His goofy grin morphed into a look of surprise when he saw her passenger. "Symon Scott? Is that you?"

No time left for warnings; Charli gave Symon one last reassuring grin before opening her car door. She was greeted at once by her five-year-old niece Meredith, who slammed into her legs, wrapping her arms tight around Charli.

"Hey, kiddo." Charli crouched so they were at eye level. "You're getting strong. One day you're going to knock me over."

"Maybe one day."

Meri gave her a kiss on her cheek before pulling herself out of Charli's arms and turning to Symon. "Who are you?"

"Meri," Craig chastised. "That's not very polite."

The little girl nodded seriously and tried again. "Who are you, please?"

Craig groaned and shook his head in apology. Charli knew it wasn't easy for him being a single dad to such a ball of energy, but he was a great father, and Meri was a fabulous kid.

"My name is Symon." He held out his hand. "I'm an old friend of your Aunt Charli's."

Meri took his hand and shook it as she eyed him. "You don't look very old."

Charli laughed, and Craig groaned again. "Meri, that's not—"

"Well," Symon smiled, "I'm older than you."

"That's true." Meri nodded. "Everyone's older than me. Even Grady. Have you met him yet?"

Symon shook his head and looked to Charli for an explanation. She lifted a shoulder. There'd been a lot of changes since he'd last been there.

"Not yet," he told her. "We just got here."

"Don't worry," the little girl said. "I'll make sure you know everyone. Come on." She took his hand and led him into the house.

Symon glanced back at Charli with a shrug, but she only shook her head with a laugh.

She started after them, but Craig grabbed her arm to stop her. "Symon's here?"

"Obviously."

"Sorry." Her brother caught himself. "I'm not trying to sound like an asshole, and it's good to see him, of course. I'm just…tonight is the…well, it's just—"

"I know. The timing isn't awesome, but to be honest, I completely forgot about the will reading."

Craig gave her a suspicious look.

Truthfully, it was pretty unbelievable, considering it was pretty much *all* Charli had thought about for the last few days. But it was the truth. "He's here now," she said. "And maybe he'll be a good distraction for everyone."

What she meant was maybe he'd be a good distraction for *her*, and they both knew it.

Craig gave her a knowing look and wrapped an arm around her shoulders for a quick squeeze. "It'll be okay, Char. Whatever it is, we'll handle it together, okay?"

"Of course, it will." She forced a cheer into her voice, the way she always did. "We should get in there and rescue Symon from his new date."

Walking into a Carlson family dinner was a strange dichotomy for Symon. On one hand, nothing had changed. The family was still loud and over the top, with everyone trying to talk over one another. It was chaotic and crazy and full of love. But on the other hand, a lot had changed. The biggest being that Michael Carlson, the patriarch of the family, was no longer at the head of the table, quietly overseeing the madness with a sly smile on his face.

Symon had been just as saddened as everyone else to hear about his passing. He'd reached out to Charli to give his condolences, but he was still angry at himself for not making a bigger effort to come back for the funeral to be there for her. But with his injury still so fresh, he'd been so preoccupied with his own stuff. He should have made more of an effort.

He snuck a glance across the table at Charli now, engaged in conversation with her younger sister, Kat.

That was another thing that had changed since the last time he'd been there. The Carlson siblings were all grown up.

Of course, he'd kept in touch with Charli and she always filled him in on what was going on with her family. And obviously, he'd seen pictures on social media. But somehow seeing everything in person was still a jolt and reminded him just how long it had been since he'd spent any real time in Trickle Creek.

Craig, the youngest brother owned his own ice cream shop *and* had his own child? It was mind blowing. Kat, the youngest of the five, had grown into a gorgeous woman with long, bright-red hair and from what he could tell, a fiery personality to match. Asher, the middle brother, was the image of his father, especially dressed in a full suit at a casual family dinner He'd heard that Asher had taken over the operations of Carlson Corp and it didn't surprise him. Asher had always been an intensely focused kid. Even at a young age, it was easy to see his drive and need to achieve.

"Sorry to hear about the crash." Craig gave him a sympathetic nod from across the table. "I saw it on the internet, and it looked..."

"Trust me. It felt way worse than it looked, man."

"I bet it did." Craig shook his head. "The doctors put you all back together again?"

Before Symon could answer, or come up with some version of the truth, there was another question.

"Is it true you're on Team Canada?"

Symon spun to see Grady, the little boy he'd been introduced to earlier. If he remembered correctly, Grady was Annie's nephew, who she and Chase were raising. They were living in the big house and were engaged to be married. Or maybe they were married? He glanced over at Chase's left hand for confirmation. *No. Engaged. Not married.*

"I am." He turned his attention to the young boy, ignoring Craig's earlier question. Technically it was true, but the kid didn't need to know the details. "Do you like to ski?"

Grady nodded. "I'm not very good yet. But I'm learning, and Chase says the only way to get better is to practice."

Symon glanced up and met Chase's gaze across the table. When they were kids, they'd ended up spending quite a bit of time playing hide-and-seek or adventure games when he and

Charli weren't off somewhere, just the two of them. But he'd only seen Chase a handful of times since those easy, innocent days before Chase moved away to boarding school when they were kids.

Seeing him in the big house now, with the rest of his siblings, was probably the biggest change of all.

Symon offered Chase a smile and focused on Grady. "He's right. That's what I did. I practiced. A lot."

"And then you made it to Team Canada." Grady nodded in appreciation. "That's so cool."

"It is cool." He reached for his glass of wine and took a sip.

"Why aren't you with the team now, Symon?" Kat asked the question, but everyone at the table grew silent as they waited for the answer. "It's the middle of the season, right?"

It was a fair question, and one Symon expected sooner or later. The ski season was in full gear and his absence was notable. "It's the knee," he answered. "It's not fully rehabbed yet." It wasn't a total lie. "Coach wanted to give me some more time before I went back into the race circuit."

"Makes sense." Craig took a bite of chicken. "Especially with the Olympic trials coming up next year, hey?"

Symon pressed his lips together and nodded. The Olympics were definitely a black cloud hanging over his head. He already had two gold medals, but earning the third would be a huge career achievement and make him the only Canadian to win freestyle gold in three consecutive Olympics. It was huge. Coach didn't think it was too late, if he could get his head back in the game. But as far as Symon was concerned, he was so far away from any medal now, let alone a gold, it hurt to think about it.

He cleared his throat and forced himself to stay in the moment and not follow that trail of thinking. Symon naturally turned to Charli, who was watching him closely. "There's definitely a lot to look forward to." He winked in her direction. "So, you all get together like this every week? Or is this a special occasion?"

The room went strangely silent. There was a clink of a fork, a clearing of a throat, and an awkward cough, but no one said a word.

"Sorry," he said slowly as he looked around the table. "Did I say something wrong?"

"Yes." Chase spoke first. "We do meet for dinner at least weekly. It was an important family tradition to have dinners together. But tonight is a little different because it's been six months exactly since the first reading of our father's will. And time for the reading of part two."

Holy shit. A will reading? Symon shot a look to Charli, who simply shrugged, her face oddly blank. "Charli didn't mention that," he said to Chase. "I wouldn't have imposed if I'd—"

"You can keep me company." Annie, Chase's fiancée, whom he hadn't had much of a chance to speak with yet, smiled at him. "It's family only in there," she continued. "You can help me clear up, and we'll get some dessert ready for after."

"And drinks." Kat groaned. "Something strong."

"It won't be that bad," Asher said, but his face didn't match his reassuring words.

Still confused, or maybe just more so, Symon looked at Charli. "I don't understand. I mean, I heard there was something with Chase and your father's will."

"I think everyone in town has heard that story."

Symon nodded. "But…there's a part two?"

For the first time, Symon saw a flicker of worry cross Charli's face, but only for a moment and then it was gone. "We all kind of think that Dad isn't done," she said. "He wasn't really the type to single out only one of us."

"Which means…"

"It's probably my turn next."

There it was again. A shadow of concern flickered on Charli's face. Symon dropped his napkin to his plate and pushed his chair back, ready to go to her and give her the hug she looked like she so desperately needed.

But before he could stand, the doorbell chimed, and Chase stood. "Right on time."

"That will be William, the lawyer," Annie explained. "And Steven. He was Michael's best friend and assistant for years. He's kind of overseeing this whole process."

Symon nodded numbly and watched as everyone stood, leaving their plates on the table. The children were dismissed and took off at full speed, presumably to get out of helping with cleanup. Charli was the last to get up, and Symon caught up with her before she could leave the room.

"Hey." He reached for her hand and turned her around. "Are you okay?"

It was a dumb question, because she very clearly was not okay.

"I'm fine," she lied. "But I'm glad you're here. I should have told you. I'm sorry. I just—"

"It's totally okay." He felt useless and had no idea what to say to his best friend whom he hadn't seen in years who was about to walk into an important meeting that could change not only the course of her life but that of her brothers and sisters, too. He settled for pulling her in for a tight hug. "I'll be here when it's over," he whispered in her ear. "For whatever you need, okay?"

Chapter Four

IT'S FINE. *It's going to be fine.*

When she opened her eyes, the room was spinning. Her brothers and sisters had erupted in a mixture of protests and sounds of encouragement, but she couldn't make out what anyone was actually saying. Nothing made sense.

It is not going to be fine.

She squeezed her eyes shut again and pinched the bridge of her nose between two fingers.

Breathe, Charli. Just breathe.

The will reading had gone just about the way she'd expected it to. Horribly.

William Evans, their father's lawyer, had read part two of Michael Carlson's will. And just as she'd predicted, it was her turn. He really was going to go through each of them in turn.

Breathe. Breathe. Just fucking breathe.

It wasn't working. Normally she was so good at self-talk and calming herself down. Then again, her world had never been spun on its head quite like this.

"Charli?"

Kat squeezed her hand, but she still couldn't open her eyes. "Charli, look at me."

Begrudgingly, she did, but the room started to spin again, her sister's head blurring in nauseating waves. So, she shut them again just as quickly.

"It's not that bad, Charli." Kat squeezed her hand tighter. "Really, you'll be able to do this, no problem."

No problem?

That was easy for Kat to say. She wasn't only incredibly talented at hair artistry, but she was legitimately brilliant. She'd graduated with honors. Hell, they *all* had. All but Charli. She hadn't even—*no!*

She really couldn't afford to let herself go down that particular line of thinking at a time like this. She needed to focus. She needed to…

Just breathe, dammit!

Finally, Charli took a breath and pulled the air deep into her lungs. She held it for a moment and released it slowly. And then did it again. And again.

Once she was feeling a bit more grounded, she tried to open her eyes again.

Kat was watching her closely; concern lined her features. "Are you okay?"

Charli nodded, although she wasn't entirely sure it was true.

The women sat on the small couch; their brothers were behind them, discussing the terms of the will in hushed whispers. Asher's frustration at the entire situation was only barely under control.

Charli ignored them and looked in front of her at her father's solid oak desk where the lawyer, William Evans, and their father's longtime assistant and best friend, Steven Larson, sat. The lawyer's eyes were averted, busying himself with reading something in front of him. Steven, however, was watching her. When she made eye contact, he offered her a smile.

"I'm here to help you," he said, just loud enough for her to hear. "Your father believed in you. That's why—"

"Can we just go over this one more time?" Asher interrupted. "This can't be legal," he continued. "Did he really do this for all of us?"

"I'm not at liberty to discuss part three of the will until—"

"So yes," Asher answered his own question. He threw up his hands in frustration and slammed his hand against the solid wood door to push it open.

"Asher, don't—"

"Let him go." Chase interrupted Craig before he could stop their brother. "He needs to calm down. But we need to help Charli figure this—"

"There's nothing to figure out." Charli took another deep breath, hoping like hell this would be the one that would help her make sense of what had just happened. "Dad wants me to start a business." The words were sour on her tongue. "And double my investment capital." She swallowed hard against the lump in her throat. "And until I do…"

There'd been a number of scenarios that Charli had entertained in her mind. Her dad could have asked almost anything of her, and she would have done it happily. That's just who she was. Agreeable, happy, friendly, *always has a smile on her face because she doesn't have a thought in her head*, Charli. But this. A business?

At least he hadn't set a time limit on this impossible task, because it was obviously going to take forever. Literally, any of her other siblings would have been better suited to such a task.

Which was exactly why he'd given it to her.

There was a reason she'd been given the cushy job at Carlson Corp and that everyone encouraged her to spend her time digging in the garden and playing with her flowers. There was a reason that no one expected more of her. Because she couldn't give it. She just wasn't capable of more. No one knew that with more clarity than her father had. Everyone else just kind of *thought* it. But Michael Carlson had *known* with certainty that his eldest daughter was funny and friendly and pretty. But she was *not* smart.

"We'll help you, Charli." Craig had moved so he sat on the other side of her. "We all have lots of experience running a business. We'll tell you everything we know and—"

She shook her head. They'd all heard William list the conditions of her task. She had to do it alone. Nothing more than general labor was acceptable. Charli was to be the one to conceive, execute, and operate the business. Including but not limited to procuring locations, inventory, or labor, signing and negotiating contracts, and any other major business decisions.

Breathe.

The word and the simple reminder grounded her.

She inhaled deeply through her nose and exhaled slowly as she ran through the situation one more time.

"Okay," she said after a moment. "If that's everything, I'm going to get going." Slowly, she stood from the couch and straightened her sweater while she waited for the lawyer to dismiss her.

"Everything else you need, including the investment check, will be with Steven Larson." The lawyer handed the other man a folder. "He will act as your advisor and oversee that the terms of the clause are carried out properly."

"Whenever you're feeling up to it, Charli. You have my number."

She somehow managed a genuine smile for the man who'd

been a part of her life as long as she could remember. "Thank you, Steven. I just need a little time. I'll be in touch."

Charli half expected one of her siblings to try to stop her, but thankfully they all let her pass. They trusted her to know that she wasn't going to treat the situation lightly. After all, each clause that was read had the same stipulation: If they failed in their task, the entire Carlson estate, including the big house and Carlson Corp, would be sold, with assets to be distributed evenly among preselected charities. They'd lose everything.

"You're sure you want to do this?"

It was the third time Symon asked. And the third time she'd nodded.

"Because we can talk—"

Charli set the shot glass down on the bar top hard enough to splash the clear liquid over the top. "If you try to suggest one more time that we talk about…" She waved her hand. "All that shit… I'm going to find someone else to drink shots with me." She narrowed her eyes and looked around the bar. "There's got to be at least one willing man to—"

"Okay." Symon conceded, as if there were any other choice. From the moment they'd walked into the Brickhouse, Charli had at least five different guy's eyes on her. She would have no problem finding someone else to drink with her, and there was no way in hell Symon was going to let that happen. Especially not with the state she was currently in.

Charli was on a mission.

She was already on her third shot, and they'd only been there for less than thirty minutes.

He'd managed to pull a few details from her about how the

will reading had gone. The gist of which was that it had been, "*Bullshit.*"

"Ready?" Charli lifted the shot glass high in the air. She didn't wait for him to reciprocate before she downed the tequila and shoved the lime in her mouth. "Woo! That was a good one."

"Better than the last two?"

She laughed, but there was no humor in it. "Are you going to drink that?"

Before he could answer, she'd grabbed his untouched drink and tossed it back as well, not bothering with the lime this time.

He gestured to the bartender for a glass of water and reached out for Charli's hand. "We don't have to talk about what happened tonight." He had to tread carefully, but maybe he could distract her enough that she didn't order any more drinks. "Why don't you tell me what you've been up to for the last few years? I've missed you."

The frown that had replaced her beautiful smile since they'd left the big house slipped a little. "You know what, Sy?" She took a deep breath. "I missed you, too." She nodded a little, as if she'd just come to a decision. "You have excellent timing, too. Because you're back just in time to watch me fail spectacularly."

Oh shit.

That was not the direction he was hoping the conversation would take.

"That's not going to happen, Char. There's a reason your father did what he did."

She shook her head, not listening.

"I'll help you. It won't be so bad. It might even be kind of fun."

He didn't know anything about running a business. Probably even less than Charli did. After all, he'd spent his entire adult life on the ski hill, chasing a dream instead of a career. *A lot of good that had done him.* He pushed the self-deprecating thought that was becoming a little too familiar away. There would be time for that later; he needed to focus on Charli and making her feel better.

"You can't help me." Her words were slurred, and she dropped her head into her hand. "I need to do it by *myself.*" She used air quotes but didn't lift her head.

"Okay." Symon tried again. "Then you'll do it yourself. You're smart and—"

"Ha!" Her head snapped up, and she shoved a finger in his face. "But that's where you're wrong. I am *not* smart."

"Just because you didn't go to college doesn't mean—"

Her laughter was sharp, short, and cutting. "College? Hell, I didn't even—hey, there's Lauren." Distracted, she spun in her stool so fast, she would have fallen off if Symon hadn't reached out and grabbed her waist.

With his free hand, he slid the glass of water the bartender had left closer. "Here, have a—"

"Remember your wish?" She flipped around to face him, her blonde hair spinning around her head. "Earlier today?"

Oh yes. He definitely remembered. Although babysitting the beautiful woman while she was drunk wasn't really what he had in mind. Somehow, he didn't think it was a good idea to point that out right then.

"I do," he said. "But what about *your* wish?"

She froze, her mouth falling open for a moment before she spoke again. "I didn't make one." Her eyes pierced him. "Not that it would have mattered. It's never worked for me."

"Ever?"

She gave him a sad smile and shook her head.

Symon wanted to ask her what she meant by that.

But there was no point asking her anything in her current state. Even if she would let him get a word in edgewise, he wasn't likely to get any straight answers out of her.

"But *your* wish can come true." Her eyes sparkled, and she twisted in her seat to look at someone over his shoulder. "I have just the beautiful woman for you."

"Beautiful woman?" He shook his head. "For *me*?"

"Yes, silly." She waved at someone behind him. "You wished for a beautiful woman to keep you company while you were in Trickle Creek, and I have just the woman for you."

"Charli." He leaned in and put his hand on her knee. "I was talking about spending time with—"

"Lauren!" Charli slipped from her barstool and threw herself into the arms of a woman. "I'm so happy to see you."

"Hi, Charli." The woman pulled back and held Charli at arm's length. "You look like you're having fun." She smiled good-naturedly. "Are you celebrating something?"

"Just the fact that my life is about to—"

"Hi." Symon jumped up and held his hand out before Charli could talk herself back into the dark hole again. "My name's Symon. I'm an old friend of Charli's."

"Yes." She wrapped her arm around Symon's waist and dropped her head to his shoulder briefly. "This is Symon. And *you* are the beautiful woman he can spend time with while he's in town."

The other woman looked visibly and understandably confused, but she'd obviously decided to play along. She stuck her hand out. "Nice to meet you, Symon. I'm Lauren."

Charli did some sort of fist pump in the air, obviously proud of her matchmaking skills, and moved back to the bar, where she called the bartender for more shots.

"Sorry about that," Symon said while they were alone for a

moment. "She got some bad news today and instead of talking about it, we're doing this."

Lauren, who under any other circumstance would be the type of woman Symon would take notice of as she was a tall, striking brunette with beautiful green eyes, nodded with understanding and shot a concerned look toward their friend. "The will reading?"

He nodded.

She grimaced and sucked in a breath. "And she won't talk about it?"

"Not unless talking involves copious shots of tequila." Symon ran a hand through his hair and tried to catch the bartender's attention, but the man behind the bar only shrugged as he poured the shots. "She's had at least three. Maybe four. To be honest, it hit her pretty hard and the last thing she needs is more."

Lauren nodded. "I've never known Charli to drink much more than a glass or two of wine. Tequila shots seem a bit extreme."

"I should probably just take her home."

"No one's going home." Charli rejoined them and thrust shot glasses into their hands. "We have to celebrate first."

"Celebrate?"

"Char." Symon turned and put his shot on the bar behind him before reaching for hers. "I don't think we need to—"

"We need to celebrate you two," Charli said, ignoring him. She reached past him for the drink he'd just put down. "To the new couple." She held up the small glass, and Symon smoothly took it from her. "I'm an amazing matchmaker." She tried to look at him, but it was clear her eyes couldn't focus on anything. "Right?"

Getting her home and tucked in with a glass of water and

an aspirin would be the best thing for her, and if he needed to agree with her to do that, he would.

"You sure are, Charli." He moved so his arm was wrapped around her, and she could lean on him. She rested her head on his shoulder again; this time, her eyes closed.

Symon locked eyes with Lauren, who nodded in understanding as he gestured to the door.

He threw some bills on the bar for the bill and started to move Charli toward the door.

"She's so nice, isn't she, Sy?" Charli's words were barely decipherable as they made their way out of the bar and into the car.

He continued to agree with her comments until she fell asleep on the short drive back to her little farmhouse on the edge of town. He'd never actually been there, but he'd remembered when she'd texted him to let him know she'd bought it.

He carried her easily in his arms up the walk and through the unlocked door—no one in Trickle Creek ever locked their doors—and up the stairs to what he assumed was her bedroom. An orange tabby cat was asleep on the pillow, but she moved to the end of the bed as soon as Symon laid Charli down.

Careful not to wake her, he took her boots off and slipped her coat from her before pulling a blanket over her. In the bathroom, he found a bottle of headache pills and put them, along with a glass of water, on her bedside table.

When he brushed the hair back from her cheeks, her eyes fluttered open. "Sy?"

"I'm here, Charli. I brought you home."

She reached for his hand and held it limply. "Thank you."

"Anything for you, Char." He tucked her hand under the blanket again.

"She's beautiful, isn't she, Sy?"

"Who?"

Her eyes weren't open, but her lips curled up a little in a drunken smile. "Lauren. She's your beautiful girl."

Symon didn't respond, but he didn't move either. He waited until he was sure she was asleep again before he bent and pressed a soft kiss on her forehead. "You're my beautiful girl, Charli. Only you."

Chapter Five

WHEN CHARLI finally opened her gritty eyes the next day to find herself fully dressed and in her own bed, she promptly squeezed them shut again against the bright mid-day sun streaming through her window.

"No." She groaned and rolled over, unwilling and mostly unable to face the day. Not with her brain pulsing as though it might burst out of her skull at any moment and her stomach churning.

Lilly, sensing she was at least somewhat awake, mewled and hopped up on the bed to nuzzle in under Charli's chin.

"Come on, Lilly." Normally the cat's purrs were comforting, but that's when they didn't sound like a jet engine preparing for take-off in her bedroom. She tried to nudge the cat away, but she was unmovable.

With a grunt, Charli opened her eyes again and spotted the bottle of painkillers along with the glass of water on her nightstand.

At least drunk me thought ahead.

But as she swallowed the pills and dropped her head to the pillow again, a flash of the night before came back to her.

Symon.

Had he put the pills there? Had he brought her home and tucked her in?

He must have.

Embarrassment flooded through her at the thought of how out of control she'd let herself get the night before.

Charli almost never drank hard alcohol because when she did, headaches, hangovers, and blackouts were what greeted her the morning after. And this occasion was clearly no exception.

Lilly curled up next to her, mercifully taking her purring away from her ear, and Charli promptly fell back asleep.

When she woke, hours later, her sister stood over her.

"What the—"

"Sorry, Char." Kat didn't look sorry. "I didn't mean to scare you. Symon called and said you might need a little...well, he said you were pretty drunk last night."

She groaned and tried to roll over again, but her bladder had other ideas.

"Meet me downstairs in a few minutes," Kat said. "I have just the thing to make you feel better."

Charli doubted that very much. Mortification for the way she'd behaved the night before—at least the bits and pieces that started to come back to her—mingled with the memory of the will reading and her task ahead, and she couldn't decide whether the hangover was making her nauseous or her life.

With little other choice left, Charli dragged herself to the bathroom.

When she finally made it downstairs, the scent of fresh coffee greeted her. Kat dropped a paper take-out bag on the table in front of her as soon as she sat down. "Eat."

Charli lifted her eyebrows, not sure that the idea of food was a good one.

"It will make you feel better," Kat insisted. "Trust me."

Charli wasn't used to letting her little sister take control, but she didn't have the energy to argue. Much to her surprise, once she finished the greasy breakfast sandwich and the cup of strong black coffee Kat had put in front of her, she felt a little better.

At least physically.

"Do you want to talk about it?" Kat joined her at the table.

"Which part?" Charli dropped her head in her hands and rested her elbows on the table. "The part where I'm single-handedly responsible for our family's future collapsing, or the part where I was a total jackass to my best friend I haven't seen in years?" She looked up. "What should we start with?"

Kat chuckled and shook her head. "Considering only one of those things is actually a thing, let's talk about Symon."

"They are both very many things."

Kat waved away her objection with a swipe of her hand. "The caveat of the will is whatever. Let's talk about—"

"What do you mean, *it's whatever*? It's everything, Kat. It's huge. It's—"

"Not a big deal." Kat shrugged. "You can do this with your eyes closed, Charli."

If her head wasn't already throbbing, Charli would have screamed in frustration. She could not handle one more person telling her how it was no big deal to start a business *and* make it immediately profitable. Or else. Businesses failed all the time. And those were started by people who actually knew what they were doing.

She took a deep breath and inhaled slowly before lifting her coffee mug to her mouth.

"You're forgetting that I'm not you," she said when she was able to trust herself not to lose her patience. "And I'm not

Craig. Or Chase. Or Asher. I'm not a businesswoman, Kat. And I've never wanted to be one."

That last part wasn't entirely true. She'd always secretly envied her siblings and their individual successes. She was also unwaveringly proud of each of them. What they'd all been able to do was nothing short of impressive.

Kat tilted her head, so her ponytail fell over one shoulder as she assessed her big sister. "Well," she said after a moment. "Looks like you get to be one anyway."

Charli groaned and dropped her head into her hand again. "You can at least let me feel sorry for myself for a full twenty-four hours, Kat. Come on."

Her sister laughed and tipped back in the chair. "No deal. You have things to do. Besides, I didn't come here to talk about that whole thing."

"You didn't?"

Kat's grin widened. "You know I didn't." She leaned forward across the table and wiggled her eyebrows. "Talk to me about Symon."

Waking up in his childhood bedroom always took Symon a second to adjust to. His grandma hadn't changed a thing since he'd left. Including the twin bed that wasn't big enough for his six-foot-two frame when he was a teenager and definitely wasn't adequate now that he was a fully grown man. As he stretched out the kinks in his back, Symon made a mental note to buy himself a new bed if he planned to stay longer than a—how long *was* he planning to stay?

He'd told Charli he was moving back for a bit, but truthfully, he had no idea how long he was going to stay or what he was going to do while he was there. Besides conquer the ski hill. That was his only goal.

That, and spend time with a beautiful woman. He shook his head, remembering his impromptu wish at the falls and the way Charli had misinterpreted it. Of course, why would she think any other way? He'd never been man enough to tell her how he felt about her when they were kids. Worse, he'd been a total asshole on the one occasion she'd tried to tell him about her feelings.

It was ridiculous and selfish to think she might still feel the same way after all these years. Why would she?

He only had himself to blame for letting her get away. And he had, for years. But time had a way of softening even the hardest things, and they weren't kids anymore. *Maybe things could be different now?*

Even as he let the thought slip into his head, he dismissed it.

It was clear from not only Charli's words at the falls but also the determined way she'd tried to set him up with her friend the night before that nothing had changed.

Symon picked up his phone and sent her a quick text.

Hope you feel okay today. Call me later.

There was a good chance that she didn't remember much about the night before anyway.

Symon could hear Gran in the kitchen, singing to herself and no doubt cooking up a huge feast for him, but he wanted to freshen up first. He'd only had the chance to say a quick hello to her the day before when he'd arrived and before he'd attempted

—and failed—to go for a ski. Symon hadn't intended to stay out so late on his first night back, but then there was the dinner with the Carlsons and…well, he owed Gran some quality time. Another reason to spend more time in Trickle Creek.

Gran wasn't getting any younger, and she was his favorite person in the whole world. She'd always been his one constant. No matter how crazy things got in his life, she was there. Steady and sure. His rock. And just like the little house where he'd grown up, with the white siding and bright-blue trim, where nothing ever seemed to change, Gran never seemed to age. At least, it was easy to think that from a distance, over his weekly Zoom calls. The reality was much harder to ignore once he came face-to-face with it.

If he looked past the surface, things *were* starting to change. It wasn't only the house that was starting to show its age.

Showered and changed, Symon was greeted with the delicious scent of freshly baked apple pie when he stepped out of the bathroom.

Apple pie?

For breakfast?

Not that he was complaining. It had been way too long since he'd enjoyed a slice of Gran's homemade pie.

"Good morning, honey." She greeted him with a hug the moment she saw him. "Did you sleep well?"

"Actually, that bed is—"

"Nothing quite like being back in your own bed, is there, hon?"

"No." Symon shook his head with a chuckle. "There's really nothing quite like it." He poured himself a cup of coffee and inhaled deeply. "It smells delicious in here, Gran." His eyes locked onto the pie, cooling on the rack next to the oven. "I can't tell you the last time I had pie for breakfast." He grabbed a fork from the drawer. "But I'm not going to say—"

"No." She smacked his hand away. "Do not touch that pie."

"It's not…" He turned to see Gran frowning at him, hands on her hips. "For breakfast?" He finished the question lamely.

"Of course it's not for breakfast, Symon."

She pursed her lips in disapproval, and Symon noticed for the first time that she was wearing lipstick. Her hair was done in what could only be described as a fashionable style, not that Symon knew anything about senior citizens' hairstyles. And she wore jeans and a silk blouse under her apron. Gran looked…good.

"You can have yogurt and granola." She moved swiftly through the kitchen, gathering things, before putting a bowl and a spoon in front of him. "Pie is not a breakfast food," she chastised him. "I taught you better than that. Don't tell me that's what they're feeding the athletes these days, because if they are I'll go down there and—"

"They're not, Gran." Symon tried not to laugh. "I promise, I'm eating healthy." He eyed the tub of plain yogurt before glancing toward the pie. "I actually can't remember the last time I *had* a piece of pie. I bet one piece won't be—"

"No." Gran stood between him and the pie. "That pie is for Jim."

"Jim." The use of their next-door neighbor's name caught him off guard. "Why does Jim need a pie?"

It must have been his imagination that Gran blushed. Gran never blushed. Especially not over a man. In fact, Symon couldn't remember his grandmother ever even mentioning a man beside his grandfather, who passed away shortly before Symon was born.

"Jim works very hard to help me out around here," she said. "He insists on shoveling the walk and keeping the lawn mowed in the summer. Just last week, he hung some shelves for me in the bathroom there, and I appreciate it very much."

"I'm sure you do." He wiggled his eyebrows and laughed when she smacked him with a tea towel. "Seriously, though." He added a healthy dose of granola to his bowl of yogurt. "I think it's great that Jim helps you out so much. It makes me feel better to know someone is looking out for you when I'm gone."

He often felt guilty for not visiting Gran more, but being hours away from a major airport, Trickle Creek wasn't exactly convenient to get to for a quick weekend visit. And when he was actively training with Team Canada, there wasn't as much downtime as he'd like.

Symon truly did appreciate Jim Muldoon. He and his family had lived next door for as long as he could remember. His kids were all about ten years older than Sy and had moved away long before he did. Gran told him when Jim's wife passed away from cancer about six or seven years ago. It had been sad, but also a blessing that she was no longer suffering. Symon always thought it was nice that he and Gran were able to keep each other company, and having someone to look out for her made it possible for Symon to stay away and follow his dreams.

Of course, he'd never considered that there was anything more than friendship between the two.

Until now.

Symon ate his granola slowly while he watched Gran closely. It wasn't just the makeup and the haircut that was different. She looked much younger than her almost eighty years. More than that, she looked happier. Maybe happiness had a lot to do with the aging process. If that was true, Symon must look at least forty.

"You look great, Gran."

She turned from the sink, a towel in her hand, and grinned. "Thank you, hon. I feel great."

"Seriously," he said. "I can't remember the last time I saw you look so…carefree and young."

Her laughter filled the room. "Age is just a number, honey."

Symon nodded and went back to his breakfast as he took inventory of the familiar kitchen.

"You look tired, Symon." The smile fell from her face, and she took the seat opposite him at the table. "Are you doing okay?"

Gran always had a way of seeing right through him. She had some sort of sixth sense when it came to him and knowing what he was going to do before he did. She'd raised him ever since he was not quite two years old, and his parents had died in a car accident. He'd been the only survivor of the two-vehicle crash on that snowy winter night when an oncoming truck had lost control on the ice and spun into his parents' vehicle. Safe and secure in his car seat in the back seat, Symon had come out of the crash without so much as a scratch. He'd been far too young to remember his parents or the crash, but on more than one occasion while driving on a particularly stormy winter night, he could swear that he could hear the familiar riff of his mom and dad's favorite song, "Take Me Home, Country Roads."

It would be so easy to confess the truth to Gran about how he hadn't been able to come back from his skiing accident the way he wanted to. How scared he was that he'd never ski again. How coming home was his last hope in figuring out how to move past his block and move on.

Instead, he put on his brightest smile and reached across the table for her hand. "I'm fine, Gran. Just really glad to be home." He squeezed her hand and hoped she believed him. There was no point in worrying her. He'd sort it out before there was anything to worry about.

She hesitated, and Symon thought she might call him out.

Instead, she smiled and patted his hand. "And it's good to have you here. The house feels better with you in it."

When she went back to fussing around the kitchen, Symon took a look around at everything that hadn't changed since he'd left. Everything was just as he remembered it, from the quirky collection of ceramic cows she kept on the shelf over the sink, to the olive-green linoleum on the floor. And even if the circumstances for his visit weren't the best, it really did feel good to be home.

Chapter Six

IT TOOK Charli just over thirty minutes before Kat finally believed her that there was nothing to tell when it came to Symon except that he was back in town for a visit. They were friends. The same way they'd always been.

Kat finally left, but she didn't look any more convinced when she did than she was the first four times Charli insisted there was nothing between them.

Truthfully, her head hurt far too much to work too hard at changing her mind. Kat had always insisted that she and Symon were made for each other, and she never could understand why her older sister wasn't in a relationship with the skier.

Maybe Charli should have attempted to explain it to her properly, but Kat was just a kid when Symon left town after graduation, and Charli didn't feel like reliving her mortification or her heartbreak by telling anyone, even Kat, that not only had she finally worked up the courage to tell Symon she had feelings for him but that she'd also put herself *way* out there by kissing him at Fairy Creek Falls.

She hadn't planned to kiss him right then, or ever. After all, she'd spent years talking herself out of ever telling Symon about her feelings, convincing herself that it was better to have him as her best friend than lose him forever because he didn't feel the same way.

It had already been such an emotional day, and for that split second as they sat side by side with their feet in the creek the way they'd sat hundreds of times before, Charli suddenly didn't care what the consequences would be.

She reached for his hand and when he looked at her, she kissed him. He was surprised at first, but only for a second before he wrapped his hand around the back of her head and deepened the kiss. It was at that moment Charli knew it would be okay. *Everything* would, because Symon felt the same way about her that she'd always felt about him, and even if that was the only thing in her life that was okay, that was enough.

Charli had kissed boys before then, but they were usually sloppy, fumbling affairs with no real feelings that left her feeling empty and more than a little awkward. But kissing Symon was different. She felt *all* the things; her body lit up in ways she didn't fully understand, and her heart felt as if it were about to burst out of her chest. But then it was over. He'd looked at her with confusion in his eyes, apologized, and run off, leaving her sitting in their special place that, in the blink of an eye, no longer felt so special. Later, she learned that he'd left town. Without saying goodbye.

It had taken her a long time to get over her hurt, but eventually, when he'd come back to visit his grandmother and they'd run into each other in the plaza, she had. In the end, she couldn't be mad at him for not reciprocating her feelings. That wasn't fair.

That was still true even after all these years. There would always be a part of her that would love him, but she was a grown woman now and fully capable of pushing those feelings down in order not to ruin their friendship. That was more important. Especially now that he was back in town, and she was...well, she was in need of as much support as she could get.

When the throbbing in Charli's head receded enough for her to think straight, she went in search of her cell phone. She only had vague memories of getting home from the bar the night before, but she remembered Symon bringing her home, and she owed him an apology for letting herself get so out of control.

There was already a text from Symon waiting for her from a few hours earlier.

Hope you feel okay today. Call me later.

She smiled and shook her head as she responded.

I'm alive. Barely. So sorry, Sy. Thank you for taking care of me.

I'll always take care of you. That's what friends do.

Friends. Right.

I'll make it up to you. Promise.

His response came right away.

How?

Charli thought for a moment before responding. She'd been pretty drunk the night before, but she hadn't forgotten everything. Symon wanted a beautiful woman to spend time with, and she'd introduced him to Lauren. Of course, babysitting your drunk friend wasn't the best way to make a connection, but she could fix that and spend a little time with her best friend.

I haven't forgotten about making your wish come true. Meet me in the plaza tomorrow at one and I'll show you everything that's changed since you left.

Charli waited while the three little bubbles appeared on the screen and then disappeared. Finally, his response came.

Sounds good.

She sent her reply quickly.

It's a date.

A date.

He laughed at her choice of words and shook his head. Charli was nothing if not good at keeping him guessing.

Logically, Symon knew she didn't mean anything by her word choice. He wasn't an idiot. It was just a turn of phrase. Something people said. It didn't mean they were going on an *actual* date. Still, she had mentioned that she hadn't forgotten about his wish. *Maybe that meant that she—*

The sharp ring of his phone cut through his thoughts. The smile on his face disappeared when he saw his coach's face appear on the screen.

He shook his head and moved to reflexively press the red circle that would send the call to voicemail. But he hesitated, his gloved finger hovering over the button while the snowflakes fell from the sky, landing on the screen.

Symon looked out across the mountain and took a deep breath. After breakfast, he'd gone for a drive and somehow ended up back at the ski hill. This time, he hadn't parked in the main lot but had instead taken the service road farther up the hill to a secret parking spot that only a few locals ever knew about. He'd left his vehicle and wandered toward the path that led straight out to the ski hill. He'd been standing in the trees, watching, ever since.

With a sigh, Symon pressed the button to accept the call. "Alan."

"Finally." His coach sounded obviously relieved. "This isn't the first time I've called, Sy."

He didn't bother answering.

"How are you doing now that you're home?" the coach asked. "Is it helping?"

Symon didn't want to lie to the man who'd been like a father to him for so many years, but he also didn't want to disappoint him any more than he already had. He took a deep breath and exhaled slowly. His silence told Alan everything he needed to know.

"Have you put your skis on yet?"

"Yes." It was an honest answer, but he didn't bother to volunteer the fact that he hadn't actually *skied* on them.

"That's excellent. How did it feel?"

"It was…" He sighed heavily. Symon was a terrible liar. "It didn't go much further than that."

"You didn't ski." It wasn't a question, and despite the fact that Symon knew Alan was trying to hide his disappointment, it was laced through his words anyway. "Sy, don't go out this way. You're better than this"

Symon dropped his head and kicked at the snow. His coach was right, and they both knew it.

"Have you thought any more about that sports psychologist I suggested?"

"I don't need a shrink, Alan."

"It's not like that. She can help you get past whatever it is that's blocking you and get you back out there."

Symon doubted it. The only thing that was going to get him back out on the hill was himself. No amount of talking to a stranger was going to help. "I'll do it, Alan. Soon."

"When?"

That was part of Alan's coaching style. He held his skiers accountable for their goals, big or small.

"I have some things I need to take care of." Symon inhaled. "Within the week, okay?"

"You got this, Sy. I believe in you." Symon squeezed his

eyes shut against the coach's words when he added, "Even if you don't right now."

Everything about Charli's home and surrounding property had been designed to create the perfect sanctuary. Her farmhouse was a heritage home situated on two acres of land on the edge of town. She'd painstakingly restored the house by herself, with a lot of help from her brothers Asher and Craig. But the design and the vision had all been hers. It had taken Charli almost five years of sanding wood floors to bring back their natural rustic beauty. Painting walls with a combination of soft whites and light blues created an airy, welcoming space. And she'd searched out just the right furniture pieces at antique stores, garage sales, and thrift stores to create her eclectic aesthetic.

As much as the inside of her home was her retreat from the world, it was the flower fields that filled a growing portion of the land around her home, and especially her greenhouse and workshop in the yard, that were Charli's favorite spaces.

Nothing grounded Charli like digging her hands deep into the earth. The smell of the fresh soil between her fingers calmed her in a way that nothing else could. With her gardens currently frozen and covered in snow, the next best thing was her greenhouse for clearing her mind.

And with the lingering effects of her hangover finally retreating, that's exactly what she needed to do. Getting drunk had served a purpose, in the sense that she was able to temporarily forget about her troubles. But they certainly hadn't gone anywhere, and with a deadline hanging over her, she didn't have the luxury of time to squander away feeling sorry for herself. She needed to think, and the best way to do that was by getting her hands dirty.

Lilly followed her into the greenhouse, disappearing as soon as they got inside. The cat liked to lay under the warming lights next to the seedlings, occasionally wandering over for pet and ear scratches. Charli pulled an empty planting tray from her shelf and put it on her workbench, where she filled each hole with her carefully blended mix of soil before moving to the box where she kept her meticulously labeled seeds. She was trying to decide between white ammi or poppies when she heard the crunching of tires on snow that announced a vehicle in her yard.

She paused, her hands on the seeds, and took a deep breath.

Charli knew without looking that it would be Chase. Besides Kat's visit earlier in the day, she'd had a check-in phone call from Craig, and a text message from Asher, letting her know that she could take as much time off from the office as she needed in order to take care of *things*.

She'd already guessed that Chase would make a personal visit. Despite her eldest brother moving away when they were still young, they'd always been close, sharing a special bond that the others didn't have. Chase and Charli were the only two siblings who had a different father. Michael Carlson loved them from day one and had adopted them both when he married their mother and raised them as his own..

Charli left the box of seeds, brushed her hands on her jeans, and called for Lilly, who lazily lifted her head before putting it back down, uninterested in joining Charli out in the cold.

"I'll be back, silly kitty."

"Hey, sis." Chase stepped from his SUV. He was dressed somewhat casually in jeans paired with his black wool coat. He'd come a long way from the suits he'd worn when first arriving back in Trickle Creek.

Charli couldn't help but smile at the more relaxed and much happier version of her brother in front of her.

"Took you long enough."

He laughed. "I heard that you might not be up for visitors this morning."

She groaned. "I suppose everyone in town has heard about that."

"Probably not everyone." He wrapped her in a quick hug when she was close enough. "But Annie heard about it at the Bean Bag this morning from—"

"I don't want to know." She held up a hand. "Gotta love a small town."

Charli shook her head because as much as she did love her small town, there were a few aspects she could very much do without. Like her drunken antics being the favorite coffee shop gossip. Still, it could be worse.

"I could use a cup of tea, sis."

A few minutes later, they were seated at Charli's kitchen table, two cups of tea in front of them. The leather portfolio Chase brought with him was a stark contrast against the white-washed wooden table. She eyed it suspiciously before turning her gaze to her brother.

"You're feeling better now?"

She shrugged, because she knew he wasn't talking about the hangover.

"It's not that bad, you know." Chase got right to the point. "I know it feels like it's—"

"It's huge." She cut him off. "All you had to do was stay in town. You didn't actually have to *do* anything."

"I had to volunteer and get involved in the community."

She narrowed her eyes at him. They both knew that volunteering had led to spending more time with Grady, Annie's nephew, which in turn led to the strengthening of their relationship. It was *not* the same situation, and they both knew it.

"Still," Chase said. "You know it wasn't easy on me."

She knew that, too. Chase had spent his entire life running from Trickle Creek and the family he'd never felt like a part of. Staying in town had been about the worst thing their father could have asked him to do. It also turned out to be the one thing Chase had needed more than anything else.

She flinched at the idea that starting and running a business would be good for her in any way. It felt a whole hell of a lot more like punishment than anything else.

Charli took a deep breath and exhaled slowly. "Do you think it's just us?" It was a thought that had popped up more than once over the last twenty-four hours. "That Dad gave us these *missions* to complete because we're not really—"

"Don't finish that thought, Charli," he warned. "Don't even *think* about finishing that sentence."

Charli swallowed hard, ashamed of herself for even thinking such a thing.

Despite the misguided feelings Chase had as a child, their father had never treated them differently from their half-siblings. They were all one family. Never in her life had Charli second-guessed that. Until the day before.

"Sorry," she said after a moment. "It's just...first you and now me. It kind of feels like we're being singled out."

Chase chuckled. "I really don't think that's the case. I suspected this might happen, but now I'm sure of it. Dad was always about fairness when it came to all of us." He held up his hands to stop her protest. "It took me awhile to figure that out, but I get it now. Which is why I'm pretty sure we're all going to have a turn. I think we all feel the same way, Char. It's not just you."

That made the most sense. "You're probably right." She

dropped her head. "I think I just wanted some sort of explanation for why he would do this to me. It's just…" She could not tell her brother her secret. Not now. Charli focused on the steam rising from her mug. "I don't think I can do it, Chase. I know you all think this isn't a big deal because you've already done it. But I'm not smart the way the rest of you are."

"Sure you are. Besides, Char. You don't really have a choice."

Her head shot up, and she glared at him.

"I mean," Chase continued, "I didn't really have a choice either, did I?"

Technically, Chase *did* have a choice. Just the way she did. *Technically.* But her brother was right. There was no choice when it came to their father's caveats, and he must have known that when he included them in his will. The Carlson siblings might have their differences, but the one thing they all had in common was each other and how much they cared about one another. There was no way any of them would let the others down.

Not trying was never an option. She'd known that from the moment the lawyer said her name, and no amount of tequila or pretending it wasn't happening was going to change that.

She pressed her lips together. "I know," she said finally.

Without another word, Chase opened the portfolio and slid out a manila envelope.

"What's this?"

"Steven asked me to bring it by for you," he said. "He also told me to let you know he's there for you whenever you need. We're not supposed to help you out, but you're not alone."

She nodded and with one finger, pulled the envelope closer. She took a deep breath and tore open the seal.

Inside was her start-up check with a note.

Charli,

You can do anything you put your mind to.

I believe in you.

Love, Dad.

She swallowed back the lump in her throat and lifted the note to see the amount of money he was asking her to double. $10,000.

Any amount seemed insurmountable, so Charli couldn't decide whether that figure was a good or a bad thing.

"Well?"

She'd almost forgotten that Chase sat across from her.

Charli slipped the check, along with the note, back into the envelope. "Well, Dad seems to think I can do it."

Her brother's smile was kind. "We all do, Charli."

Chapter Seven

"THERE'S REALLY nothing else you need me to do?" Symon came up from the basement where he'd just spent the last hour moving boxes from one shelf to another. A make-work project if he'd ever seen one. He wiped his hands on his jeans. "I want to help you out, Gran. Put me to work."

"You are such a big help, hon." She smiled in a way that was suspiciously similar to patronizing when she looked up from her crossword puzzle. He couldn't help but feel that Gran was digging deep to find Symon chores to do that would make him feel important and keep him busy. It turned out that Jim next door was a whole lot more helpful than Symon had originally thought.

In fact, Symon was very quickly getting the impression that Jim spent quite a bit of time at Gran's house. He didn't say anything, but he'd noticed the men's slippers tucked into the front closet, and the bottle of whiskey—that he knew his grandmother didn't partake in—in the kitchen cupboard.

Not that he cared. In fact, Symon thought it was a good thing. Jim was a nice guy and Gran deserved to be happy. Still, he'd wait for her to tell him about it when she was ready. After all, they were both allowed their secrets.

Still, if Gran didn't have anything major for him to do, he was going to quickly run out of excuses to stay away from the ski hill.

"Maybe tomorrow I can take down the Christmas lights."

"You will do no such thing." She put her puzzle down and stared at him. "You know very well I like to enjoy the lights through the month of January."

He tried not to smile.

"Winter can be so dreary. You absolutely will not take my lights away from me."

Symon laughed. "You know I wouldn't." He moved to kiss her on the forehead. "But if you can think of anything else at all you need doing that Jim hasn't already seen to," he added with a wink, "put it on my list so I feel useful while I'm here."

"Symon, you are always useful." She reached for his hand, which he took in his. "I love having you around. I missed you so much."

"I missed you, too, Gran." He sat on the couch next to her. "I'm sorry I've been gone so long."

She waved away his protests. "Your job is to go out and live your life, hon. That's how it's supposed to work. You were never meant to stick around just to look after me. You were always supposed to go out into the world and follow your dreams."

She had a way of looking right through him, as if she already knew the real reason he wasn't with the team in the middle of the race season. He tried to pull away because if she couldn't look into his eyes, she wouldn't be able to see the truth.

"I like having you home right now, Symon. And you should stay as long as *you* need to."

Her grip was strong; he couldn't look away.

"But it's only temporary. Your injury was only a setback, not a permanent state."

She knew.

Maybe she didn't know exactly what the problem was, but she knew there *was* a problem. Gran knew him in a way that was unlike anyone else.

Even so, Symon knew she wouldn't push. And he was grateful for that.

"Thanks, Gran," he said after a moment. "And if you're sure there's nothing else for me to do today, I'm going to head down to the plaza for a bit. I'm meeting up with Charli so she can show me some of the changes since I've left. Do you remember—"

"Don't insult me." She sat upright and dropped his hand, the serious mood gone. "You know very well I know who that dear girl is. She is absolutely the sweetest woman, and just like her father was, a true gem of a person. You know, I always thought that one day you'd—"

"We're just friends." Symon cut her off as he jumped up and moved for the door. There was no point in trying to explain their relationship to Gran—again. He'd tried once when they were teenagers. It probably didn't help that he couldn't fully explain why they'd never dated. Still, it wasn't a conversation he wanted to get into minutes before seeing the subject of discussion. "Call or text if you need me to pick anything up from the market, Gran."

He closed the door behind him before she could say anything more. But he did catch the trail of her laughter before the door clicked behind him, reminding him for the second time how well she knew him and the things he didn't have to say.

The walk into the plaza only took a few minutes, and with the sun warming his face and taking the chill out of the day, Symon was glad he'd decided not to drive. Particularly because this way he could take the treed trails down the hill and avoid looking at the ski hill.

He let his thoughts drift to Charli's last text message. *It's a date.* Logically, he knew she hadn't meant it that way. But then again, she had also mentioned that she hadn't forgotten about his wish to spend time with a beautiful woman.

Despite every reason not to read anything more into it, Symon couldn't help but let his thoughts run away from him a little bit.

Despite the stupid way he'd run away from her all those years ago, Symon *did* have feelings for Charli. He had for years. Feelings that he'd been too young and stupid to articulate. Which was why he'd run. After graduation, when Charli suggested they go to Fairy Creek Falls, Symon agreed. Not because he thought Charli was going to kiss him or declare that she had feelings for him. But because he'd been trying to find the perfect time to tell her he'd been asked to join the junior team and was leaving for training camp the next day.

He'd been sitting on the news for weeks, trying to figure out how to tell her. He'd planned it out a million different ways in his head. But nothing seemed right, because up until he'd received the call that he'd made the team, Symon had been trying to figure out how to work up the courage to tell Charli how he felt about *her*.

But when she'd kissed him, every single thought in his head vanished. All he could think about was her lips on his and how soft they were. And then the little gasp she made when he deepened the kiss. And then there was no thinking at all, just doing because it was all he'd ever wanted to do. He'd never wanted it to end, but even through his teenage-boy lust and love-filled brain, he knew it had to.

So, he'd pulled away and then, like a total asshole, he'd run off and left her there without so much as a word. The next morning, Gran drove him into the city so he could catch a flight to Vancouver to start training.

For weeks after, he'd picked up his phone to call her or text her, but he could never think of what to say that would make it okay. Next to Gran, Charli was the person he cared most about in the world, and he'd hurt her because he was too scared not to.

Had the past fifteen years made him any braver?

He wasn't meant to meet up with Charli until one, and the walk had taken far less time than he'd expected, which meant once Symon got to the plaza, he had twenty minutes to kill. Before he could decide what to do to kill time, the decision was made for him.

"Symon? Symon Scott?"

He spun around at the familiar voice. "Brody?" Symon's face split automatically into a smile at the sight of his old friend. "Brody Lyons? Holy shit. It's been years, man. What the hell are you doing here?"

The two men moved into a back-slapping hug.

"I think I should be the one asking that question, don't you?" Brody took a step back, the same wide, toothy grin Symon remembered from when they were kids on his face. "What the hell are *you* doing here, Sy? Shouldn't you be winning gold for our country right about now?"

Symon forced a chuckle. "Not this year," he said. "I'm still in recovery training for the knee injury." He slapped his knee, the lie getting easier and easier to tell. Hell, maybe if he told enough people, he'd start to believe it himself.

"Damn, that was one hell of a crash." Brody shook his head. "But you're young and strong enough, you should be back in the mix by now. What gives?"

Symon worked to keep his face as neutral as he could. "Just not up to full strength yet, I guess."

Brody eyed him strangely, but fortunately didn't push. "And they let you come home to train on your home hill? Damn. I can't think of anything better."

"Right? I can't wait to get out there." Another lie.

"You're living the dream, Sy." Brody flipped his mop of hair off his face.

They'd been on the ski team together growing up, along with Brody's four other brothers. But because Symon and Brody fell into the same age group, they spent most of their weekends racing each other through the trees and moguls and flying over jumps, just like the kids he'd seen in the lift line the other day.

"Sure am. But what about you? What are you up to these days?"

"What am I doing? Dude!" Brody pretended to look shocked. "Come on, I'll show you. I mean, it's not skiing for Team Canada, but it's a pretty sweet gig. Come on in."

"In?" Symon turned around to see the storefront he'd been standing in front of. "Peak to Path?"

"Welcome to the shop." Brody held the door open, and Symon walked in, his old friend behind him. "About five years ago, I had this idea to open a store," Brody began as Symon took in the rows of skis and snowboards, shelves of boots and helmets, and racks of clothing and gear. "With tourism picking up, it seemed like a wasted opportunity not to give the people what they wanted."

"Skis and boards?"

Brody nodded, beaming. "And in the summer, bikes. As you

know, the trails around here are killer. We do sales and rentals as well as tune-ups and repairs, of course."

"Of course." Symon shook his head in wonder. The Brody he'd known as a kid spent more time on the mountain than in the classroom. The fact that he'd grown up to run what looked to be a thriving business was impressive. "You've done this all by yourself, Brody? Damn. I'm impressed."

"Thanks, man. But no, I didn't do it totally by myself. Preston's my business partner."

"Preston?" Symon remembered the youngest of the Lyons boys as the annoying little brother that he and Brody were often tasked with taking up the chairlift on the weekends and making sure he didn't get lost on the ski hill. Not that they hadn't tried to lose him. At least a little. "I don't think I've seen him in years."

"Probably not," Brody agreed. "You've been gone a long time, man. But it's good to see you. How long are you sticking around for this time?"

Symon didn't know how to answer that honestly; instead, he shrugged. "A little bit, anyway. Until this old leg can start to keep up."

The lies were getting way too easy to tell.

"Sounds like that'll give us time to hit the hill and get a few runs in, for old times' sake. And you'll never guess who took over the coaching gig for the junior freestyle team."

"Don't tell me it's you."

Brody laughed. "You got it. The kids would love to see some of your moves."

"For sure."

The idea of skiing with Brody sent ice through his spine. There was no way. He couldn't even get on the friggin' chairlift. The last thing he needed was to have a panic attack with his old friend standing there. Never mind the drama if he actually made it to the top of the mountain and had to come *down*. Just thinking about the possibility sent his heart racing, and the store became unbearably hot. He unzipped his jacket and took a deep breath. Symon knew from experience that if he could just slow his breathing, he would have a chance at hiding his anxiety.

He turned, pretending to examine a row of skis, and took another breath before responding with yet one more lie. "Gran is keeping me pretty busy with chores around the house and I'll have to check with my rehab schedule, but——"

"You say the word, Sy. Anytime. I only need five minutes' notice to get up there. And really, if you're going to get back out there with the team…"

"You're right. I'll need all the help I can get." Symon nodded and his heart rate slowed, the panic attack avoided for the time being. Although, standing in a shop surrounded by reminders of the sport that had cost him everything probably wasn't the best idea. "But I should probably run. I'm meeting Charli any minute and——"

"No shit? Charli Carlson?" Brody wiggled his eyebrows. "Don't tell me that after all these years, you two finally——"

"Are friends." He interrupted him. "Just as we've always been." It obviously wasn't just Gran who had ideas about the two of them. Still, the last thing he needed was people talking about them as if they were a thing. At least not until there was a *thing* to talk about. And that definitely remained to be seen.

"In fact, she introduced me to a friend of hers last night," he added in an effort to stop whatever rumors were about to start swirling. "Her name is Lauren. She's quite——"

"Lauren?" Brody looked as if he'd been slapped. "Lauren Westfield?"

Symon shrugged. "Maybe? I don't know. I didn't catch her last name. In fact, I——"

"She owns Earth's Own, just down the way."

"Oh, you know her?" It was a stupid thing to say. Everyone knew everyone in Trickle Creek.

Brody nodded slowly. His eyes had a far-off look, but he didn't elaborate.

"You're not dating her or—"

"Nope." Brody shook his head and busied himself behind the counter. "Definitely not dating. She's a nice girl. Have fun."

Symon had the distinct impression that he should press his old friend for a bit more information about the situation because there clearly *was* a situation there, but at that moment he caught a glimpse of Charli out the front window. Besides, it had been awhile since he and Brody had been at the *talking about women* stage of their friendship. A long while.

"Okay," he said after a minute. "It was great to run into you, Brody, and congratulations on the store. Really."

The broad grin once more returned to his old friend's face. "So good to see you, man. And I can't wait to hit the slopes with you. Soon, okay?" He pointed his arm at Symon, who mirrored the gesture as he backed out of the store without answering the question or committing to anything he couldn't get out of.

Chapter Eight

CHARLI'S favorite place in the plaza was the gazebo that had been placed directly in the center of the main square. The Carlson siblings had it constructed a few months earlier and dedicated to their father, who'd been the savior of the town of Trickle Creek years earlier when he championed the arrival of tourism to what had once been an industrial town. Ever since the dedication ceremony, Charli found herself drawn to the huge wood structure whenever she was in town. It always felt as if her father was there with her when she sat beneath it.

Now, though, it felt different.

Chase was right: she didn't have a choice when it came to her father's request; she never had. And she'd already wasted enough time trying to drink it away. That wasn't her style. Maybe she didn't have the skill sets of her siblings when it came to business, but the one thing she did have going for her was her positive attitude. Charli had optimism in abundance, even if it had taken a brief little holiday. She'd figure this out.

And the sooner, the better.

The day before, after Chase left, she'd worked first in her greenhouse and then her workshop well into the night, but she was no closer to an answer on what she should do that would have the potential to double her money than she was before. The only business experience she even remotely had was running her flower stand at the summer farmers' markets, and that wasn't about making money. She only charged a few dollars for her bouquets because people insisted they couldn't take them for free. If she could give them away, she would. Flowers were meant to bring happiness and smiles to the faces of the people who saw them. It was her hobby, and she loved to be the creator of those smiles.

She closed her eyes and tipped her head up to the wooden beams overhead. "I wouldn't object to a little guidance here, Daddy."

"How come every time I see you these days, you're talking to yourself?"

Charli's eyes flew open to see Symon standing under the gazebo, his hands stuffed in the pocket of his parka and a grin on his face.

"Don't get me wrong… I think it's kind of cute."

Cute? A flush warmed her body, and she was glad she had a scarf wrapped around her neck to bury her face in and hide her blush. "Are you saying you think I'm cute?"

His laugh echoed. "I said the whole talking to yourself thing was cute. In a kind of crazy for a grown woman talking to herself, sort of way."

Charli rolled her eyes and moved forward to give her friend a hug. He smelled good. Like a familiarity she couldn't quite pinpoint. Unwilling to let herself linger in his embrace, she pulled back quickly.

"Hey, I wasn't trying to eavesdrop." Symon shifted from side to side. "But were you just talking to—"

"My dad?" She nodded. "Yup. I know it's silly, but I feel kind of close to him here and sometimes, I just…"

"Hey." He held up a hand to stop her. "You don't need to explain anything to me. I was too young to remember my parents, Char. But it's still hard." He reached for her hand. "I'm really sorry about your dad. I know how close the two of you were."

She felt tears pricking at her eyes, and she did not want to cry. "Thank you," she managed. "It is hard. I thought it would get easier with time, but it's been six months and it still feels like it was yesterday that he was here."

Before she could protest, he pulled her into his arms again and squeezed. "It's okay. And there's no timeline for these things.

She tried to shake it off. "Well, now that he's given me this impossible task, I guess I have something else to focus on besides the fact that he's gone."

"It's not impossible." He tilted his head and gave her a look. "I've never known you to be so pessimistic about something like this. What gives?"

For a minute, she thought about confiding in him that she wasn't smart enough and never had been and her father knew it, but she didn't want to dampen the spirit of their afternoon any more than they had.

"It's a lot right now, and I really miss him." It wasn't a lie; it just wasn't the full truth. "And...I really don't want to talk about it anymore." She gave him her brightest grin. "Unless, of course, you want to tell me why exactly you're really back in Trickle Creek right now in the middle of ski season when you should be out there winning races."

Symon froze, swallowed hard, and nodded once, a small smile on his face before he shook his head. "Why would you think there's a reason other than I need to rehab my knee?"

"Because I know you, Symon," she said without hesitation.

"And I know something else is going on. You're just not talking about it."

"And I don't want to, either."

She wasn't going to push it, just like she appreciated the way he wasn't going to push her. "Fair enough. But when you're ready to talk about the real reason, you know where to find me."

"I sure do." He clapped his hands together. "Now, can we start this tour or what?"

"Let's start from the beginning then." She cleared her throat and waved her arms with a flourish. "So, Symon. Are you adjusted to being back in Trickle Creek yet?"

Symon shrugged and lifted his arms dramatically. "Of course. It's like nothing's changed." They both laughed, because that was the furthest thing from the truth. "I bet you see that, too, hey? Not much is changed in all the years you've been here."

She felt the smile slip from her lips, but she looked down before Symon noticed. In fact, forgetting about everything that *had* changed, even for a little while, would be a good thing. A *very* good thing.

"Hey. I wasn't trying to—"

"You didn't do anything." She stopped him quickly. "It's fine."

"It's not fine." He put his hand on her arm. "I know it must have been hard." He shook his head. "No, I know it's still hard. And now with this—"

"Let's put that on the list of things we're not talking about today." She tried, and failed, to make her voice light.

"I didn't realize we had a list going."

"Seems we do." She nudged him with her elbow. "You talk and I'll talk." It was a safe promise because she knew him well enough to know he wasn't going to talk about whatever was going on with him. At least, not yet.

"Maybe later." He shrugged. "But for what it's worth, I don't know why you're nervous about your dad's request. You're smart and—"

"Let me stop you right there." She held her hand up. "All this fresh air must have affected your memory. Because I was never the smart one. I left that to my siblings."

It was so long ago that Symon likely didn't even remember the way she struggled in school, or the barely average grades she got, never mind the failing grades she got in math. She'd hid it well back then, focusing her energies on school council and spirit events, but she'd never dwelled on her low grades, and she'd certainly never advertised them.

"Well, for what it's worth, it's going to be fine, and I know you're sick of hearing it, but it will be okay, Char. You've got this."

"You're right." She looked up to see him watching her with concern in his eyes. "I am sick of hearing that." Despite herself, she smiled. "And before you ask, no. I haven't come up with any earth-shattering ideas about how I'm going to pull it off. But I will." She bit her lip before she added, *Because I have to.* "Now... since we've both established that we don't want to talk about our problems right now, can we just get on with our afternoon?"

"Our *date*, you mean?" He wiggled his eyebrows, and she rolled her eyes.

"Anyway," Charli looped her arm through his, "are you ready to see all the things that have changed since you've been gone?"

"We could start with this." He used his free arm to encompass the huge wooden gazebo they stood under. "I've never seen this before and it clearly has magical powers that rival

Fairy Creek Falls. I've never seen you—oh no." Symon pulled away so he could turn and look at her. "Are you crying? Don't cry. I was kidding…I didn't…just don't cry."

"I'm not crying."

Symon tilted his head and tried not to smile. "It sure looks like you're crying."

"I'm not." She still wouldn't look at him as the tears continued to fall.

She turned away and pressed her mittened hands to her eyes, in an effort to will the tears that had been threatening all afternoon to stop. This was not at all how she'd hoped their afternoon would go.

"Charli?" He dragged out her name. "Look at me."

She shook her head like a child, and he laughed. But she still wouldn't look at him. It was ridiculous. She hated crying in public, and she especially hated crying around Symon on what was supposed to be their fun afternoon together. She took a deep breath, but the tears just kept coming.

"Charli."

This time when he said her name, it was softer. He put a hand on her shoulder and forced her to turn toward him, where he pulled her into another hug. This time, she didn't try to cut it short or pull away from his embrace. She let herself sink into him, inhaling his familiar scent. *Soap. Ivory, or something traditional like that. It must have been what his gran used.* She breathed deeply and pressed her head against his chest while he held her.

The tears slowed, but they still didn't stop. Finally, when she thought she might have a bit more control over her emotions, she took a step away. "I'm sorry, I don't really…I'm fine now."

"Hmm…" He lifted her chin with one finger and used

another to wipe her cheeks. "If you say so," Symon said slowly, never taking his eyes from hers.

Something about the way he looked at her calmed her. She let herself take a deep breath and then another. Finally, the tears stopped completely. He wiped her cheeks again. It was such an intimate touch that it sent flutters through her core and warmed a spot deep inside her.

"This gazebo..." She took a big breath and continued. "We put it here in honor of my dad at the kick-off to the Carlson Classic this fall, and I always feel a little closer to him when I'm here, which I know is dumb. But then today I felt—" A sob choked her words. "Ugh, sorry." She shook her head. "Today I felt kind of mad at him."

Instead of telling her that was ridiculous or that she shouldn't be angry at the dead, or that her father loved her or any of the other platitudes that Charli knew to be true but didn't want to hear, Symon simply nodded. "That makes sense."

"I know I—wait. What?"

"It makes sense," he repeated. "I know how much you loved your dad and how special he was to you. No one would ever challenge that. But it's okay to feel a lot of different things, too. Especially considering..." He waved his hand and shrugged. "You know."

"I do know." She laughed a little and sniffed hard. "I'm sorry about all...well, it's been an emotional few days. I guess, I—"

"Don't apologize," Symon said.

His hand cupped her cheek now. It was such a natural, comforting touch, Charli closed her eyes a little and sank into it.

"Your ability to feel so deeply is amazing," he continued. "I've always loved that about you, Charli."

Her eyes sprang open at the same time that he dropped his hand from her face.

"I just meant that I love how you're not dead inside, like me." He laughed a little, and the moment was gone.

For a split second, Charli let herself wonder what it would have been like if Symon hadn't moved away. *Would they be together now? What if he hadn't run away from her that day and instead, he'd stayed and—no.* There was no point in letting herself go down that path again. It had taken her too long to come back from it once before. The truth was, they were friends, and it was better that way because it would hurt a whole lot less when he left again.

"You are *not* dead inside." She pressed a hand against his chest. "There's a heart in here, I just know it."

"Careful." He snatched her wrist and pretended to look shocked. "I can't risk my secret getting out."

She rolled her eyes, but Symon had accomplished his mission and her tears dried up completely.

"Better?"

"Much." Charli nodded.

"Are you sure we're not talking about the—"

"My offer still stands." She eyed him seriously. "If you're talking, I'm talking."

He laughed, breaking up the moment. "I guess we're not talking."

"Sounds like a deal to me." She took his hand and squeezed. "Now, can we go have some fun and pretend that neither of us have any worries at all?"

Spending the afternoon with Charli made two things crystal-clear for Symon. One, his hometown had grown and changed more than he'd even realized while he'd been gone. There were so many new shops, restaurants, and cafes that Charli assured him were filled with tourists all year round. The transformation had begun when Symon was still young and living there, but it hadn't seemed as noticeable at the time. Probably because he was a teenager and completely self-absorbed with his own life, which consisted primarily of skiing.

And, two, he still enjoyed spending time with Charli as much as he had when they were kids.

Maybe more.

No. Definitely more.

Being with her was easy and comfortable but at the same time, it felt new and exciting. She constantly made him laugh, and he found himself smiling more than he had in months as she pointed out each new storefront and spent hours browsing through shops, laughing and teasing each other. He ran into a few familiar faces, but there were more people he didn't know. A detail Charli was determined to change as she introduced him to what felt like every single person they came across. If he'd wanted to keep a low profile, there was no hope for it now. Charli proudly introduced him as Trickle Creek's skiing superstar. Considering that the real reason he was in town was because he *couldn't* ski, it wasn't a title he deserved, not even close, and more than once Symon considered breaking their pact not to talk about their problems and just telling Charli the truth about why he was in town. That he'd been given an extended recovery period, not because his knee still needed rehab but because he had some sort of mental block and was too much of a chicken shit to even get on a chairlift, let alone ski again.

But he couldn't bring himself to ruin what was turning out to be a very good afternoon by telling her anything close to the truth. It could wait. Besides, he hadn't forgotten her tears from earlier. She had her own worries and stress, and she very obviously didn't want to talk about them today either. Never mind the fact that he knew Charli well enough to know that she'd take on his worries as if they were her own, and it would only add to her worries.

"So?" Charli said when they finally managed to sneak away from the Bean Bag and the half dozen familiar faces inside that they'd been drawn into conversations with for the last hour.

"So, what?"

"What do you think about Trickle Creek?"

Symon could see the pride in her eyes as she asked the question. Truthfully, no one loved this town the way Charli did. "I think I've had a lot of fun with you this afternoon," he answered honestly. "I missed you, Charli." Worried he'd said too much, he quickly raised his paper cup of hot chocolate to his lips and took a sip. "Is it just me, or did this get even more delicious since I've been gone?"

She laughed. "Don't tell me in all your international travels you haven't found a better hot chocolate than this?"

He shook his head and took another sip to keep himself from saying something completely inappropriate. He really *had* enjoyed every moment he'd spent with Charli. He may have made some big mistakes recently, but screwing up this friendship after only just rekindling it was not going to be one of them. Which meant he needed to keep his mouth shut when it came to whatever it was he was starting to feel for her—again. Even if he really, really didn't want to.

"Hey," he said as he turned, his drink still on his lips. "What's this? You said every shop in town was thriving."

They stood across from a storefront he'd only vaguely registered earlier. There were giant signs in the window announcing a closing-out sale. "Everything must go?" He turned to Charli. "That doesn't seem to be thriving."

Charli moved so she stood shoulder-to-shoulder with him. "That's Marta's shop," she said, as if he should know who Marta was. "She's a potter?"

Symon shrugged and pressed his lips together, making her laugh.

"Marta was definitely here when we were kids," she said. "But she sold mostly at the market in the summer. And I could see how pottery wasn't high on your radar back then."

"Can't say it was."

"Too bad," Charli said. "She makes beautiful things."

She looked back to the shop, and Symon followed her gaze. "So, if her stuff is so great, why is she going out of business?"

Symon didn't know anything about running a store, but from what he could gather from Charli's enthusiastic tour, every single shop, with very few exceptions, that started up in Trickle Creek did extremely well.

"She's ready to retire and spend more time with her grand-children," Charli said. "She's had the shop for a few years now, and I think it's done really well, but apparently she doesn't love the business side of things and just wants to focus on pottery." She took a sip of her drink and nodded. "I can relate," she added wistfully.

It was a strange comment, and Symon waited for her to elaborate, but when she didn't, he asked, "You can relate to wanting to spend time with your grandchildren?"

Charli almost spat out her drink as she spun to face him. "No, silly," she said when she recovered. "I can relate to not wanting to focus on the business stuff." The smile quickly faded from her face again. "Not that I'm going to have a choice."

"Why don't you take the shop?"

"The shop?" Her eyes wide with question, she gestured to the store in front of them. "You think I should take the *shop?* And do what exactly, Sy?"

He didn't think it was nearly as crazy an idea as she seemed to. After all, she needed a business, and there was one right in front of them. "I don't mean to bring it up because I know we're not talking about it today," he said carefully. "But you do still need a business idea to make a bunch of money on, don't you?"

"I'm not a potter, Sy."

"I know that. And I didn't mean that you should take over *her* shop. I just thought maybe you could..." He didn't know what he thought. In fact, he really didn't have any advice at all, but the store going out of business seemed like a bit of a sign. "Maybe we could think about it together," he finished lamely.

She stared at him and then back to the picture window before shaking her head in resignation. "I wouldn't know the first thing to put in there," she said. "And *that* is the whole problem."

He wanted to say something to fix it and make all her troubles go away. More than anything, Symon wanted to wave a magic wand and make it all better for her. "Hey." An idea popped into his head. "Maybe we should go back to Fairy Creek Falls, and *you* can make a wish."

She looked at him incredulously. "You're kidding, right? Please tell me you're kidding."

He shook his head as seriously as he could. "Not at all."

"I don't mean to burst your bubble, Sy. But the wishes..." She shrugged and pressed her lips together. "They're not really real. They never come true."

"I beg to differ."

She took a step back, her eyes still wide with skepticism. "Is that what happened for you? Did you wish to be on Team Canada?"

He swallowed hard but he couldn't deny it. He *had* wished for that.

"Huh." She took a moment and assessed him. "I stand corrected."

"But to be fair..." He took a breath and exhaled slowly. "Not *all* of my wishes have come true." He tapped his left knee. "And now maybe they won't." They'd made a promise not to talk about their troubles, at least not now, but it felt like the right time. And the more time he spent with Charli, the more he wanted to open up to her. "The truth is, Char, I don't know if I'll ever win another race, let alone gold at the Olympics."

"Don't say that, Sy."

"It's true. The crash was so..." He shook his head to clear the memory of the pain that had ripped through his leg when he'd landed in a twisted mess.

"Hey." She wrapped him in a tight hug. "I can't even imagine how hard it must have been to work your way back from that. And I saw the..." She shuddered. "It looked awful."

"It was."

"But you're strong."

Not strong enough.

"And you'll get back to where you need to be, Sy. I know it."

"I had to come back here because—"

"You're going to win, Sy. It will be a wish that comes true."

"I sure hope so."

She smiled but it didn't reach her eyes the way he knew it could. "Char." Symon took her mittened hands in his and squeezed. "My wish came true today, too."

"Your wish?"

"I wished to spend my time with a beautiful woman." He pulled her a bit closer. *Maybe it was time, after all these years, to stop dancing around it once and for all? If he just told her how he felt about her, how he'd always felt about her, then maybe they could finally—*

87

"Oh my goodness!" She pulled back and pressed a hand against his chest. "You're right."

He reached for her again. "See?"

"I can't believe I almost forgot, Sy. All this talk about wishes and it totally slipped my mind. Thank you for reminding me."

He tilted his head and narrowed his eyes. "Reminding you of what?"

"I promised to make your wish come true."

"You already have, Char."

"That doesn't count."

"I assure you, it very much counts."

She looked at him for a moment, as if she were trying to figure out exactly what he was trying to say. Hell, he'd make it crystal-clear if that's what she needed. After an entire afternoon with her, hearing her laughter, seeing her smile, and the way she lit up at the simplest things when she showed him around, had brought up feelings he hadn't felt in a very long time and every single reason he'd told himself about why it couldn't work between them didn't matter. He needed to shoot his shot.

"Charli, today has been one of the best afternoons that I can remember and—"

"Just wait." She clapped her hands together. "It's about to get better, because remember Lauren?"

"Lauren?" He shook his head. "No. That's not what I…I mean, yes. I remember her. But—"

"That's her shop." Charli spun around and pointed to the natural food store they hadn't been in yet. "I know you met her the other night, but I was…well, it didn't count. And I *did* promise you a beautiful woman for you to spend time with, so let me introduce you properly."

He studied her face for any traces that she understood what he'd been trying to tell her.

"You want me to get to know your friend? Really?"

He watched her carefully, but the smile on her face only got brighter. "Of course I do, Sy." She shrugged and the knit cap with the ridiculous, but super cute pom-pom on top bobbled. "I just want you to be happy."

That was the moment that he should have told her he *was* happy. That *she* made him happy and more than anything, he wanted to make her happy and maybe together they could—

"You're my best friend, Sy."

And there it was. The reason he wouldn't say anything. He'd had his chance years ago, and he'd blown it. It was his own damn fault, but he wouldn't screw it up again. If having Charli as a best friend was the best he could hope for, he'd take it.

He'd made a mistake once that changed everything; he wasn't about to do it again.

"It'll make you happy?"

"It will." She nodded; the pom-pom bobbled, and her eyes sparkled. "Are you ready?"

As if he had a choice.

He pasted a smile on his face that he hoped like hell was convincing.

"To dazzle her with my charm?" He stood straight and wiggled his eyebrows. "She doesn't stand a chance."

She rolled her eyes. "I guess we'll see."

Symon froze when she hesitated and bit her bottom lip. "What's the—"

Words failed him as she tugged her mitten off, reached out, and used her finger to wipe at the corner of his lip. A shiver rippled through him, but he wasn't cold. Quite the opposite. Her simple touch sparked a flame deep inside him. His cock twitched, a completely inappropriate response as his thoughts instantly moved to sucking her finger between his lips, even for a brief moment before he pressed his lips to—

No.

Friends. *Best friends.*

He swallowed hard and forced the image from his mind.

"There." Her voice wavered a little.

Or was it only his imagination?

"You had a little chocolate just there," she said, her voice quieter, the humor from earlier gone. She swallowed hard. "But I got it."

Symon reached out and grabbed her hand by the wrist, holding it for a moment. "Thanks."

Their eyes locked, and Symon once again had to remind himself that no matter what he *thought* he was feeling, there was nothing more between them. Hell, she was mere moments from setting him up with her friend. If she were in any way interested in him more than just the best buddy he'd always been, Charli wouldn't be so damn excited for him to meet another woman.

He dropped her hand and shrugged. "I guess I'm ready then."

Chapter Nine

OKAY. Maybe it hadn't been the best idea to play matchmaker with Symon when she was already so emotionally raw. Charli could admit that. In fact, she'd almost had second thoughts about going through with the reintroduction after the fun afternoon they'd spent together. She didn't want to share Symon. But that was selfish, and she knew it. Symon deserved to be happy, and having a beautiful woman like Lauren, who was not only gorgeous but smart and funny and interesting, to spend time with while he was visiting, would make Symon happy.

It was his stupid wish, after all.

There'd been a moment right before they'd gone into the store when she'd been sure that Symon was going to stop her and tell her that *she* was the one he was wishing about. But then the moment was gone, and she was happy she hadn't said anything at all because, frankly, she'd had enough emotional turmoil for one day, and the last thing she needed was to make anything awkward between them. If she was going to survive the next few months, she needed the support of her best friend. She did *not* need him running off again, leaving her in the lurch. Or worse, treating her any differently.

No. She needed Symon on her side. As her friend.

And if that meant swallowing her feelings *again*, she'd do it.

There really wasn't much matchmaking involved at all. Lauren and Symon hit it off at once. Of course, they'd met the other night. Maybe they'd bonded over their drunken friend. Either way, they jumped into easy conversation almost immediately, as if they'd known each other for years. Charli hung around for a few minutes before casually drifting away to check out the new arrivals shelf Lauren had recently updated.

Charli pretended to be immersed in smelling every single one of the essential oil blends that were new since the last time she'd been in the store. She took her time painstakingly unscrewing each lid, lifting the bottle to her face, and inhaling deeply. But she wasn't registering any of the scents. All of her attention was focused on trying to listen to the conversation happening at the back of the store by the till.

Lauren's laugh rang out, and Charli glanced over her shoulder to see her friend flip her hair back. Her gorgeous smile lit up her face.

Charli tried not to feel inadequate, but the feelings of not measuring up began to sneak in the way they always did when she let her guard down. When she was younger, she'd worked hard at developing coping strategies to fight her feelings of not being good enough or measuring up to the success of her siblings. Over time, she'd settled into an easy acceptance of who she was and all those *less than* feelings kind of faded into the background.

Until very recently.

The will reading had most definitely brought them all rushing back in vivid Technicolor. Never mind the conversation that was currently happening on the other side of the shop. Only, in that particular case, she was the one to blame for that.

"I'd love to learn how to ski."

Lauren's voice was an octave higher than normal, and Charli didn't have to look to know that she was probably leaning into Symon and maybe even touching his arm. She had absolutely no reason to care about her friend flirting with Symon. In fact, she should be happy that her matchmaking was on point. After all, they were both great people and they deserved to be happy. That was the idea.

Wasn't it?

"I can't believe you don't know how to ski," Symon replied, his voice laced with a matching flirtation that made Charli wince. "You live in a ski town. That's totally unacceptable."

Charli absentmindedly lifted a bottle of new hand lotion tester that she'd never seen before and squirted some into her hands.

"Maybe you can teach me one day?" Lauren asked.

Charli took a deep breath, held it, and squirted more lotion into her hand. It wasn't until she exhaled that she realized she now had a small mound of the cream in her palm. With her free hand, she dug out a tissue and wiped the minty mess away before rubbing the rest in. She shook off the unexpected jealousy and moved closer to the door. She'd done her duty; she didn't need to stick around and listen to every excruciating moment of it. Besides, there were things she *should* be doing. Like saving her family.

"I think I should get going," she called over to her friends.

Lauren looked over, a hand on Symon's arm and her bright smile firmly in place.

They really did look good together.

That thought shouldn't bother her as much as it did. Charli swallowed hard.

"Wait up, Char. I'll come with you." Symon lifted a hand and quickly turned back to Lauren. "It was really nice meeting you again," he said to her. "Maybe I could give you a call sometime?"

"I'll be outside." There was no way she was going to wait around while they planned a date. In fact, Charli had no plans of waiting for Symon at all. It may be true that she'd set it up, but she'd had enough of witnessing it.

There was only so much one person could take.

The moment she'd set foot into the plaza, she started to walk, but she didn't get far before she heard Symon call her name.

Charli forced a smile on her face and turned to see Lauren next to Symon at the door of her shop.

"I thought we were spending the afternoon together?" He pretended to look wounded, and Charli couldn't help but smile.

She walked back toward them. "Sorry." She shrugged. "I didn't know if I should—"

Symon wrapped an arm around her shoulders and squeezed. "Are you kidding? I've been waiting for years to spend time with my favorite girl. I'm not ending our day early." His eyes flashed with warmth, and she couldn't help feeling ridiculous for any shades of jealousy she'd felt a moment ago.

"Oh, hey, Charli, I've been meaning to ask you about those window boxes you did for the Bean Bag," Lauren said. "They're absolutely gorgeous."

"Thank you. Annie said they wanted a change after the Christmas season, so I tried my best to give them a happy new year/winter wonderland feel."

"They're absolutely perfect," Lauren said. "Don't you think, Symon?"

Dutifully, Symon looked to where Lauren pointed. He nodded appreciatively before addressing Charli. "You did that?"

She shrugged. "It's not like it's a big deal."

"Nonsense. You know I'm not really one to notice that type of thing, but Lauren's right. They're beautiful. I'm impressed, Charli."

She flushed at the compliment. "You know I've always loved plants and flowers, and in the winter, I just..." She shrugged. "I work with what I have."

"I think it's a very big deal," Lauren said. "In fact, I'd really like one for the front of my own store. Different, of course, but if you had time, I'd really love something to display. It's so inviting. I'd pay you, obviously."

"Pay me?" Charli laughed loudly. "For a display?" Her laughter cut off abruptly, and she swallowed hard when she realized no one else was laughing.

"Yes," Lauren said seriously. "It's a product *and* a service. And a damned good one."

Charli waved a hand dismissively. "Anyone can do it."

"Not true."

Symon shook his head. "I certainly couldn't."

The idea of accepting money from Lauren for doing something she loved to do seemed ludicrous.

"Seriously, Charli. Let me know how much you'd charge for something like that, and I'll happily pay you."

"I couldn't take money for—"

"I insist."

Her friend was so serious about it that Charli didn't bother to try to dismiss her again. Instead, she nodded and tucked her hands into her pockets. "Okay," she said. "I mean, let me come up with a price and I'll text you, okay?"

Lauren's face lit up. "That's perfect. Thank you." She directed her smile at Symon. "It was so nice to see you again, Symon. I hope to see you soon."

Charli was only half listening as the two of them flirted

their way through their goodbyes. Instead, she started to wander slowly through the plaza, an idea beginning to take form in her head as she looked at the storefronts there. *Was it really that crazy of an idea that Lauren would pay her for a window box display? Would anyone else pay for one? And if they would, how much? Could it be enough? Was it even possible that she could turn her love and talent for flowers and displays into a* business?

The thought stopped her in her tracks.

Beyond the farmers' market, which she loved because of the vibe and energy of all the people milling about, smiling and laughing and looking for community connection, Charli had never considered selling her flowers. But she'd never had to. But now…

Her mind spun.

She'd only ever charged a few dollars for a bouquet and even then, she'd do it for free to see the smiles on their faces that the beautiful flowers created.

But if Lauren was right…if people would actually *pay* her for her arrangements, then maybe…

Charli had stopped walking and was staring at the boughs of pine with silver snowflakes that she'd done for the cafe when Symon caught up with her.

"She's actually pretty—"

"Do you really think people would pay for this?" She cut him off. "I mean, really? Tell me the truth. It's important."

Symon looked confused for a moment as he glanced between her and the window boxes, but he finally nodded. "Yes," he said. "I do think people would pay for it. I mean, Lauren would. I think others would, too. They're really nice, Charli. And…this is it, right? This could be your business?"

She answered him with an absent nod as the ideas flashed through her head. There was still so much to think about, consider, and plan for.

But at least now she had an idea.
More importantly, she had hope.

Chapter Ten

IT HAD BEEN two days since his plaza date with Charli, but Symon still felt a boost from their day together that he hadn't felt in a very long time. He'd texted her a few times to see whether he could help out with her business idea in any way. There was something he still couldn't put his finger on with her. She'd been excited about having an idea to run with, but at the same time she'd seemed so skeptical that she could pull it off.

When Symon looked at her, he saw a smart, brave, creative, and talented woman who could do anything. Charli clearly didn't see that in herself. But why?

Of course, the same argument could be made for himself. Charli believed in him, far more than he believed in himself, and he was smart enough to know that things weren't always as they seemed. After all, he was doing his best impression of a talented, champion freestyle skier, yet here he was, back in his hometown in the middle of the ski season, lying to everyone—including himself—about why he was really there.

When they'd parted ways, they still hadn't actually discussed what was really going on in their lives. But maybe it was time to have those hard talks. Their relationship had always been—*friendship*.

He corrected himself.

They had a friendship. Not a relationship.

A point she'd once again made in her last text to him.

Did you call her yet? When are you going out?

It took him a minute to remember that Charli was talking about Lauren. And really, why was he waiting on that? She was beautiful and smart and funny. Maybe it wouldn't be a love match, but Charli had made it clear that *she* wasn't going to be his love match. And really, it had been awhile since he'd enjoyed a woman's company. And as much fun as he was having with their *Law and Order* marathons every evening, Gran didn't count.

Before he could change his mind, Symon picked up his phone and pulled up the number Lauren had typed into his contacts a few days earlier.

She answered on the second ring. "Symon? I was hoping you'd call."

"Well, then I'm certainly glad I did." A smile crossed his face. "I was wondering if you ever get any time off from that store of yours? And if you might like to grab…" He thought quickly. "An ice cream someday."

"An ice cream? In January?"

He couldn't have said coffee? Or a drink? He shook his head at his lack of game. Clearly, he was out of practice when it came to women. More the reason to ask Lauren out.

"Yes," he said with as much confidence as he could muster, deciding to just run with it. "Charli took me into the Sugar

Shack the other day and there were too many yummy-looking flavors. I've been meaning to go back."

It wasn't a total lie. Charli *had* taken him into her brother Craig's shop. Besides ice cream though, the Sugar Shack had also branched out into specialty hot chocolate drinks and other warm beverages that would be much more suited to the weather.

"I love that place," Lauren said, although he was pretty sure she was just agreeing with him to be polite. "Ice cream sounds perfect. When were you thinking?"

"Well…considering I really have no plans…"

She laughed. "How's this afternoon work for you?"

"This afternoon?"

"I know it's last minute, but my part-time employee is in, and I can sneak off for a bit. Unless you have other plans?"

Symon's gaze went to the window. Again. And the ski hill in the distance. He *had* been trying to work up the courage to give it another try. Maybe the motivation to see Lauren afterward would be a good incentive? Lord knew he needed something to push him to get out there. "What time works?"

"Three?"

That gave him enough time to get in at least one run before he sampled the mint chocolate chip. And that's all he needed. Just one.

"I'll see you then."

"It's a date."

Her choice of words took him off guard.

Get over it.

It was stupid. Charli had no business occupying space in his head, because the key difference between his afternoon with her and ice cream with Lauren would be that one of them was an *actual* date.

Charli had no idea what she was doing. And she still had zero idea how she was going to double any kind of investment. But at least she had even a sliver of an idea. And hope. And that was a whole hell of a lot more than she'd had a few days ago.

She'd barely slept for the last few days, retreating into her workshop, where she'd taken inventory of her supplies and what she'd need to source in order to make a few window displays so she could get started. Working Using what she already had, Charli got to work, creating what would be a spectacular display for Lauren. She used pine boughs mixed with some cedar that she trimmed from the edge of her property as the base.

Lauren used a lot of bright green in her shop logo, so Charli spray-painted oversized pine cones with a grass-green paint that was bright enough to pop against the evergreen foliage and eucalyptus sprigs. And then, for texture, she found some dried twigs in the back of her shed.

It was simple.

Clean and bright. And perfect for Lauren's shop.

Charli still hadn't told her friend how much she'd charge for such a thing and a few internet searches turned up figures that were much higher than anything she was comfortable charging. But to be fair, Charli was uncomfortable charging at all. Her supplies hadn't cost her anything. She'd already had all the pieces. And the arrangement and creative energy to put it together…well, how did you put a price on that?

She needed help.

Steven had already checked in on her and reminded her that although she wasn't able to let her siblings *do* any of the actual work for her, she could ask them general questions or for some advice. And that's exactly what she was going to do.

"Come on, Lilly." She scooped up the cat, who'd been sleeping on her worktable. "We have some work to do, and maybe your Auntie Kat can help me out a little bit."

She left the cat behind and made the drive into town, her basket of supplies in the back of her SUV. She still needed to find some type of container for the front of Lauren's shop, because she didn't have any actual window boxes. Charli envisioned some big metal wash buckets that could be repurposed for future displays as the seasons changed. That was assuming that her friend liked the first display and actually wanted Charli to do more.

Maybe she should offer some sort of subscription or deal? Like, buy three and get one free. That way, the shops would have a steady stream of fresh displays out their front doors, and Charli would have an ongoing business.

Business.

A shiver went through her. *Were window displays really a business? Could it really be that easy? And even if it was, she didn't want anything to be ongoing.*

Charli made a quick stop at Tony's Treasures, the old heritage home that had been turned into an antiques shop. It truly was a treasure trove of all kinds of goodies and had been one of Charli's favorite places to shop when she was looking for just the right pieces for her renovation. It had taken some time to win Tony over. He was known to be a crotchety old man, set in his ways, and it was even rumored that he hated to actually sell anything from his shop, preferring to hoard all his treasures. But Charli had slowly started to earn his trust. It hadn't taken her long to learn that although he might be grouchy and set in his ways on the outside, he was a sweet, lonely old man, who only wanted someone to talk to about the old days and what all of his possessions meant to him.

"Hi, Tony!" She called out her greeting as she pushed hard

against the old squeaky door and let herself into the shop. When he didn't appear right away, Charli wandered through the rooms, checking for any new additions.

Tony's shop was truly a passion project for the old man. Each room in the house had a theme, with the items all arranged in a natural way. In the sitting room, there were old bookcases carefully filled with records and old record players off to one side, while the other had an antique piano with stacks of classic sheet music. In the kitchen were all kinds of old crockery on display, a churn for making butter, and quite a few cooking implements that Charli didn't recognize at all.

Each room was like that, giving the store a cozy feel.

As Charli moved through the shop, she periodically called out for Tony until finally, she heard his answer from upstairs.

"Charli Carlson, is that you?"

"It sure is." She couldn't help but smile. No doubt he was organizing some new finds or rearranging one of the rooms. "Should I come up?"

"No, no," he called. "Be right down."

While she waited, Charli wandered toward the back of the shop, keeping her keen eye out for something she could use either in her house or for future arrangements. She was hoping she'd find what she needed for Lauren's window box display in the back, and she wasn't disappointed.

Three large metal washtubs were stacked, along with an old washboard. Charli carefully moved the washboard and was examining the tubs when Tony finally appeared.

"Charli. It's so nice to see you."

She gave the old man a hug, noticing as she did how thin he felt under his sweater.

"Tony. Are you taking care of yourself?" She stepped back to assess him. "You're eating more than those frozen meals, aren't you? Because I'll have something sent over if you need—"

"Don't push your nose in where it doesn't belong." He was gruff, but he winked at her as he spoke. "I'm fine. Just getting old. And there's no fix for old, Charli Carlson." He pointed past her. "What did you find?"

She spent the next few minutes telling him about what she was hoping to do with the window displays, leaving out the part about the caveat in the will and the pressing timeline she had to pull it off. "So, if you have anything that you think would work well as a container, keep it aside for me, okay?"

He readily agreed, and they moved to the old-fashioned till in the front room so Charli could pay for her items.

"You know." Tony moved slowly and methodically as he typed in the numbers on the old keys. "I like this idea of yours. It's about time you started something of your own."

"Something of my own?"

He didn't look up, so he couldn't have noticed the surprise on her face as he spoke. "Your brothers and sisters, they're all good people."

She nodded but held her tongue.

"And they're all quite smart."

She couldn't disagree with that.

"But you have something they don't, Charli."

"And what's that?"

Tony finally looked up and into her eyes. "You have heart and soul," he said gently. "It's been a long time since I've met someone who cares as much as you, young lady, and that is what will set you apart. No matter what you do."

Charli's first instinct was to brush him off, but his words lingered with her as she packed the tubs into her car and headed toward the plaza.

Heart and soul. Sure, she had that. But was it going to be enough?

Symon parked in his secret spot, halfway up the hill in order to avoid the chairlift and the crowd at the base. He carried his skis to the edge of the run and clipped his boots in the bindings. No problem.

"You got this, Symon. It's just skiing. As natural as breathing. No big deal."

He kept up a running commentary as he used his poles to gently push away from the tree line out onto the run. Instead of tilting his skis down, he froze, parallel on the hill. Fortunately, there wasn't anyone coming.

His breath came fast; sweat began to pool under his arms and run down his back.

Breathe.

Just fucking breathe.

He squeezed his eyes shut. But that was a mistake, because the moment he did so, memories of the accident rushed back. He didn't have enough speed. He wasn't going to have enough air to attempt it; he knew that. Still, a split-second decision to go for it anyway. His skis hit the edge of the jump, and he was in the air. Flying. It felt like slow motion as he forced his body into the flip and then the twist. And then—nothing.

With a gasp, Symon's eyes flew open. He tugged the zipper of his parka down and pulled the goggles from his face as he gulped the air .

"Fuck this."

He planted his pole into the snow, made a quick turn, and slid on his skis back into the safety of the trees, where he quickly unclipped from his bindings and headed back to his waiting truck.

It was progress anyway. He'd actually made it on the hill.

Fuck.

Maybe Alan was right, and he should phone the sports psychologist after all.

Something had to give, and he was going to have to make a call, either way. The question was, would it be to the shrink? Or to his coach when he officially quit the team?

———

The snow had just started to fall by the time Charli lugged the buckets and her basket of supplies to the plaza. She'd decided to create the display in place instead of heading back to her shop. It didn't take long to put it together and when she was finished, she stood back to admire her work and was more than pleased with the final product. The washtubs had been a great idea, and they looked amazing in front of Lauren's shop. She knew her friend would be happy with them, but she still had no idea what she should charge.

The tubs had only cost five dollars each, and she'd already had the supplies on hand. It didn't seem right to charge more than ten dollars for both, but she'd ask Lauren for her opinion, too. Just as soon as she got back. The employee at the till had told her Lauren was out for a bit, and she expected her back within an hour or two. The arrangements would be a nice surprise for her friend when she returned. With time to kill, Charli gathered up her things and headed to the opposite end of the plaza and her sister's hair salon.

Strands was warm and smelled like her sister. A mixture of shampoo and coffee.

"Hey, Charli," Kat greeted her from the chair where she worked on curling a client's hair. "I didn't expect you today."

"I was nearby and thought I'd pop in to say hi to my favorite sister."

Kat threw a grin over her shoulder. "I'm almost finished here and then, if you like, I can give you some waves?"

Charli's blonde hair spent most of its time pulled back from her face when she was working in the gardens or in the greenhouse, but she usually tried to style it when she went into the office. Still, she never could get her own curls as nice as the ones her professional sister could give her. "That sounds nice, Kat. Thanks." Charli took a seat in the empty chair next to her and grabbed a magazine while she waited. But she couldn't focus on the articles and instead pulled her notebook from her purse and started to scribble down some more ideas for arrangements she could potentially sell.

A few minutes later, Kat walked up behind her and pulled Charli's hair from her elastic. She used her fingers to comb it out over her shoulders. "This is a nice surprise." Kat picked up a brush and started to gently pull it through Charli's hair. "You don't usually pop in."

"I'm not usually in the plaza in the middle of the day."

"Something bring you here? Or maybe…" Kat wiggled her eyebrows. "It was *someone.*"

"What are you talking about?" Charli groaned because she knew exactly what her little sister was going on about, and it was ridiculous.

"Is there a certain gorgeous skier keeping you busy, sis?"

Charli glared at her sister's reflection in the mirror. "Symon is—"

"Don't even tell me that he's too busy skiing, because from what I hear, he hasn't even been on the ski hill."

Her comment stopped Charli. "What do you mean?"

"It's a small town…people talk." Kat shrugged. "And from the sounds of that talk, Symon hasn't been skiing. Don't you think that's kind of strange?"

Charli thought it was very strange. Especially when she factored in the way Symon hadn't wanted to talk about what was really bothering him the other day.

His knee.

She'd suspected there was more to his injury and why he was home than he'd let on, but now she knew it.

"That's not why I'm here," Charli said. Even if she did suspect that something was going on with Symon, her sister didn't need to know that. "I was actually hoping I could pick your brain a little." She met her sister's gaze in the mirror. "About the whole will thing." She used air quotes.

"Is that what we're calling it?"

Charli laughed. "It's better than some of the other things that come to mind."

"True." Kat lifted a hank of her hair and twisted it up in a clip to get it out of the way while she worked on the other section. "So how's that all going, anyway?"

"I think I have an idea. Well, the start of one, at any rate. I actually need some advice."

Kat raised her eyebrows.

"Don't worry," Charli added. "I don't want any help. Just advice. You're allowed to give me that."

"Okay." Kat grabbed the curling iron. "Tell me what you're thinking."

Charli spent the next few minutes telling her little sister about her idea for the window displays, including the small list of businesses she'd put together who might be interested.

"And you want to charge ten dollars for these? Hold on."

Without another word, Kat put the curling iron down, left Charli in the chair, and disappeared out the door of her shop without even bothering to put a coat on. She was gone only a few minutes.

"It's freaking cold out there." She grabbed at her arms and gave herself a hug, rubbing at her bare arms.

Charli spun in her chair to face her. "It *is* January, Kat, and you aren't even wearing a sweater. What was that all about?"

"I needed to see these displays for myself." She grinned. "And I want one. Put me on the list." She picked up her curling iron again and spun Charli so she was once more facing the mirror.

"You like them?"

"Of course I do. They're gorgeous." Kat twisted a piece of hair around the iron and held it. "But there's no way I'm paying ten dollars."

Charli's heart dropped. "Too much?"

"Are you serious right now?" In the mirror, Kat's mouth fell open and she stared at her sister. "I mean, I get that you don't have any experience with a business," she used air quotes, "but you're not stupid, Char. How did you even come up with a price of ten dollars?"

Shame burned at her cheeks, and she ducked her head so she wouldn't have to look at Kat. This was exactly what she'd been worried about with the whole *business* thing. She didn't know what she was doing. She had no clue where to begin, and if she couldn't even figure out this one simple thing, there was no way she was ever going to be successful. *It was all just a big waste of time. She should just give up now before anyone got—*

"Charli." Kat spun the chair so they faced each other and squatted so when Charli finally opened her eyes, her little sister was right in front of her. "Talk to me. I'm not trying to make you feel bad. I want to help you be successful. Obviously. And for what it's worth, I think this is the start of what's going to be a great idea."

"The start?"

Kat nodded. "Window arrangements are great, but it's too limited. How many shops are on your list?"

"Maybe ten." Charli shrugged. "I was going to offer a buy three, get one free deal."

"Okay." Kat dragged out the word. "And with that math, at ten dollars an arrangement, how long is it going to take you to hit your goal?"

Do the math.

It wasn't even hard math, but Charli froze. Numbers were going to be her downfall. She just knew it.

"We're allowed to give advice, right?"

Charli nodded.

"My first piece of advice, assuming you want it, is to stop limiting yourself. I know you don't think you're good at math."

Thinking had nothing to do with it. She *knew* she wasn't good at math.

"But it doesn't have to be complicated," Kat continued. "Keep it simple. Make a list of your products and assign them a value. Notice I said, *value.* I'm going to go out on a limb here and say that you chose the price of ten dollars because of what your supplies cost, right?"

"How did you—"

"Because I know you. And it's the same reason you price your bouquets practically for free at the farmers' market during the summer."

"But they don't cost me much to grow. And as for these shop arrangements, the bins only cost a few dollars each and—"

"That's your problem, right there." Kat stood and paced to the other side of her shop, where she grabbed an album. Returning to where Charli sat, Kat flipped it open to a picture of a woman showcasing a shoulder-length dark haircut with blonde highlights. "How much do you think I charged for this?"

Charli opened her mouth.

"Before you answer, I should tell you that the product I used in her hair cost about…twenty dollars."

It had been awhile since she'd had anything more than a trim done to her hair, but even that had cost her about forty dollars, and Charli knew that was the sister discount. "I have no idea."

"Cut, color, and style," Kat said. "One hundred and twenty dollars."

Charli's mouth fell open. "But, it didn't—"

"And this one." Kat flipped to a page with long blonde hair styled into an elaborate braid for a bride. "I didn't use any product except a few bobby pins. One hundred and fifty."

"What?"

"Want me to keep going?"

Charli shook her head. Kat had made her point.

Her sister dropped the book on a nearby table and resumed curling Charli's hair. "The thing you need to remember is that people will pay for talent and convenience. It's not just the flowers or the foliage you're providing. You need to account for that cost, along with how much time it takes you to grow, tend, and care for your plants. But when you're doing your pricing, remember that when someone like Lauren or Annie asks you for a display for their shop, they're asking for your experience. Your eye for what will look good and how to arrange it so it's all beautiful. And they're also asking you to do it for them so they don't have to. And that's worth something as well. Factor *all* of that in along with your cost of supplies to come up with your price."

Charli's head spun. She hadn't stopped to consider any of those things.

Finished with the curls, Kat put the iron down and ran her fingers through Charli's locks, fluffing them out into beautiful waves that fell perfectly over her shoulders. "And don't forget." She picked up a can of hair spray. "People also equate value with price. Like if you charge twenty dollars for a bouquet of flowers, psychologically, they assume they're better flowers than the very same bouquet that's priced for only five."

"That's not true."

"It is." She nodded smugly. "Are you going to sell bouquets, too? I miss your flowers."

Value. Time. Talent. Charli scribbled in her notebook. "They don't really grow in January." She shrugged. "I have a few things, but not enough."

"Too bad. It would have been a nice addition to your product line."

Product line?

"I don't have another client for thirty minutes. Let's go see if Craig is busy. He'll back me up and might have some good advice for you, too."

With her brain already on overload, Charli would have rather retreated to her workshop to think about things, but it was clear that she needed all the advice she could get.

"Ice cream is on me."

Chapter Eleven

SYMON PROBABLY SHOULD HAVE CANCELED his date with Lauren after his spectacular failure at the ski hill, but after a few bites of the maple walnut—he didn't feel he'd earned the mint chocolate chip—he felt better.

Plus, Lauren's smile and easy company didn't hurt either. It didn't take him long to put his problems from his head and focus on the beautiful woman in front of him.

"You know what?" He put another spoonful in his mouth. "I think ice cream in the middle of winter is completely under-rated. I mean, why should it be a warm weather only thing?"

"Right?" Lauren's tongue slipped from her lips and swirled around her cone, catching the drops of melted chocolate before they could fall.

Oh yes. Ice cream could definitely be a year-round treat as far as he was concerned. Not that he had any business thinking dirty thoughts about a woman he'd just met. Especially when nothing was going to happen between them, no matter how much Charli tried to play matchmaker.

The reality was, despite the fact that Lauren was beautiful and smart and funny and really good company, he was having a hard time thinking of her as anything other than a friend—despite the ice cream cone lick.

But why shouldn't he?

There was only one reason Symon could think of. Or more specifically, one *person*.

Charli.

He couldn't get her out of his head. And as much fun as he was having with Lauren, and he really was having a good time, his thoughts kept slipping to his best friend.

"She's something else, isn't she?"

"Pardon me?" Symon's head snapped up. *Had he spoken out loud?*

"Charli." Lauren laughed. "I was just saying how not subtle she was in trying to set us up."

"Oh."

"She's really something else, isn't she?"

Symon nodded and took another bite of his ice cream. "She really is." *In so many ways.*

"You two have been friends for a long time?"

Symon was out of practice when it came to dating, but he knew enough to know that talking about the woman he couldn't get off his mind with the woman he was currently on a *date* with was probably not the best way to move forward.

"Pretty much most of our lives." A smile came to his lips. "And she's always been that way. Kind of like a force of nature. In a good way," he added. "Charli always has this super positive energy about her that makes you want to do whatever it is she wants to do. Ya know?"

"I do know." Lauren laughed. "She was one of the first people I met when I moved to town a few years back. But it didn't take long for her to introduce me to every single person she knew." Lauren leaned in. "Except you. But then again, it sounds like you've kept your distance from Trickle Creek for the last few years."

"It wasn't on purpose." That was true. At least, it had been mostly true. There'd been a brief period after he'd moved to join the junior team that he hadn't wanted to return to town, but that had more to do with his immaturity than anything else.

He'd felt like an ass after running away from Charli and their kiss without even telling her that he was moving. A huge, first-class asshole, and he was too young to understand how to handle the situation properly. So he'd ignored it. Eventually, enough time had passed that when he did come home, he could act like nothing had happened; Charli didn't seem interested in bringing up the past either, and they'd just kind of carried on. Maybe it hadn't been the most mature way to deal with it. But it seemed to have worked.

Or had it?

"That was just kind of the way it happened," he said as his thoughts returned to the present moment.

"Well, it seems to have all worked out now."

He wasn't sure he could agree.

Symon took another bite of ice cream, but it no longer held any satisfaction. He dropped the spoon and pushed away the cup. The truth was, it *hadn't* worked out at all. He was back in town because he'd failed at the one thing he'd been good at. And instead of being with the one woman he'd ever had real feelings for, he was on a date that *she* had arranged for him.

No. Nothing had worked out at all.

"I'm glad we're doing this." Lauren smiled, and Symon instantly felt like an asshole. He had no business leading her on in any way. "But I have to be honest," she continued before he could stop her. "I'm not really looking for anything serious. I'm kind of coming out of a…well, I don't think you can really call it a relationship." She blew out a breath. "Not that you need the details, but I just wanted to be upfront with you. I think it's better if we just stay friends."

"That's great." Relief washed through him. "I mean, it's not great that you're coming out of a...well, that came out wrong." He really did suck at this. "What I'm trying to say is that I'm not really looking for anything serious right now either."

She laughed. "That makes sense."

"It does?"

She shrugged. "I mean, it's none of my business, but you and Charli seem to be..."

"We're just friends." The word sounded wrong on his lips. Of course, they *were* friends, but...

"If you say so."

Something in her voice made Symon push a little more. "What do you mean by that?"

"Can I be honest?"

"Well, we are friends now, right? I expect honesty."

"Makes sense." She took another bite of her ice cream cone before continuing. "It's just that I think it's pretty easy to see that you both...well, you both seem to me to be two people who are a whole lot more than friends and just haven't admitted it to themselves yet."

Symon took a moment to let her words settle in. He opened his mouth to object but closed it again because maybe there was a layer of truth to what she'd said.

"I didn't mean to speak out of turn," Lauren said. "But, honestly, I didn't think it was a secret. If it is, neither of you hide it very well. But then again, maybe I'm wrong. It's happened before."

She laughed, and Symon forced thoughts of Charli from his head to join her in the laughter. It was a ridiculous idea, anyway, that his best friend felt anything more than friendship for him. She'd made that clear to him. Lauren had just read it wrong. After all, a closeness like theirs came with a certain level of familiarity. That's all it was. She was just seeing a deep friendship. He was sure of it.

Almost.

"Changing the subject," Lauren said. "As your friend, I should probably do this, too."

She leaned across the table between them and used her finger to wipe at a spot in the corner of his lip, just like Charli had done a few days earlier.

Only, unlike when Charli had done it, Symon's body didn't react. He didn't want to capture her hand in his and suck her finger into his mouth before—

"Got it."

Lauren held up her finger, but Symon was no longer looking at her. His gaze had gone instinctively to the door when the bells rang, announcing new customers. Two women walked in, brushing snow from their coats, but his eyes locked on only one of them.

Charli.

———

"Oh." Charli tried and likely failed not to look surprised when she walked into her brother's ice cream shop. "Symon. And…" She took a breath, forcing cheer into her voice. After all, what she was witnessing, and what she had *just* witnessed as they walked in, was entirely because of her. "Lauren. What a nice surprise."

She was vaguely aware of Kat behind her, who mumbled something she was probably better off not hearing as she made her way over to where her friends sat. Symon stood to greet her. "I knew the two of you would be a perfect match." She gave him a brief hug and moved quickly away.

She may have practically pushed the two of them together, but she didn't need to stick around to witness it. Well, to witness any *more* of it than she'd already seen. She'd seen Lauren wipe Symon's lip clean right before she'd pulled the door open and walked in, and it had made her guts churn to see such an intimate gesture between them.

"Well, I don't want to interrupt." She didn't make eye contact with either of them as she spoke. "I guess Kat and I weren't the only ones who thought ice cream on a cold day sounded good." Her laughter sounded hollow and tinny, even to her own ears, and Charli knew if she looked, Kat would be rolling her eyes.

"You're not interrupting at all." Lauren pulled out a chair. "Do you two want to join us?"

No. She did *not* want to join them. She wasn't much for torturing herself. *But on the other hand, maybe if she hung around, she could get—*

"No." Kat appeared at her side and put her arm around Charli's shoulders. "But thank you." She smiled at each of them in turn. "We actually have some pretty important business to talk about with Craig."

For the first time, Charli turned to look for her brother, who just appeared from the back room.

"This is a nice surprise." He raised a hand in greeting. "Who knew it would be such a popular day for ice cream." He laughed. "I guess the snow outside just kind of inspires the need for a frozen treat."

Kat groaned at her brother's attempt at humor but didn't remove her arm from Charli's shoulders.

Charli turned back to Symon and, in a low voice, said, "Let's talk soon. I need to talk to you about something." Just because her matchmaking had clearly worked out, didn't mean they'd stopped being friends and as his friend, she needed to figure out what was going on with him and his skiing.

"I think that's a good idea," Symon said.

She didn't have time to read anything into his words before Kat led her to the table in the corner that was farthest away from the happy couple and sat her down. "Do *not* turn around," Kat whispered in her ear. "Let them have their date."

Date. The word stung.

"This is a nice surprise, sisters." Craig joined them at their table. "What can I get you two?"

Kat eyed her suspiciously, as if she thought she might jump up from the table and run back over to the happy couple, but she needn't have worried. She wasn't going to do that. At least, Charli didn't *think* she was going to do that. Truthfully, she wasn't sure what she was going to do. She'd never before felt a surge of jealousy like what she'd just experienced.

"I told Charli I'd buy her ice cream," Kat said. "Cherry cheesecake, Char?"

Charli nodded.

She needed to get hold of herself.

"Plus, our big sis has an idea for her business, and I think she could use a little brainstorming help."

"Really?" Craig clapped his hands together sharply.

Instinctively, Charli turned in her seat despite Kat's warning not to. Symon was looking in her direction. He smiled when he caught her looking, and she spun around again to face her brother.

"That's great news," he said. "Let me get the ice cream and then you can tell me all about it."

The ice cream was delicious, but the brainstorming session with Craig and Kat turned out to be exactly what she needed.

In more ways than one. As soon as she started talking, she'd forgotten all about the date going on behind her.

Well, she'd *mostly* forgotten about it.

She outlined her initial plan, the same one she'd explained to Kat, with a few modifications based on their earlier conversation. She still wasn't sure what her pricing should be. Kat had some very valid points about value, time, and talent, but it was hard to wrap her brain around it all.

"What do you think I should charge?" she asked Craig, who'd been listening intently.

"Well, first, I think this is the start of a great idea."

"Why does everyone keep saying *start*?"

She looked at Kat, who only shrugged.

"Because it is a great start," Craig said. "But there's so much more you can do with this. You need to think bigger."

"I can hardly even think small about it." She shook her head. "And if I can't even figure out what to charge for the shop arrangements, there isn't going to be anything else to think about anyway."

She hated letting herself get down about anything, but Charli was only barely keeping it together as it was. She pinched the bridge of her nose and inhaled deeply before blowing it out slowly.

"Don't panic, Char. You've got this."

Kat meant well, but she was getting seriously sick of hearing those words.

"We're here to help as much as we can. Right, Craig?"

"Absolutely. Do you have a picture of these arrangements? I can give you my opinion as a shop owner what I'd pay, and hell, if it's not a conflict of interest, I'll order some."

She looked up at her brother, who grinned broadly, and couldn't help but smile, too. "I don't have a picture. I should."

"You should." Her sister agreed. "Go look, Craig. There's one outside of the Bean Bag, and Lauren's shop, too."

"Be right back."

Kat watched him go and glanced over at Symon and Lauren, who were deep in conversation again. "You didn't tell Lauren."

"She looked busy."

"You're being dumb." Kat raised a pointed brow, and Charli knew she wasn't talking only about the arrangement. "I'll tell her."

Before Charli could stop her, Kat called across the mostly empty shop. "Lauren, the display outside your shop looks amazing. I really like it."

Lauren looked confused for a second before it registered. "Is it…you did…I have to look." She jumped up from her seat and, leaving Symon behind, ran out the front door.

"You're welcome," Kat whispered with a giggle.

"Sorry," Charli called over to Symon before shooting her sister another glare. Seriously, she had enough to worry about without having to concern herself with…well, getting in the middle of her best friend's love life. "We're just sorting out some—"

"Holy shit, Charli!" Craig rushed back into the shop with a blast of snow. "Those are great. Seriously. And yes, I want some. It's embarrassing that I don't have any yet and my sister is the talent behind them. Maybe with little ice cream cones, or something to encourage this trend of eating ice cream in the snow. Or maybe—"

"Whatever." Kat stopped him. "What would you pay for that, Craig?" Her eyes darted to the door, but Lauren hadn't returned yet. "Quick. Honest opinion. If someone else, not your sister, came in here offering that service and showed you examples like the ones you just saw, what would you be willing to pay?"

Craig didn't take long to think about it. "A hundred. Easy."

Charli didn't have time to digest that information because a moment later, Lauren burst through the door. "Charli! I love them! They're absolutely perfect. What do I owe you?"

"I was thinking maybe—"

"A hundred and fifty." Kat cut her off.

"Kat, that's too—"

"That's all?" Lauren shook her head in what could only be described as wonderment. "In the city, something like that would go for way more. I don't have my checkbook with me right now. Would you be willing to take an e-transfer?"

"Oh…um…"

"E-transfer works perfectly," Kat answered smoothly. She put her hand on Charli's shoulder and guided her slowly to turn around again. "That wasn't too much help, was it?" she asked with a grin. "Don't tell Steven."

"Cheers, sis." Craig lifted his almost-empty ice cream cup. "You just made your first sale, and I have a feeling it's only the beginning."

Chapter Twelve

ONE. *Two. Three. Four.*
  Breathe.
  In.
  Out.
  Visualize.

The voice on the recording was calming, almost rhythmic. And just the way he'd been practicing for the last week, Symon let himself get drawn into the instructions to relax. He'd finally called Doctor Jan Sanders, the sports therapist Alan had recommended. The woman had clearly been waiting for his call and had immediately set them up on a twice-weekly video meeting schedule.

In the first meeting, she hadn't even mentioned skiing, which both concerned Symon and relieved him. The focus was on getting Symon to relax and meditate, something he'd resisted heavily at first. But he had very few choices left, unless he planned to quit skiing altogether—and as much as that idea appealed on the worst days, he wasn't ready to give up on the dream. Yet.

So he was meditating.

Well, he was trying to meditate.

Breathe.

Symon gave himself over to the process and before he knew it, the twenty minutes had passed, and his eyes were opening but he didn't feel as though he'd fallen asleep. In fact, he felt refreshed and…good.

As instructed, he quickly typed a text to Doctor Jan.

I meditated. It was unexpectedly good.

She replied immediately.

Of course it was. Do you feel ready to move on to the next step?

Symon hesitated. So far, they hadn't discussed the accident in detail or why he wasn't ready to get back out on the skis, but he knew it was coming. It had to be. That was the entire point. His first instinct was to text her back that he wasn't ready and he didn't want to rush things, but when he started to type, something different came out.

Sounds good.

Symon stared at the words he'd typed. *What kind of black magic was in those meditations?*

A moment later, his phone rang, and Doctor Jan's name

appeared on the screen. With a laugh, he answered the call. "What have you done to me?"

"I assume you're talking about the meditation."

There was a smile in her voice that Symon appreciated. One of the reasons he'd connected with the woman was her easygoing approach. Having never seen a therapist before, he wasn't sure what to expect, but it wasn't the friendly, casual banter that made him feel like he was talking to a friend. And he definitely hadn't expected to meditate. Or journal. The other strange thing Doctor Jan had asked him to do.

"The meditations are designed to allow you to relax and get out of your head in order to access your subconscious. By putting yourself in a meditative state, your brain is able to do the work you can't do when you're overthinking things," she explained. "And that's actually a very basic way of explaining it, but it works. Doesn't it? I think it's great progress that you're willing to move on so soon. It also demonstrates your willingness to move past this situation."

He couldn't disagree with that. "So, what's next?"

"Next we're going to find your fun."

He was glad they weren't on a video chat so the doctor couldn't see him rolling his eyes. "Find my fun?" he repeated.

"Absolutely. Are you ready for your homework assignment for the weekend?"

"Sure." He rubbed a hand over his face before answering. "Why not?"

"Why not indeed. And don't worry, your homework should be easy. I promise."

Symon listened to the doctor's instructions, agreed to get his homework done by the end of the weekend, and ended the call.

"Okay." He spoke aloud in his empty bedroom. "This shouldn't be too hard."

The doctor told him his homework was to *have childlike fun*. The key word was *childlike*. His job was to seek out an activity, preferably with a companion, that he would have participated in when he was a kid. Apparently, the idea was to bring back the same kind of joy that you could only feel when there were no pressures or stresses.

It seemed easy enough. Symon might be new to the concept of therapy, but he did know enough to know that if something *seemed* easy enough, there was probably a catch.

Still, he'd committed to the process.

Now all he had to do was find something fun to do.

"How's your therapy going, hon?" Gran looked up from the stove, where she was stirring a pot of something that made his mouth water as soon as he walked into the kitchen a few minutes later.

"My what?" He froze, despite wanting a taste of whatever was in the pot. He hadn't told Gran about the therapy. He hadn't told *anyone* about the therapy because that would mean telling them that he was too broken to get out on his skis anymore.

"Your knee." She pointed with the wooden spoon. "The physical therapy. You did say you had more therapy to do, didn't you?"

Oh shit.

"Oh, of course. Yes." He caught himself quickly, and Gran went back to stirring. "What are you cooking, and can I have some for lunch?"

"My famous chicken noodle soup."

"Mmm." He snuck around and tried to dip a spoon into the pot, but Gran smacked his hand away. "I'm hungry."

"You're a grown man," she chided. "Make a sandwich."

He stepped back and let the spoon drop to his side. "Are we having soup for dinner?"

"*We* are not." Gran turned around with a sly smile on her face. "I have a date."

"You have a what?"

She laughed, and the smile on her face was so bright and genuine, Symon swallowed the follow-up comments that were on the tip of his tongue.

"Jim and I have been wanting to watch that new movie with the big guy."

"The big guy?"

"He waves a hammer around or something."

Symon laughed. "You mean Thor?"

Gran spun around and giggled. "That's the one. Have you seen his arms?" She wiggled her eyebrows. "And he's so funny."

"The perfect man." Symon tried not to roll his eyes.

"I don't know about perfect," Gran said. "But he is pretty entertaining."

"That he is, Gran." Symon moved around her to the pantry and grabbed a box of crackers. They weren't going to be nearly as satisfying as the soup, but they would do until he could get a real meal.

"What are you going to do this afternoon? It's a beautiful day." She waved her arm toward the window. "The sun is shining, and I haven't seen the sky that blue since, well…last week." She laughed at herself. "Seriously, Symon. You know how I feel about wasting gorgeous days."

"Don't," he said simply.

"Good boy." She moved to the fridge and started to pull items from the well-stocked shelves. "I knew I taught you well." She pressed a kiss to his forehead. "So?"

Symon moved to look out the window at the snow-covered world outside. *Fun. Childlike fun? What did that even look like?*

"Hey, Gran?" He turned to see her slicing cheese and

pieces of sausage, arranging them on a plate. "Can I ask you a question?"

"Anything." She handed him the plate and wiped her hands.

"Thanks." He dumped some crackers onto the plate and sat at the table. "When I was a kid, what's something I used to like to do for fun?"

She tilted her head and eyed him suspiciously. "You're not that old, hon. You don't remember?"

He shrugged.

"Besides skiing I assume?" She gave him a pointed look but didn't push. He nodded. "Well, let's see. You used to like to skate on that rink they flood in Creekside Park."

He had enjoyed skating when he was young. The pickup games of hockey with the other boys had been a favorite after-school pastime until Jason Perry decided girls weren't allowed to play. If Charli wasn't playing, neither was Symon. So they'd left the rink behind and—

"And then there was Baker's Hill," Gran said, reading his mind. "The two of you would play back there for hours and hours. I always thought you'd get tired or cold and come in, but up and down you'd go. Sledding over and over on that old hill."

A smile crossed his face as he remembered the way he and Charli would race down the hill on their sleds.

"Do you remember how you used to beg me to buy you a new toboggan?"

"The only one we had was that baby one," he protested. "I had to sit on my knees in it and even then, it was so slow."

"And then Michael Carlson bought you both those fancy racer things. I thought you would crack your heads open."

Gran shook her head at the memory, but Symon couldn't stop smiling.

"That *was* fun."

"The two of you certainly did have a good time together."

"We sure did." His eyes drifted to the window again as his idea came together.

It had been over a week, and Charli had hardly left her workshop unless it was to get more supplies or deliver her latest orders. With Kat and Craig's guidance, she'd created a simple flyer with pricing that included photos of the displays she'd already done, and had secured four more orders. It wasn't much, but it was a start.

She still had a very long way to go to create an actual profitable business and she was nowhere near doubling her start-up costs, but she was finally doing something and moving in the right direction, and that was a win as far as she was concerned.

"What do you think of this one, Lilly?" Charli took a step back from the display she'd just finished, this one in a wicker basket with birch logs as the feature. It was perfect for Ax and Arrow, the clothing boutique in the plaza.

Lilly got up from where she'd been napping, stretched deeply, and wandered over to the arrangement. She took her time to scratch her back on the side of the basket, purring in appreciation.

"I'm going to assume that means you like it." Charli laughed and scratched the cat under her chin before scooping her up in her arms. "Okay, it's time to get to work."

The cat mewled in protest and squirmed to be put down.

"I get it, Lilly. I thought we were done, too." She should probably be concerned with how much she was talking to her cat over the last few days, but Lilly was turning out to be a great business partner. She took payment in treats and catnip, agreed with most of her ideas, and didn't protest when Charli sang along to Taylor Swift while she worked.

"The work is just beginning," she said to the cat as she pulled the door to the workshop closed and blinked in the bright afternoon sun. "We still need to figure out how to turn this into an actual business and make up some sort of a price list for the summer bouquets."

It was an idea Craig had planted in her mind when he was talking about his ice cream shop and how he'd assumed it would be a seasonal business, but that he'd been surprised by the amount of traffic he was getting in the winter months, too. Maybe she shouldn't assume that people only wanted flowers in the summer season when they could buy them at the farmers' market.

She'd never considered turning her hobby into a business before, but the more time she spent thinking about it, and creating arrangements for more clients, the more it felt right. Was it possible that her little idea had been under her nose all along? What would her father think about it?

He'd always loved Charli's flowers, but had he ever seen them as more than just a hobby that kept her busy? She didn't think so. Not really.

But did that matter now, anyway? Because he wasn't there to give her any input in *what* she did. Just *that* she did it.

Charli sighed and was about to head to the house when a black truck pulled into her yard. Immediately, a smile came to her face and when Symon finally stepped out, it only grew wider.

"What are you doing here?"

"What are you doing outside?" he called back. "It's freezing."

"Is it?" She walked toward him. "It's a gorgeous day."

"It is."

He moved to give her a hug in greeting, but she side-stepped. He eyed her strangely as she snuggled the cat closer, using Lilly as a shield. It was stupid, she knew that. She also couldn't help it. She'd been unexpectedly jealous when she'd seen Symon with Lauren the other day, and rational or not, Charli didn't have the capacity to unpack those particular feelings at that moment. Avoidance was best.

"Did I catch you at a bad time?"

"No," she said. "I actually just finished up with a few orders. Can you believe I got some? I mean, that was the idea I guess, but I didn't really believe that I could. And for that price? It's all a little—"

"Incredible." Symon grinned. "I had no doubt that you'd get more orders," he said. "And I still don't think you charge enough, Char. You're so talented."

She waved off the compliment, but his words hit a spot deep inside and warmed her. "I haven't done anything yet. There's still so much work, and I need to figure out how to actually make a business out of this so I can make sure my family is okay, and—"

"Hey." He put his hand on her arm and squeezed. "You will. I believe in you."

She stopped, took a breath, and looked him in the eye. "Thank you, Sy. Really. And you know, I believe in you, too."

Taken aback, Symon shook his head a little. "What do you mean?"

Maybe she was crossing a line, or maybe she'd read something into the situation that wasn't there. But judging by the way he looked at her just now, she was pretty sure she hadn't. "Just what I said. I think you're talented and amazing and that you can do anything you set your mind to."

"Is that right?"

He bit his bottom lip, and Charli's stomach flipped before

clenching in a tight ball. It was completely unfair that her best friend was so damn sexy.

"Well, in that case, if you have a bit of free time, I was hoping I might be able to borrow you this afternoon for a little…well, it's actually kind of a homework assignment."

"Oh? That sounds intriguing." Lilly squirmed in her arms, and she set her down. "I'm sure I can spare some time. But only if you help me brainstorm later."

"Deal."

Chapter Thirteen

SYMON SETTLED IN BEHIND HER. He put a leg around either side of Charli and scooted forward until she was nestled between his legs. When he'd thought about asking her to join him, he hadn't considered that they would be so physically close. Or that his body would react to that closeness. He swallowed hard and shifted a bit on the sled. Hopefully, she hadn't noticed that particular reaction. He didn't remember tobogganing being so sexual.

Of course, the last time they'd done this was long before either of them had hit puberty.

"Are you ready for this?"

Charli twisted around a little. Her eyes sparkled with excitement. Her blonde hair in two braids stuck out from her knit cap, and matched with the excited grin on her face, she looked just like she had when they were younger. "I can't believe we're doing this." She shook her head. "I don't think I can remember the last time."

"I think I do." He pressed his lips together. "It was that time I tried to beat you on our snow racers, remember?"

Her eyes widened, and she laughed. "Oh my goodness. Yes! But you hit that jump and—"

"Crashed," he finished for her. "Hard."

She laughed, but the memory stopped him. Symon had forgotten about that crash that had broken the snow racer that Michael Carlson bought for him two years earlier, until right then. No one had been hurt, luckily, but his sled hadn't survived the impact with the tree.

Another crash.

Shit. Had he made a mistake with this homework assignment? It wasn't going to be fun for anyone if he had a panic attack doing something that was supposed to bring joy.

He looked past Charli to the hill that lay beyond, expecting to have the same tightness of breath or flash of panic he had on the ski hill the week before, but it didn't come.

"Sy? You okay?"

He blinked and nodded. When his eyes locked on Charli's, he smiled. "Totally. Let's do this."

"Let's do it."

Symon put his hands out on the snow and pushed them forward. And then again. And just like that, they were sliding and flying. He wrapped his arms tight around Charli's waist and pulled her back into him, not worried about anything except the moment.

"Whee!"

"Holy shit!"

And then they were both laughing as they gained more speed. Snow flew into his face, but he didn't dare move his arms. Nor did he want to.

"Oh my—"

"Hang on!"

The snow grabbed onto the sled and spun it, turning the entire toboggan sideways and before he knew it, they were tumbling and rolling in the snow. Charli slipped from Symon's grasp in the crash. He finally came to a stop, lying on his back. With a mittened hand, he wiped the snow from his face and looked up to see Charli not too far away, lying facedown in the snowbank.

"Charli! Are you…"

He watched as she pulled herself up and turned in his direction. Her cap had come off in the crash, her entire face was covered in snow, and…she was laughing.

"Okay?" He finished unnecessarily before getting to his feet and going to her.

"That was amazing," Charli managed to say when she got her laughter under control. She sat on her ass in the snow, her legs wide. In her snow pants and ski jacket, she looked adorable and sexy all at the same time.

He reached out with a gloved hand and wiped some snow from her head.

"Hey!" She pretended to be offended. "That was part of my look."

"It was, was it?"

She shook her head. "You're just jealous because you don't have the same snow chic look." Before he could react, she scooped up two mitts full of snow and tossed them directly into his face before once more breaking out into hysterical laughter. "That's so much better."

"Ohh, you're going to get it now." Symon wiped his face clear and lunged for her, tackling her backward into the soft snowbank. "You just started something you—" The words died on his lips when he realized he was lying on top of her, his mouth only inches from hers.

She'd stopped laughing and stared up at him with a look in her eyes he was pretty sure he understood.

For a second, neither of them moved. And then Charli's

tongue slipped from her mouth and licked her bottom lip, and there was nothing else he could have done.

He kissed her.

She must have hit her head in the crash. She was probably unconscious or had a concussion or some sort of brain injury because Symon Scott was kissing her. And holy shit, it was amazing.

Whether it was a dream or a concussion, Charli didn't care. She'd waited a very long time for this kiss—she was going to enjoy every second. She closed her eyes, but then as soon as the kiss began, it was over.

Her eyes snapped open as Symon jumped up and off her.

Charli sat up, half expecting Symon already to be on his way back to the truck by now, but he stood close, his back to her, his hand on his head, like he was thinking hard about something.

Was there really something to think about? And if there was, there shouldn't be. Charli may not have ever gone to college, but she had a master's in pretending everything was fine when it was exactly the opposite. There were a million other things she'd rather say to him in that moment to get to the bottom of what had just happened between them. Instead, she pasted a smile on her face and as cheerfully as possible, said, "Well? Are we going to go again?"

Symon turned and opened his mouth to say something, but she stopped him.

"I mean we came all the way out here." She got to her feet. "We might as well do it again."

Charli didn't wait for his answer. Instead, she gathered up her cap, brushed off the snow, and shoved it back on her head before grabbing the rope on the wooden sled Symon had bought for the occasion and began to haul it up the hill.

"I got it." Symon ran up beside her and took the rope from her hand. "Race you."

And just like that, the awkwardness was over.

They climbed the hill and slid down four more times before finally, Charli flopped into a snowbank, her arms outstretched, and declared she was done. "I'm exhausted," she groaned.

"Me too." Symon flopped down in the snow next to her. "We had way more energy when we were kids."

"I can't disagree with that." She laughed and flipped to her side in the snow so she faced him. "Can I ask you a question?"

They'd had a good time. A really good time. And the last thing Charli wanted to do was ruin what had been the most fun she'd had in recent memory. She'd tried to ignore what had happened between them earlier, but she couldn't erase the feel of his lips on hers from her brain.

Symon sat up. "Of course."

This was her chance. All she had to do was ask him why he'd kissed her. Why he'd run away from her all those years ago and left without so much as a word. She could ask him all those questions that had spun around in her head for way too long and finally get the answers she needed. "Why tobogganing?" *She was such a chicken shit.*

Surprise crossed Symon's face, as if he, too, expected a harder question.

"What kind of homework assignment do you have that requires tobogganing? And why me?" She doubled down on her questioning. "I mean, not that I'm complaining. It was a lot of fun and—"

"Honestly?"

She sat up. "Always, Sy."

Charli waited and watched. Something was going on with

her friend; she could see the war in his eyes as he battled with whatever it was. She'd been so caught up in her own drama that she hadn't seen it until now. And then again, it had been so long since they'd spent any real time together, would she have really known anyway?

She reached for his arm. "Sy? You can tell me anything."

Like why you kissed me.

A slow smile flickered on his lips. "I know I can, Char. It's one of the things I've always loved about you."

The word floated through the air between them. Again, her real question was on the tip of her tongue.

"How about I tell you over a cup of hot chocolate?" Symon jumped up so quickly, he sent snow flying around him. "Besides," he said as he held a hand out for her. "I promised you I'd help with some brainstorming."

"Hey!" Symon swatted away the cat for the third time. "Cut that out." He was trying, but not having much success dealing with their wet clothes in the mudroom while Charli got started making hot chocolate in the kitchen. He'd volunteered for the task, partly to give himself a minute to gather his thoughts. Or, more specifically, to figure out what exactly he was going to do about the feelings that were getting to be damn near impossible to ignore anymore.

Being with Charli was just...good.

Everything about being with her felt right and made him feel things he hadn't felt in years. She made all his stress and worries disappear. And when she'd looked at him and told him she believed in him...well, shit. She lit up parts of him he didn't even realize were inside him. And that kiss. Damn. He knew he shouldn't have kissed her. Not when she so clearly had put him in the friend zone, but he couldn't have stopped himself if he'd wanted to. And he hadn't wanted to.

Her lips had melted into his, and he knew he hadn't imagined it when she'd started to kiss him back. And he definitely hadn't imagined that sweet little sound she'd made.

But it wasn't right. He couldn't just kiss her like that in the snow with no warning. Not after all these years when she'd more than made it clear that they were *friends*. Symon didn't even realize until he got back to Trickle Creek just how much he'd valued that friendship, either. And he'd taken it for granted for way too long. Even after he'd been a huge asshole and taken off, and the last thing he deserved was her friendship, she was there.

He didn't want to ruin that. Not for anything.

Which was why he'd pulled away from her before the kiss had really gotten carried away. If he was going to go there with Charli, and it appeared he was, or at least that he was going to try, he was going to do things the right way. He just needed to figure out what that was.

"Okay," he said to the cat, yanking a mitten from its grasp. "Enough already."

Symon scooped up the cat, who mewled in protest, and went to join Charli in the kitchen.

"Are you hungry?"

When he walked in, she turned from the counter where she was scooping chocolate powder into two mugs.

Damn. She was so pretty. Even with her hair in two tangled, wet braids, that were dripping down her back and the thermal shirt she wore, she was gorgeous. Her leggings hugged her curves in ways that made Symon very hungry indeed.

"Symon?" She stared at him. "Are you hungry?"

"Oh." He attempted to scratch the cat behind the ears to

distract himself from her ass, but the cat squirmed, demanding to be let down.

"I don't think your cat likes me."

She laughed. "Lilly doesn't really like anyone but me. But she's sweet." She bent to pet the cat, who threaded her way through Charli's legs. "So?"

"I'm a little hungry." He finally answered the question. "I guess I didn't realize how late it was. Why don't you let me take you out? We can go to the—"

"Out?" Her hands flew to her head. She pulled her braids out to the side. "I look awful. Like I've been rolling around in the snow."

"To be fair, you *have* been rolling around in the snow." He stepped toward her, closing some of the distance between them. "And, for the record, you look beautiful."

She froze, a question in her eyes.

"Charli, I—"

"So, you never told me why you wanted to go tobogganing today." She interrupted him and turned her back to him, once more focused on preparing the hot chocolate. "You said it was a homework assignment."

He didn't want to talk about the homework. Or the tobogganing. Not unless they could talk about how good it felt to have her pressed up to him, his arms wrapped around her waist, and how his entire body came alive when she was close. Never mind how much he wanted to talk about that kiss and hopefully get another one.

But once again, she was closing herself off. He could take a hint.

For now.

Besides, when he agreed to tell her about it, he'd meant it. Plus, when Doctor Jan found out that he hadn't told anyone in his life the truth about his injury, she'd had a few very choice, but also very professional, words to say about that before she'd insisted that coming clean with someone he could trust was an important part of the healing process.

"It's kind of…well, do you have any Irish whiskey for that hot chocolate?"

Charli flashed him a grin over her shoulder. "You know I do."

A few minutes later, they sat across from each other at the table, sipping their drinks. Symon took a deep breath and told Charli the story. He started at the beginning with the accident and how he'd gone at the rehab exercises like it was his job so that he was stronger and in better shape than he'd ever been. If he wasn't so focused on what he needed to tell her, he might have called out the way she scanned his body at that comment, her eyes widening with appreciation at just how good of shape he was in.

"So, I don't get it."

Charli took a sip of her drink, and Symon watched as her tongue slipped between her lips to lick up the traces of chocolate on the edges. He swallowed hard and looked away.

"I still don't understand the homework."

"It's part of…well, I haven't told anyone this and…"

"Sy." She reached out and put her hand on his. "You know you can tell me anything."

Charli's touch grounded him and gave him the strength he needed. "I'm too scared to ski, Char. That's why I'm here. I'm blocked and I just can't…well, I don't know what's wrong with me. Coach gave me leave to sort it out, but if I don't figure it out, I'm not going to be able to—" He dropped his gaze to the table. Besides Doctor Jan, Symon had never said the words out loud. Now that he had, it all felt a whole lot more real.

"I knew there was something more going on."

Charli nodded, and Symon wasn't surprised. Of course she knew.

"Just like I know there's something more going on with you."

She tilted her head and gave it a quick shake. "We're not talking about me right now, Sy."

"No. We're not." He dropped his head. "But we will."

They sat in silence for a moment until Symon took a deep, shuddering breath.

Charli was at his side, her arm around him, pulling him into her until he was fully in her embrace. "Hey," she said. "It's okay."

"It's not, Char. That's the whole thing. It's so not okay."

She pulled back and looked him straight in the eye. "Maybe it's not right now," she said. "But it will be, Sy. I promise you. It will be more than fine."

"You can't know that."

"I can. Remember when I told you I believed in you?"

He'd never forget it. Symon nodded.

"Well, I said it because I believe it, Symon. And I know that you'll get through this, and I'll do whatever I can to help."

Chapter Fourteen

CHARLI BELIEVED what she told Symon. It *would* be okay. She had no doubt in her mind that he would ski again. Not only that, but he'd compete again. And win. She knew it in her heart. In the past, she'd been accused of being overly optimistic. A bit of a *Suzie Sunshine*. It was a label she never fully understood because Charli truly believe that things would always work out for the best.

Over the last few weeks, however, her blind optimism had morphed into something a little more based in reality. She understood that *yes*, things still could and would work out. But maybe it wasn't quite as easy as she used to naively believe.

When Symon was done explaining how he'd tried and failed to take himself skiing and had finally broken down and called the sports therapist, Doctor Jan, who'd given him the homework assignment, their hot chocolate was empty.

"You're very brave, Symon."

He shook his head with a chuckle. "That's the exact opposite of what I am, Char."

"Not true." She'd moved into her own chair, but she still sat next to him. Close enough to reach out and tilt his head in her direction. "And I believe in you. So, that's enough of that." She used her best *I mean business, so don't mess with me* voice. "Does it suck that you hurt yourself? Yes. Does it super suck that you're having some kind of mental block? Absolutely. But does that mean that you can't get past it and move on? No. Not at all. And that's the part you need to focus on, Sy." She squeezed his cheeks a little. "From this moment on, I need you to only think positive thoughts and banish all that bullshit negative self-talk, okay?"

When he didn't say anything, she used her grip on his face to move his head up and down and mimic his voice. "Okay, Char." She deepened her voice. "You're right. I'll do whatever you say."

Her plan worked, and Symon started to laugh. She joined in, the seriousness of the moment gone.

"Now can we talk about you?"

She froze.

"I know you don't want to, Charli. But the thing is, I know you're still hurting from losing your dad, and now with this whole business thing…it's a lot."

That was an understatement.

"But you can do anything you put your mind to. The same way you look at me and have blind faith, I have that with you."

"It's not the same."

"It is." He grabbed her hand from his face and held it until they were simply staring at each other. "And I'm not going anywhere, Charli. Neither of us have to do this alone."

Under the table, their knees touched. Maybe it was the secrets he'd shared with her or the afternoon they'd spent together. The kiss they'd shared earlier. The whiskey they'd just had in their drinks. Or maybe it was just a build-up of every-thing, but something had shifted between them. And it scared the hell out of her.

He'd kissed her. But then…*no.*

She was not going to let what was so obviously a slipup ruin them. Not again.

Charli pulled her hand away and jumped up from the table. "I'm absolutely starving now, and no," she added. "I'm not going out anywhere. I need a shower and my hair is a total disaster." She moved to the freezer and dug around inside, looking for something besides a tub of ice cream that she could cook. "I'm sure I can find something in here that will work for dinner. As long as you aren't picky and don't mind something simple. I'm not really the best cook, but I can pull something basic together." She was aware that she was rambling, but she didn't dare turn around. Mostly because she needed the sharp cold of the freezer to cool the flush on her cheeks.

"Charli?"

"You're not okay with basic?" Still, she didn't turn around.

"No," Symon said behind her. "I'm very okay with whatever. I just wanted to—"

"Great." She found a bag of frozen tortellini in the very back of the freezer. "Can you check in the pantry there for some kind of sauce I can pair with this?"

"You don't have to go to any trouble, Char. I'm just happy to be here with you."

"I'm happy—" Charli whirled around, a package of frozen tortellini in her hand. Symon stood close. Very close. His proximity caught her off guard, and she completely lost her train of thought. "I'm happy you…trusted me to tell me the truth."

He nodded simply and reached for the pasta still in her hand. "Thank you for…well, for being you, Char. You made it easy to open up. You always have." He still stood so close, but neither of them moved. "I feel so much better for talking about it, and I know you're right. It *will* be okay. Thank you for believing in me."

"Always."

"And today was a lot of fun. Thank you."

"It was fun."

It was the most fun she'd had in recent memory. She couldn't remember the last time she'd laughed so hard. Symon always did have that effect on her. Just being around him made her feel good.

"Well, maybe we can have fun together tonight, too."

Charli's eyes widened and her mouth dropped open at the exact same moment that Symon must have realized what he'd said.

"I mean, we can have fun, but…not like…oh my God."

She burst out laughing. "Oh, I'm sure you'd like that, wouldn't you?" she teased and spun away from him before her eyes gave anything away. Like the intense attraction that was no doubt being reflected in her own eyes. She'd always been terrible at hiding her feelings. Especially when it came to Symon. The last thing she needed was for him to read anything more into it than what it was. Or worse, see what it actually was.

Because that was the difference. What he'd said was only a slip of the tongue, an unfortunate stringing together of words. That was it. Symon didn't feel that way about her. He never had. And despite everything else that had changed, that hadn't.

Just like that kiss on the hill had been a mistake. A slip because he'd been caught up in the moment. It didn't mean anything.

Before he could respond and say something that would surely only hurt, Charli moved past him for a pot of water and set to work, getting dinner ready. "Don't worry, Symon. I won't hold you to any crazy expectations."

Charli swallowed hard. It would be so easy to tell him that she still thought he was insanely good-looking and just as funny and kind as he'd been when they were kids and that her feelings for him hadn't dulled at all. What would it hurt if she just told him the truth, that every man she'd ever dated never stood a chance because she always compared them to him?

She knew exactly what it would hurt.

Their friendship.

Which was why, after that humiliating moment when they were kids, she pretended like nothing had happened, and she would do it again. She valued their friendship too much to make a fool of herself or put him in the awkward position of having to tell her to her face that he didn't feel that way about her and he never had.

"Do you really think it would be so crazy?"

She spun around so fast, she almost splashed the water from the pot onto the floor. "What did you say?"

"Nothing." He shrugged. "I was just…it's nothing."

"You didn't tell me." She spoke without thinking, needing to put an end to the awkward moment. "What did Lauren say? About not skiing?"

She regretted the question the moment it came from her mouth, but especially when Symon froze and the smile fell from his face. "Lauren? You think I told Lauren? But I just finished telling you that no one knew."

Oh.

"I just thought that since you're dating, you might have—"

"Dating?" Symon's lips flicked up into the tease of a smile. "Oh, I see. You think I'm dating Lauren?"

"Well, I…" Of course she thought that. She'd *seen* them together. She'd seen the way Lauren had leaned over and intimately wiped Symon's lips clean. She'd seen the way they laughed and cuddled close together over ice cream. She'd set them up, for goodness' sake. "I mean, I just assumed."

"Because you set us up?" He took another step toward her.

"Well, yes. And I mean, you're both…and you were so…"

"And you're such a good matchmaker?"

Charli nodded. "And that."

"You are good," he said as he got even closer. "And Lauren is an amazing person."

She swallowed hard.

"But I hope you think better of me than that, Char."

"What are you talking about? Think better of—"

"Do you really think I would have kissed you if I was dating someone else?"

Oh.

"Do you really think that little of me?"

She shook her head. "I don't know why you kissed me, Sy." It was the truth. One she'd been avoiding all day. "And I don't think anything but highly of you."

He was so close to her now that she could smell the sweet chocolate on his breath, mixed with the light, soapy fresh smell that had always been his.

"Charli, I kissed you because, just like now, there was no way I couldn't."

Before she knew what was happening, his lips were on hers again. She was no more prepared for this one than she had been for the last one.

The kiss didn't last long, but it didn't have to. When he pulled back, Charli was shaking a little and was more confused than she'd ever been.

"Symon, I…" Words failed her, because how could they not? After all these years of loving him, of wanting him when he'd been the one to reject her…and now he just kept kissing her…it was all too confusing. She needed to think. She needed a second without him touching her, or looking at her with that completely new expression in his eyes. Or kissing her like he…

Charli pulled away and turned so she could press both

hands on the countertop. She dropped her head and sucked in a deep breath.

"Charli?"

"Can you please go see what you can find in the pantry for sauce?"

Sauce? She wanted him to look for sauce?

How the hell was he supposed to think about dinner after that kiss?

After he'd just opened up to her. After he'd shown her exactly how he felt about her and she'd just…

"Charli?"

Slowly, she turned. Her face was flushed. "Did you get the sauce?"

"Fuck the sauce."

"We need sauce with the—"

"Charli, I—" He took a step toward her, but she held him off with an outstretched hand.

"Look, Symon. I don't know what…well, I don't really understand…" She took a breath and tried again. "I can't do this. Not right now."

"Do what?"

She gave him a look. "This."

"Us?"

"There is no us."

"There should be."

"Symon." There was an edge to her voice he'd never heard before. "You didn't want us. You ran away. You were—"

"Eighteen, Char." He reached for her hand. "That was a lifetime ago. It doesn't count."

"It counts. I still remember."

He saw the hurt in her eyes. The hurt he'd put there so

many years ago because he'd been too damn stupid to handle things like a man. Because he'd been too scared to tell her exactly how he felt about her and how those feelings scared the hell out of him because he thought he'd have to choose between his dreams and her. So, instead, he'd run like the chicken shit he was.

"I never answered your question earlier." He twined his fingers in hers and pulled her close. "I told you why I wanted to go tobogganing, but I never told you why I asked you instead of someone else."

Charli looked up. He held her gaze.

"It had to be you because it's always been you, Charli. It's only ever been you. And it will only ever be you."

Damn. It felt good to say those words out loud after all these years. It was also the scariest thing he'd ever done in his entire life. Especially because she still wasn't talking.

"Charli, I've loved you since I was twelve years old, and I didn't even know what I was feeling." She shook her head, but he wasn't going to let her stop him. Not this time. "No," he added quickly. "It's true. We were in the sixth grade, and we had to do those stupid presentations about our family. The whole time you were standing in front of the class talking about your crazy, big family, all I could think about was how I felt like I was your family, and it didn't seem fair that you hadn't even mentioned me."

"And then I did."

"And then you did."

She smiled at the memory. "I said you were family but not like a brother. Better."

"That's right." He nodded. "Better than a brother. But it wasn't until we were older that I finally started to understand what those feelings meant. By then I was too dumb to know what to do about it, and then you kissed me that day and for the first time, everything made sense."

"No." She shook her head. "You left, Sy. You ran away from me and left. Nothing made sense about that."

"I hate that I hurt you, Charli." He lifted her chin with his finger. "And if I could go back in time and take back that moment, and so many moments after that, I would. I would give anything to change what a giant asshole I was."

She closed her eyes.

"Look at me, Char. Please." He waited until her eyes opened again. "I ran because I was scared, and I didn't know how to love you and follow my dreams at the same time."

"And now?"

"Now? Now I don't know how to follow my dreams without loving you."

It was the most honest thing he'd ever said and as soon as the words came out of his mouth, Symon knew it without a doubt.

It felt like forever before Charli spoke again. "You love me?" She bit down on her bottom lip in an effort to hide the smile that was starting to twist her lips up.

"Woman. You know I do." He cupped her cheek in his hand.

"Say it again."

"I love you, Charli Carlson." Now that he'd started saying it, he never wanted to stop. "I love you. So. Fucking. Much." He leaned in to once more press his lips to hers, but she stopped him with a finger to his mouth.

"You ran away."

"I told you why. I was an idiot. I was young and I didn't—"

"No." The smile slipped from her face. "Earlier, at the hill. In the snow, you…I can't do that anymore, Sy. I can't do this thing where we kiss and then you run."

"I didn't run." True, in that moment he didn't know *what* to say, but he sure as hell hadn't run away.

As if he hadn't spoken, Charli continued, "If we're going to…well, if we're going to do whatever it is that we're going to do here, then I need to know why you keep doubting your feelings."

"Doubting my feelings? Is that what you think that was today?"

She nodded.

"No." He put his other hand on her cheek so he cupped her face in his hands and she couldn't look away. "That wasn't about me doubting my feelings, Char. That was me trying to figure out how not to fuck this up again."

"Yeah?"

"Yeah."

"So you're not going to run away again?"

"Never."

"Good." Her smile returned, lighting up her face. "Because I love you too, Symon. It's always been you."

Chapter Fifteen

HE WASN'T RUNNING.

He loved her.

And Charli couldn't remember ever loving anyone *but* Symon.

It might have felt like a dream if it weren't for his hands on her body and his lips on her mouth. That all felt very, *very* real.

He left one hand on her cheek, holding her in place while his other hand slid down the length of her body. A moan escaped her, and she pressed her body into him, needing more of his touches, more of *him.*

Their kiss deepened, each of them hungry for the other. After so many years of waiting and wanting, they were greedy and impatient.

Charli's hands slipped up his back. Her fingers clawed into his strong muscles, pulling him closer to her. She pressed her breasts into his chest, and a strangled sound slipped from his throat.

He yanked his mouth from hers. "I don't think I'm going to have any self-control when it comes to you, Charli." His voice was husky and thick with need. "If you want me to stop, speak now."

"No stopping." She threaded her fingers through his hair and tugged him back to her mouth. "Absolutely no more stopping."

"You don't need to tell me twice." A sound very much like a growl came from him. He lifted her top from her, pulling it up and over her head. His eyes widened as he took in the sight of her in her bra.

The idea that she should feel self-conscious around him flashed through her mind, but it just as quickly vanished.

How could she feel anything but sexy with him looking at her as if she were the most desirable woman in the entire world?

"Fuck, Char. You are so fucking perfect." He buried his face between her breasts.

She giggled, but her giggles turned to moans as he turned his attention to first one breast, and then the other. Without pushing her lacy bra out of the way, he sucked one hard nipple into his mouth. He flicked his tongue over the hard nub, the lace providing friction that made her groan and drop her head back. Moisture pooled between her legs when he pinched her other nipple before giving it equal attention.

"If you keep doing that, I'm not going to make it to the bedroom."

Symon lifted his head from her chest. "Who said anything about a bedroom?" He used his head to nod toward the table.

A thrill ran through her, landing directly between her legs, making her squirm with the promise of what he was implying. "Here?"

"Babe, I've waited over fifteen years for this. There is no way I'm going to make it to the bedroom." To make his point,

Symon pulled her tight against his hips so she could feel the hard length of his desire.

She slipped a hand between them and into the waistband of the track pants he'd worn under his snow pants. She wrapped her hand around his girth, her eyes widening in the process. "You're huge."

He laughed. "Damn, Charli. You do know how to make a guy feel good."

Her cheeks heated. It's not that she'd never been with a man. She'd had a number of relationships over the years. Some were more serious than others, but most were casual. But none of the men she'd ever been with had measured up to Symon. In more ways than one, it turned out. She shivered in anticipation of everything they were about to do. But there wasn't even one doubt. Nothing had felt more right.

She stroked her hand up the length of him, and he vibrated from her touch. "Careful." His hand stopped her. "Your touch feels a little too good."

"There's no such thing as *too* good." She kissed him hard and stroked him again. "And the last thing I want to be is careful."

Her touch was too much. And not enough.

He needed more of her. He needed *all* of her.

Never had Symon felt so on the edge of control with a woman. Then again, he'd never been with Charli. And none of his many, many fantasies had come even remotely close to what he was feeling at that moment.

He needed to slow things down. There was only going to be one first time with them. And after so many years of pent-up need between them, there was no doubt it was going to be explosive. And he was going to enjoy every second of drawing that explosion out of her.

Symon managed to pull away from her touch before he lost control completely. He took a tiny step back, giving him just enough room to pull her leggings down. She stepped out of them and stood in front of him, wearing only her pink lacy bra and purple panties. She looked like a delicious candy confection, and he was ready to eat up every bit of her.

He reached for her panties, but she slipped to the side. "Oh no."

"No?"

"Well…yes." She shrugged. "But first, your turn." She put a hand on her hip and waved a finger up and down as she bit down on her bottom lip.

Damn. She was so fucking sexy. His fingers twitched, needing to touch her again. Every second was turning out to be an exercise in restraint. But if she wanted him naked, who was he to deny her?

With no further hesitation, Symon pulled his sweatshirt over his head and threw it somewhere behind him.

"Ohh." She eyed him appreciatively. "You weren't kidding when you said you were in the best shape of your life."

"Did I say that?"

"More or less." She reached out and ran her hands over the muscles on his chest, sending electric sparks flying through him. "Holy shit, Sy. You're…"

"I'm…"

He shivered under her touch. She had no idea the effect she was having on him. Especially with the way she was looking at him, as if it were her turn to eat him up.

"You don't need me to tell you how hot you are."

"I don't *need* you to…"

She laughed. "Show me the rest and then I'll make my judgment."

He did not have to be asked twice. With a flash, his track pants and boxer briefs were off, and he kicked them behind him. "Well?"

"Hmm..." She took her time assessing him. Her finger tapped at her lips, as if she were contemplating what she saw. "I think you're in very good shape here..."

He let her play her little game and stood stock-still while she slowly began to walk around him. He thought he might come completely unhinged when she reached one finger out and let it trail across his abs, around his hip and to his ass cheek before circling him completely and coming to rest on his throbbing cock. "Yes," she said, as she came to a stop in front of him. "You are incredible."

"Oh no, babe. *You* are incredible." Symon grabbed her wrist and spun her so her back was to him. "And I think it's about time we got rid of the rest of these clothes."

She murmured her approval, and he didn't waste any more time. He unhooked her bra, discarding it on the floor while his hands properly explored her glorious full tits. But he wasn't anywhere near done with her. With one hand cupping her, he used his other to push her panties down over her hips, stopping himself before tearing the skimpy garment off altogether.

And then he was kissing her neck, touching her everywhere. In response, she ground her buttocks back into him. He was already impossibly hard; it was going to take a fucking miracle for him to hold off taking her for much longer. But, at the same time, he wanted to—he *needed to*—take his time and remember every single second of her.

"Sy." His name was barely a breath on her lips. "I...we..."

"I couldn't agree more."

Again, he spun her around and caught her mouth in his,

kissing her as if they both needed it to survive. She squirmed against him, her wet heat pressing into him with need.

"Condom." He managed to get the word out. "We need a—"

"My room."

It looked like they were going to make it to the bedroom after all.

She slipped away from him and took off toward the stairs. Symon was right behind her, so when she handed him the condom from her nightstand, he didn't waste a second. Using his teeth, he tore the foil package open and quickly sheathed himself with a small groan before once more reaching for her.

"I need you so bad, Char."

Their mouths crashed together as they tumbled onto her bed. Symon lifted himself with one arm, holding himself up over her so he could look her in the eye when they finally came together. His cock pulsed against her center. She shifted her hips to welcome him. With restraint he didn't know he was capable of, he took his time, sliding into her heat, and she held his gaze until he completely filled her.

"Oh…my…" Charli's eyelids fluttered closed.

She felt beyond amazing, and he desperately needed a moment to get control.

"Sy?"

She opened her eyes again. Her pupils were dark with desire as she looked up at him.

"I just needed a second, babe. You feel…well, you are…dammit."

She reached up with one arm and pulled him down to her kiss. Her tongue twisted with his as she lifted her hips to meet him, and there was no more slowing down or turning back.

She matched him thrust for thrust until he felt her body tighten and tense. Moments later, she crashed over the edge.

She cried out as she shattered beneath him. Seconds later, he joined her, his own intense orgasm slamming into him. Not once did Symon close his eyes, unwilling to miss one second of their time together.

When Charli finally opened her eyes again, she smiled shyly. "That was...well..."

"Fucking amazing, Char." He stroked a strand of hair from her cheek. "*You* are fucking amazing. Every single part of you."

"Mmm. So good." She turned her head to the side before looking back at him. "You don't think that...what if..."

"Just say it. What are you thinking?"

She swallowed hard. "You don't think this is going to change things between us, is it?"

Symon rolled off her, to the side, and with one hand on her hip, pulled her close. "I sure as hell hope so." And then he kissed her.

Chapter Sixteen

HE WAS STILL THERE.

Every day for the past three days, Charli had woken up in her bed with her best friend next to her or, more specifically, wrapped around her, after a night of lovemaking and sex like she'd never experienced before. Maybe it was true, that sex really was better with someone you loved? Because she did love Symon. The past few days had made that clearer than ever.

She wiggled backward in his arms, pressing herself against him. Symon groaned in his sleep and tightened his arm around her, pulling her close. His morning erection pressed into her back, and she thrilled at the way he was always so ready for her.

It hadn't taken long for them to establish that Charli was on birth control, and they were comfortable without using condoms, which turned out to be a good thing, because Charli had lost count of how many times they'd made love already.

With anyone else, it might have been awkward to turn a lifetime of friendship into a sexual relationship, but with Symon, it just felt natural. As if they'd worked their entire life to get to this moment together.

There hadn't been any fumbling or weird times while they tried to figure each other out because they already knew each other so well. The connection they'd always had, despite so many years apart, hadn't faded over time; it had only strengthened.

"Good morning, gorgeous." Symon's voice was thick was sleep and lust. He kissed the tender spot behind her ear as his hand slipped over her hip and between her legs, where she was already wet and ready for him.

She'd been in a perpetual state of arousal for the last three days, and if she had it her way, she didn't plan on it ending anytime soon.

"Mmm." She wiggled back into his dick. "Good morning indeed."

"It's about to be a fucking fantastic morning." With his hand still between her legs, Symon shifted them a little and with a long sigh, slipped easily into her heat.

"Oh, yes. It is."

It was slow and lazy and perfect.

Symon held her close, kissing the back of her neck while his thumb pressed slow circles on her clit until finally, she was moaning her release. He took his own a moment later with a long, deep groan.

When she flipped over and laid on his chest, Symon brushed a stray hair back from her face and stared up into her eyes. "That is exactly how I like to start the day. And it's exactly how I'd like to spend the rest of my day, too." He reached up and pulled her down for a kiss, but she squirmed away from his grasp.

"No can do, darling."

Before she could be convinced to stay—and she was pretty sure she could easily be convinced—Charli hopped from the bed.

"You're killing me." Symon sat up against the headboard and dropped his head back. "Bring your sexy body back here."

She did a little shimmy and shake for his benefit, which only caused him to groan louder, but she made no move to get back in bed because if she did, she knew they'd lose hours to each other. It wasn't a bad way to spend a day, but they'd already spent the majority of the past three days lost in each other. *Making up for lost time.* And she had work to do.

Work.

It still felt odd even thinking about that word in relation to being in the greenhouse or workshop, but she was getting used to it. Not that she thought of it as *work*. She loved every minute of it.

"I have to make my deliveries today, remember?"

Symon's lips curled up into a sexy smile. "Of course I remember. You've been working so hard."

"You've been helping." She moved across the room and pulled her robe from the hook behind the door.

"Oh. Don't cover up that beautiful body."

She laughed. It was a huge turn-on how much he enjoyed her body. For the last three days, Charli had felt like a bona fide goddess. And he was definitely her god. She hesitated before pulling the robe up over her shoulders, letting her eyes roam over his defined abs and strong shoulders. *Damn.* If she'd known he was hiding that under his clothes all this time, she might have made a move sooner.

Not that it was her who'd made the move. She couldn't let herself think of all the time they'd wasted because of miscommunications and misperceptions. It would drive her crazy, and she had way too many other things to concern herself with.

Like getting her deliveries done.

With a sigh, Charli pulled her gaze away from the incredibly sexy man in her bed and pulled her robe over her shoulders.

"That's the last of them." Symon handed Charli the bucket of pine boughs and ornaments from the back of her SUV. This one had miniature skis tucked into it, which was a nice touch for Brody's shop, Peak to Path. He blew her a kiss when she took it from him and headed through the covered walkway that led from the parking lot into the pedestrian-only plaza.

"I'll meet you up there," he called after her. "I'll buy you an ice cream to celebrate."

He'd offered to carry the displays for her, but Charli had insisted she do the deliveries herself. She'd worked hard over the last few days on making each of them special, and she'd nailed it. She was uniquely talented in a way that she didn't even understand. Symon tried to help her as much as he could, but mostly that consisted of taking quick trips into the woods that surrounded her property to gather more pine and cedar branches, hauling the displays from one spot to another and massaging her shoulders after she'd spent too long hunched over her workbench.

She'd been impressive to watch, and he was so proud of the way she'd dedicated herself to it.

He locked up the car, tucked his hands into his pockets, and headed into the plaza himself. Symon glanced in the direction of Brody's shop. His old friend was admiring the work Charli had done. He turned in the opposite direction before Brody could see him. It's not that he meant to avoid his old friend, but also…he was avoiding him. He still hadn't been on the ski hill, and he still wasn't ready to admit the reason why to anyone but Charli.

Doctor Jan had been impressed with how successful his first homework assignment had been, especially when he told her that he'd confessed everything to Charli. It was a positive step in the right direction, but it wasn't enough. Doctor Jan was pushing him to get back on the skis again and try, but only for fun. She recommended taking Charli and treating it like their day out tobogganing.

"Just have fun with it," she'd said.

They'd had fun tobogganing. And they'd had even more fun afterward. Although he'd spared his therapist those particular details.

Symon smiled to himself with the memory of just how much fun they'd had after, and in the days following.

"That smile better not have anything to do with my sister."

Symon spun around to see Asher Carlson frowning at him. A few years younger than him, Symon didn't know Asher very well growing up and had only seen him the night of the family dinner that Charli invited him to, but they hadn't exchanged more than a few words. Asher didn't look all that chatty now, either. He stood with his hands shoved into his black wool dress coat that he wore over his suit. His blond hair was combed to the side, and he looked more suited to a boardroom in the city than in front of the shops of a snowy mountain town.

And what the hell did he mean with that comment? Symon and Charli had hardly left her house for the last three days. Besides a quick trip to Gran's to gather some things and tell her where he'd be, not that she was very surprised, the two of them hadn't been out in public. There was no way Asher could even know about him and Charli, and even if he did…he was not going to be intimidated by her little brother.

Suitably recovered, Symon stuck his hand out. "Asher. Hi."

"Symon." The other man nodded at the hand but didn't take it.

"Okay." He drew the word out and tucked his hand away. "Well, this is a nice surprise, but I was just about to buy Charli some ice cream to celebrate." He pointed over Asher's shoulder, to Craig's store. "You're welcome to—"

"Listen." Asher cut him off. "I don't want to come off like a dick."

Too late.

"But when it comes to Charli—"

"When it comes to Charli, what?"

The subject of conversation appeared with exceptional timing and put her arm through her brother's, giving him a hug. "What are we talking about?"

Asher looked between her and Symon. He opened his mouth, but Charli cut him off.

"Because I would hate to hear that you're giving my very best friend in the whole world a hard time, Asher." She looked up at her brother and fluttered her eyelashes.

"Your best friend?"

"We've been best friends for years, man." Symon nodded. "That's hardly news."

"That's all you are? Because Kat said—"

"Kat shouldn't tell stories that aren't hers to tell."

Kat. Of course Charli would tell her sister about them.

Not that they were a secret. He looked at Charli, who still smiled at her brother, but neither confirmed nor denied anything. *Did she want them to be a secret? Did she want a them?*

They'd done a lot of talking over the last few days and they'd covered all kinds of topics, mainly why he'd been an idiot at eighteen and why she'd tried so hard to push him toward her friend Lauren and why both of them were too stubborn to admit to their feelings earlier. But the one thing neither of them had brought up was how they wanted to move forward. Was it a secret? Was it a *relationship?* Was it going to be something serious?

Symon couldn't speak for Charli, but he knew exactly how he felt and he wasn't going to waste any more time playing games.

"Your sister and I are together." Symon stepped up and took Charli's hand in his, pulling her to his side. "A couple. That's what we are."

Charli looked at him with surprise written all over her face.

"Together," he said directly to her.

"Together." She nodded, her smile growing wide. "We are very much together."

And then, in case there was any more doubt, he took her face in his hands and kissed her, right there in the middle of the plaza.

Ice cream in the middle of January had never tasted better, and it had everything to do with the man sitting at her side, his hand on her thigh under the table. That and the amazing feeling of accomplishment Charli had from delivering her first real orders successfully.

"Cheers, sis." Craig, who'd joined them, along with Asher at a table by the window, raised his cone in a toast.

"I'm so proud of you." Symon squeezed her leg while he, too, lifted his cone.

Asher shook his head in their direction before he, too, raised his paper cup of hot chocolate.

Charli tried not to laugh at his reaction to seeing her with Symon. After all, it was kind of cute that he was feeling so protective of her, even if that protection was totally unwarranted.

"You're doing great, Charli," Asher said. "Cheers to that."

"Thanks, guys." She raised her paper cup of ice cream. "I will absolutely toast to that." She took a scoop of the sweet cheery cheesecake before speaking again. "I've been thinking of a few ideas on what else I can do."

Asher tipped his head in question. "You want to do more?"

She nodded. Both Kat and Chase had mentioned that her idea was a *good start* and the more she thought about it, the more she agreed with them. Over the last few days, Symon had helped her brainstorm some other things she could do to increase her revenue faster and ultimately fulfill her requirements so she could put this whole caveat behind her as soon as possible and get back to her life.

"The window displays aren't enough?"

She shook her head at Craig's question. "Not unless I want to be doing this for years. And I don't. I want to get this thing done so we can move on."

"There wasn't a time limit on Dad's request, Char." Asher shook his head. "You don't have to rush it. Not on our account."

She looked between her brothers. Both of whom shook their heads. "Thank you," she said. "I appreciate the support. I do. But I really want this done with so I don't have it hanging over my head."

Under the table, Symon rubbed her leg in support. She leaned in toward him. Not for the first time in the last few days, she caught herself marveling at how quickly things had changed between them. If it had been anyone else, in any other circumstance, Charli would be pumping the brakes and pulling back because it was moving too quickly. But this was Symon and that made everything different.

And it was just one more reason to finish up with her father's crazy request, so she could focus on the future. On *their* future. Whatever that would look like. It didn't matter. But she couldn't move on at all until this *thing* was finished.

"Well, whatever we can do to help," Asher said. "You know we'll do whatever we're allowed to do." He added the last part with a grin. "But I'll admit that I'm not really in a rush for part three of the will reading."

"That's right." Craig pointed across the table at him. "You're next."

Asher shrugged, but Charli could see her typically cool and always in control little brother was trying not to look affected. "What if you're next?"

"He's going in order."

"We don't know that," Charli pointed out. "Of course, we don't really know anything. I mean, as far as we know, it could be over with me." She hadn't meant to say anything, especially after Chase had shut down her idea that their father might have singled the two of them out.

"No way." Asher shook his head. "He wouldn't have left us out of this."

"Left out?" Craig laughed. "I don't know, I think I would be pretty happy to be left out of this particular family activity." He finished his ice cream in one bite. "And speaking of family activities. I need to go grab Meri from kindergarten and get her to ski lessons." He stood and pushed his chair in. "Stay as long as you want. I'll tell Kristie not to kick you out."

"I think she'd be happy for the chance to do something." Charli shook her head. "Did you actually give the poor girl some duties around here?"

Craig had finally broken down and hired a part-time employee to help him out around the shop, but it was no secret that he was a control freak and had a hard time letting go and actually giving her something to do around the shop. It was big news that Craig was even leaving her in charge of the shop for a few hours.

"Very funny." Craig stuck out his tongue at his sister before turning to Symon. "Hey, I was telling Meredith that you're a super star skier, and she didn't believe me. I was thinking that maybe as a treat for her when she passes this round of ski lessons, I could convince you to join us on the hill and show off some of your moves?"

Next to her, Symon tensed. They'd only discussed his situation a few more times, but beyond talking—and the homework assignment of tobogganing, of course—he'd been pretty tight-lipped about it in general.

"Come on, Craig," she said before Symon could answer, wanting to defuse the situation before it got awkward. "Sy is on a break right now."

"Well, yeah." Craig looked between them. "I was just thinking—"

"It's no problem at all." Symon's smile was genuine. "I'd love to get out on the hill with you guys. We'll have to set something up."

"Sounds great. Thanks, man." Craig pulled his jacket from the hook by the door. "I'll see you guys in a few days at the family dinner."

"I should run, too," Asher said after Craig left. "I'm still not totally sure how I feel about the two of you together." He shook his head. "It's a little weird."

"In the best possible way." Charli kissed Symon on the cheek, and Asher groaned.

"Okay, okay." He laughed. "I'm happy for you guys, okay? But I don't need to see my big sister getting all mushy."

Symon and Charli followed him out, calling out a goodbye to Kristie, who was mopping the already clean floor.

Once they were out in the fresh air, Charli grabbed

Symon's hand and pulled him to a stop. "Hey," she said when he turned to look at her. "You don't have to…I mean, I don't want you to feel like you need to go skiing with Craig or my niece or…"

He put a finger on her lips to quiet her and then moved her, so she stood with her back against his chest. He wrapped his arms around her and pointed in front of them. "Look at that."

She followed where he pointed, past the row of shops in the plaza and beyond the arch that marked the beginning of the shopping square to the mountain that stood as the center-piece of the entire town and the ski hill.

"It's beautiful."

It was. The setting sun reflected from the mountains across the valley, casting a stunning pink and orange alpenglow over the ski hill, lighting it up in a way that only Mother Nature could pull off.

She nodded against his chest, agreeing with him before he spun her around to look into her eyes.

"Will you do me another favor, Charli?"

Her stomach clenched in anticipation, and she wiggled her eyebrows. "Are we going skiing?"

Chapter Seventeen

"WE'RE REALLY GOING to do this?"

Charli looked at him with mischief sparkling in her bright eyes. She licked her lips and nodded slightly. "Oh yeah. We're doing this." She pulled her goggles down over her eyes and turned toward the hill. "Are you ready?"

"No."

He wasn't trying to be dramatic. He *wasn't* ready. But after another call with Doctor Jan the night before, and a meditation session earlier in the morning, he was as ready as he was going to get.

"You got this, Sy." She reached for his arm with her ski glove. "And even better…"

She wiggled her hips, which looked ridiculously cute in her pink ski suit. Even covered head to toe, the woman was crazy sexy, and his body reacted instantly.

"You have me." She blew him a kiss.

"I'll have you, all right. Later." She was proving to be a good distraction from the thoughts that were usually taking over at this point.

"Down, boy." Her laugh was downright magical. "I'll tell

you what," she added. "You do this." Charli used her pole to gesture to the ski run they stood on the edge of. "You ski with me today and have *fun*, then I'll reward you by—"

"Deal."

"You didn't even wait to hear what I was going to say."

"If you're promising me rewards that come in the form of sexual favors, then I am absolutely in." Symon knew he'd made a good choice in asking her to accompany him skiing. Sexual rewards from Charli were exactly what he needed to get back on the hill.

"I didn't say it was a sexual reward," she teased. "But why don't we wait and see? You want me to go first?"

She pushed herself closer to the hill, and the fear he'd been fighting off rushed back.

It was time.

"No." Symon swallowed hard and forced himself to focus on Charli. "I'll go."

"I'll be right behind you."

He knew she would.

Before he could talk himself out of it, Symon pulled his goggles down onto his face, took a breath, and pushed off with his poles until he was on the groomed ski run. The skis slid easily under him, pulling him across. Instead of stopping himself the way he had last time, he planted a pole next to him, hopped a little, and made the first turn.

And then he was moving, picking up speed. Muscle memory took over as he made another turn and then another.

Behind him, he heard Charli hoot and holler. It was only then that he relaxed his jaw a little.

Fuck yeah.

He wasn't going fast, but this wasn't about speed.

Soon, he caught a flash of pink in his peripheral vision as Charli caught up with him. She matched him turn for turn as they made their way down the hill. When the run flattened out a little, Charli held her arms and poles up and over her head and hollered, "Whee!"

Caught up in the moment, Symon completely forgot he was supposed to be afraid and followed suit, yelling as loud as he could.

He stopped himself before the last steep section that would lead to the base and the chairlift and let himself watch Charli, in her pink suit, easily carve up the rest of the run. She stopped at the entrance to the chairlift line, and that was his cue. This time when he pushed off, the nerves were gone; he was focused only on the woman in front of him. And fun.

Symon could see her huge smile as he approached and for a moment, he felt mildly guilty about what he was about to do. But only for a second, and then he cut deep, pulling both his skis together as he came to a hard stop in front of her, causing a wave of snow to crash over her, covering her completely.

"Symon!"

She screeched, but he could hear the laughter in her voice. He looked over as she pulled the goggles from her face and used her mittens to wipe the snow away.

"I can't believe you did that."

"Damn, you look hot, all frosty like that."

"Oh yeah?" She scooped up two mitt fulls of snow and threw them at him, and then it was on.

It was clumsy with their skis still clipped to their feet, and the snow fight didn't last long before they ended up in a tangled mess of equipment and each other on the ground. They were both laughing too hard to care, and when Charli kissed him, he only had one thought in his head.

Symon managed to pull himself up to stand before helping her up. He slipped his skis between hers so he could kiss her properly, not giving a damn who was watching and what they might think of the ridiculous couple who'd just been rolling in the snow. "Now," he said when he pulled away. "What was that about a reward?"

She made him wait until they'd done three more runs down the hill before she agreed to give him his reward, although Charli was pretty sure the reward was already evident in his eyes. He'd done it. Symon had taken the first huge step toward conquering his fear of skiing again, and she couldn't be more proud of him. Not that she'd doubted him. She hadn't. Not for one second.

When he first confessed the problem to her, she'd seen the fear in his eyes. But she'd also seen a determination there, too. Symon loved skiing too much to walk away from it, and she agreed with what Doctor Jan told him. He needed to make it fun again.

She watched him now while he put the skis in the bed of his truck, and even from where she stood, she could see the grin on his face. It had been fun. Symon had fun. It was just a matter of time before he was back to full power and back with the team.

Back with the team.

The thought hit her hard. What would happen when he'd completely conquered his fear and was ready to go back to training with the team? He'd leave, that's what would happen. He'd leave her. Again.

She shook the thought clear of her head, because she was just being dumb. He belonged on Team Canada. He said himself that he was in the best shape of his life. He'd never been stronger. It was just his brain that needed fixing, but once he mastered the mental side—which he would—he would be a force. She wanted that for him. Of course she did. But the idea of saying goodbye to him again so soon, especially now, was too much for *her* to wrap her head around.

"Ready to go?" Symon stood next to his SUV in only his long-sleeve shirt and ski pants.

He was in his element at the ski hill. She'd seen it in their afternoon together, the same way she'd seen it when they were kids.

"I'm ready." She walked over and kissed him on the lips, hard.

"What was that for?" He laughed. "Not that I'm complaining. Not even a little bit." He kissed her again, softer this time.

"I'm proud of you." She pulled away and moved to her car door. "You're going to the Olympics, Sy. I know it."

"Don't get ahead of yourself. I have a lot of work to do still," he protested, but she could see the grin on his face and the sparkle in his eyes. "Now, come on. I'm ready for my reward."

"You have a one-track mind." She smacked him lightly on the arm as she climbed into the truck. "But don't go home. We need to stop in the plaza first."

"My reward is in the plaza?" He navigated the car out of the lot and started the short drive down the hill into the town center. "I had something a little different in mind."

"I'm sure you did." She slipped a hand on his upper thigh and squeezed. "And that particular reward is coming later. But today was a big day for you and…well, you kind of inspired me."

"I inspired you?"

Charli nodded. It was something she'd been thinking about in the vaguest way for a little while, but she hadn't been brave enough to even speak it out loud. Their situations were totally different, but watching Symon overcome his hurdles had given her a push.

A few minutes later, she took Symon's hand in hers and led him into the plaza.

"We're going for coffee?" Symon looked toward the Bean Bag, but Charli stopped him in front of a different storefront. "Oh." He looked at her, confused. "We're getting pottery?"

"No." Marta's store was almost completely empty now. There were only a few things left in the window display beside the *Everything Must Go* signs and the new, red *For Lease* sign in the corner. "I was thinking of getting the store."

Speaking the idea out loud sent a shiver rippling through her and down her spine. It was scary as hell. But also exciting.

"You want the store?" Symon turned to her, understanding slowly registering on his features. "For your business?" He said the words slowly, a smile crossing his face. When Charli nodded, he pulled her into a hug. "That's amazing, Char. Really. And it's a huge step."

"The hugest."

She faced the window and took a deep breath.

"I've already discussed the terms with Cathy. She's the listing agent, and she told me they're looking for a long-term lease arrangement obviously, but since she knows my situation, and our families have known each other for so long, they would consider a short-term temporary situation, too."

"Temporary?"

"Of course." Charli nodded. "I just need to hit the mark for Dad's request, and we can all move on." And she could put this whole stressful nightmare behind her. That was the whole point of the storefront. Get it done quickly and maybe she could put all this behind her before anyone discovered how completely inept and unqualified she really was. "The sooner the better, right?"

"But you've had so much fun working on this, Char. I guess I thought you might…I don't know…keep going with it. It's kind of the perfect business for you, Charli. I mean, you love this."

"Business is the keyword there, Sy. I love the plants and the flowers and the arrangements and the creativity, yes. But *business*?" She shuddered. "No thank you."

Charli spun away from the window and put her hands on his arms so he faced her. "But enough about this. I just wanted to tell you before I chickened out. This is your day. What do you say we go celebrate?"

His pupils darkened, and he pulled her close. "I like that idea very, very much."

Chapter Eighteen

SYMON KNOCKED BEFORE he opened the door to Gran's house. It had been almost two weeks since he and Charli had finally taken their relationship past the friend zone, and he hadn't been home much since then, choosing to spend as much time with Charli as possible. Which, in turn, made him feel guilty for not spending as much time with his other favorite woman.

"Gran, I'm home." He was greeted with the familiar scent of an apple pie baking. This time he knew better than to assume it was for him. Still, the delicious smell led him straight to the kitchen. "Another pie for Jim?" Symon kissed Gran on the cheek and helped himself to a cup of coffee from the pot that was perpetually fresh.

"This one's for you."

"What?" Symon almost splashed coffee all over the floor. "A pie? For me?"

Gran laughed. "Don't look so surprised. I'm allowed to bake a pie for my favorite grandson, aren't I?"

"I'm your only grandson, Gran. And yes. You are most definitely allowed." He moved to the counter and the cooling

178

pie. "Do you think it's cool enough?"

"Only if you're willing to risk a burn."

Symon grinned. "It's a risk I'm willing to take."

Gran declined a slice of her own and sipped at her coffee until he joined her at the table. Steam rose from the pie, so he forced himself to wait before diving in. "So, what did I do to deserve this, Gran? I mean, not that I'm complaining. But I was really starting to think that a certain neighbor gentleman had taken over my spot as the favorite man in your life."

She blushed. His grandmother actually blushed. It wasn't something he'd ever seen before.

"Gran? Is there something you need to tell me?"

"I don't need to tell you anything, Symon. I'm a grown woman."

"You are." He tried not to chuckle and focused on the pie, breaking off a small piece with the side of his fork. "But if there was something you wanted to tell me, I, for one, would think it's great."

She tilted her head and raised her eyebrows as she took a sip of her coffee. "You would, would you?"

"Absolutely." Symon blew on the steamy piece of pie.

"Just like I think it's absolutely wonderful that you and Charli finally got over yourselves."

He grinned. "Me too." He put the pie in his mouth and immediately closed his eyes to enjoy all of the deliciousness. "Oh. This is amazing. So good, Gran. Thank you."

"I'm glad you like it," she said. "Be sure to save some for your girlfriend, too."

Girlfriend.

The word sounded foreign in relation to Charli. But what other word was there? Girlfriend didn't feel *important* enough, because she was so much more than that.

"I know how hard you've been working in your *therapy*." Gran interrupted his thoughts. "You deserved a treat."

"My therapy?" Symon froze, his fork hung in the air as he assessed his grandma. *How much did she know? And did it even matter if she did?* "I have been working hard," he said cautiously. "It's been a much harder recovery than I ever expected."

"And it's going well now?"

He nodded. "So much better."

"I'm glad to hear it, hon. Sometimes it's not the physical recovery that can be the challenge."

She *did* know.

"How did you know, Gran?"

She shook her head with a laugh. "Symon, I think you should know by now that there's nothing I don't know."

Symon put his fork down and clasped his hands together in front of him on the table. "Why didn't you ask about it?"

"I knew you'd tell me in your own time. And I knew if you weren't telling me, it's because you had something you needed to work through. I didn't want to rush you."

He blew out a breath. "I didn't want to let you down, Gran. I didn't know how to tell you that I couldn't get on skis again after the accident. I didn't know how to tell you that I was scared. You've sacrificed so much for me to ski."

"No." She stopped him. "Everything I have ever done or sacrificed, as you say, was for you to be happy, Symon. If skiing made you happy, then so be it. But let's be clear: I have never looked at you or your dreams as a sacrifice. It has been my life's greatest pleasure to raise you."

He reached for her hand and squeezed. "Thank you, Gran. For everything."

"You never have to thank me." She covered their grasp with her free hand. "Whatever you need, you know that." She nodded to the pie. "Eat, while it's warm. It's always better while it's warm."

Symon finished his pie and hung a new picture for Gran that he suspected she'd purchased only to give him something to do, but he didn't bother saying anything. He left with promises to be back soon and to bring Charli, too.

He hadn't officially moved in with Charli; it was way too soon to even think about such things. *Wasn't it?* But they had spent every single night together since they'd finally made their relationship well...a relationship, and it wasn't just her king-sized bed that he preferred over sleeping at Gran's house.

Instead of heading back to Charli's right away, Symon drove up to the ski hill. After his first attempt at getting back on his skis with Charli, he'd made a point to go for a few runs every day. Each time he did, it got easier and easier, and to his surprise and delight, it was just as fun as it had been with Charli. He still hadn't attempted any moguls or skills and definitely not a jump, but he'd get there. Alan was pleased with his progress and wanted to start discussions about his return to training with the team, but Symon couldn't even think about that. Not until he knew he could perform the tricks.

Tricks and jumps were a huge part of mogul skiing. Not only did you have to have perfect form blasting down the hill in the bumps, but a big part of the scoring was executing two tricks of various degrees of difficulty. Skiing was one thing. Throwing himself full speed off an icy jump and launching himself into the air so he could twist upside down multiple times before landing...that was a whole different thing.

Doctor Jan, who was quickly becoming one of his favorite people, had walked him through multiple visualizations, and Symon had been using her downloaded meditation at least once, sometimes twice a day. He was ready.

It was time to tackle the next challenge. But he was going to need help, and he knew just who to ask.

———

Another week had passed since she'd first talked to Symon about the idea of leasing the storefront for her shop. It was as if just saying her idea out loud had given it power because things started to move quickly after that.

She'd once more reached out to Cathy, the real estate agent in charge of the lease. There were a few issues to work out, but Cathy promised to do her best to move through them and get Charli the space she needed.

It was almost Valentine's Day, the one day of the year besides Mother's Day, where flower sales went through the roof. There was so much about business that Charli had no clue about but lining up a flower business with Valentine's Day seemed like a no-brainer.

Steven had helped her with some of the details that she hadn't even considered, mainly a business license. He also agreed to look over the lease for her, and Chase and Annie had offered to help design some flyers and advertisements, something else she hadn't thought of. And through it all, Charli worked hard at silencing that little voice in her head that kept telling her that she was too stupid, and far too under-qualified to even attempt something of the magnitude she was.

But she didn't have a choice. She'd looked at the numbers every which way, and it was going to be tight, but if she could just pull this off, it would be done, and she could put this night-mare behind her.

"Charli. Thank you for meeting me here." Cathy burst into the cafe on a gust of cold winter wind. "I'm so sorry I'm late, but I wanted to make sure I had all the details of the agreement in order."

"Of course." Charli waved over at Annie, who was waiting to bring them fresh cups of coffee. "And is it all a go?"

Her entire plan hinged on getting the short-term lease for the shop, something that was far from a sure thing. Cathy warned her the owners might not agree, especially if a potential tenant came forward before then. She held her breath while Cathy pulled a stack of papers from her case.

Annie appeared and delivered two cups of coffee. Charli thanked her with a smile and held her breath while Cathy took her time getting settled.

Finally, the older woman tapped the papers in front of her and looked up at Charli with a look she couldn't quite decipher. "Okay," she said slowly. "I have good news and bad news."

Charli's heart sank. She took a deep breath and blew out hard. "Just tell me."

"A long-term tenant has put in an offer for the shop."

"What?" She thought she was going to be sick. She shook her head and looked down at the steaming drink. "But…how…"

"Charli, we always knew it was a possibility."

"We did. But…" She didn't bother saying that despite Cathy's warnings, Charli hadn't let herself believe that it was ever a possibility. She'd been so sure that if she could just get the shop space, she could sell enough product and it would all be done. "You said there was good news, too."

"I didn't think you were ever going to ask." Cathy grinned. "Because of the move-in date for the new tenant, I was able to negotiate a very short temporary lease arrangement."

"How short?" Her plan had involved leasing the shop for a month. It didn't get much shorter than that.

"Before we talk numbers, I want you to understand that in order to make this happen, I had to negotiate heavily and the owner is taking a risk as well, so the pricing may not be quite in line with what you were thinking. But it really is the best I could do, Charli. And if it weren't for our history and our families knowing—"

"Cathy." Charli tried and likely failed to hide her growing frustration. "Just tell me."

Cathy pressed her lips together, pulled a piece of paper from her leather portfolio, and slid it across the table. "It's for a one-week lease, starts a few days before Valentine's. That should give you enough—"

"A one-week—"

The rest of her protest died on her lips when Charli saw the number written on the top of the paper. The length of the lease would be a hurdle to be sure, but the price…it was…

"It's high," Cathy said.

"High? It's ridiculous, is what it is." Charli was finally able to swallow. Her mouth was so dry it was hard to swallow. "They want this much for *one* week? *One?* How am I going to do anything in one week, Cathy? It's…impossible."

Her optimism failed her. It was starting to become a disturbing trend. *Is this what her father wanted for her? The stress and pressure and soul-killing negativity of starting a business all by herself?* It didn't make any sense at all. Maybe her dad hadn't been of such sound mind after all.

"It's not impossible, Charli." Cathy looked at her sternly. "I would never negotiate a deal for you that wasn't reasonable. And yes, this isn't exactly what you had in mind, but you did tell me you wanted a short-term solution so you could, and I quote, get in and get out. You can do that with this deal."

Charli shook her head. "It will eat up too much budget. I wanted to have a bit of a cushion, just in case…well…" *In case she didn't pull it off.* That was the real reason, one she wasn't willing to say out loud. Truthfully, Charli didn't think she *could* pull it off. And if she didn't, she was in trouble. *Big* trouble.

"I know it's not something you generally see in a town like Trickle Creek." Cathy was still talking. "But you have to think of it like a pop-up shop."

"A pop-up what?"

"I love pop-up shops." Annie, who was walking past the table with a handful of coffee mugs, stopped. "Chase and I found a really cute one that was selling photo prints last time we were in the city. I wanted to come back when we had more time, but they told me they were only there for the day. The day, can you believe it?"

Charli shook her head.

"So, Chase bought it right then," Annie continued. "I don't know if it worked the same way for other people, but for us, it was very much a get-it-while-you-can kind of thing." Annie looked between the two women. "Sorry," she added. "I didn't mean to eavesdrop."

"It's fine." Charli waved away her apology because she'd given her something to think about. "Do you really think it adds urgency?"

"One hundred percent."

Cathy nodded her head in agreement, too. "Have you dialed in what product selection you're going to offer?"

Charli sat back with a shrug. She knew mostly what she wanted to do. It would all be Valentine's themed, obviously. With bigger outdoor arrangements and some centerpiece options as well. She was fairly limited in what kind of fresh flowers she offered considering most of the plants in her greenhouse had only just started sprouting. And she didn't have time to start anything that was faster growing, which was too bad because she really wanted to offer a fresh flower option. There was only one other alternative she'd been thinking about. There was a flower wholesaler out of the city who'd told her there was still time to put in an order for Valentine's Day if she did it right away, but it was pricey. Really pricey. And with the increase in the cost of the lease, it was going to be even tighter than she'd expected. Still…if she was going to do this, she had to go all in. She knew that. She felt it in her bones.

"It's going to be a mixture of evergreen arrangements and fresh displays, including bouquets and centerpieces. Everything you need for Valentine's Day."

"That sounds great."

It did. It sounded perfect. She just needed the location.

"When it comes to the lease, Charli, I just need—"

"Okay."

"Okay?"

"You look surprised."

Cathy recovered quickly. "I'm not surprised, just…okay, yes. I'm surprised. You didn't even let me finish."

"It doesn't matter." Charli pinched the bridge of her nose. A headache was starting to build at the back of her head at the idea of what she needed to pull off in mere days. "It doesn't give me much time, but hopefully I won't need much. But what I do need is the space to pull this off. I don't really have another choice."

"Are you sure, Charli?" Annie set her coffeepot down and sat next to her. "You don't need to rush into this. Maybe in the spring, you'll have your own flowers ready and—"

"I can't wait till spring." She let her gaze drift out the window to the vacant storefront. The idea of having this hanging over her head for months to come was too much. "No. I can't wait until spring." She took a final deep breath. "I'll sign it. Let's do it."

Chapter Nineteen

THE AFTERNOON HAD CLOUDED IN, with a huge dump of snow forecasted. The conditions were perfect on the mountain for skiing. Especially for what Symon wanted to do.

He'd done a few warm-up runs already. Nothing too strenuous. Just enough to warm up before he made his way to the part of the ski hill where the junior freestyle team practiced. Symon knew it well. He'd spent some of his happiest days training there when he was young. Some bad days, too, when things didn't go quite the way he wanted them to. But that was all part of learning and training. And it was exactly why he was there now.

He'd been watching the kids for about thirty minutes from the side of the hill. Every single one of them reminded him of when he was younger.

Fearless.

Hell, it hadn't even been that long ago since he hadn't a care in the world every time he launched off those jumps and hurled himself in the air. With any luck, it wouldn't be much longer until he was that way again.

"Thanks for making time for me, man." Symon bumped

fists with Brody after he wrapped up practice with the kids. "I really appreciate it."

"Are you kidding me? I'll always have time for you, Sy. Especially if I can convince you to show these kids a few moves." He used his head to gesture to the team that had devolved into horseplay and snowball fights as soon as their coach released them.

"Just like we used to be." Symon shook his head with a laugh. "And I would be happy to show them a few things. But not today. That's actually why I wanted to see you, man. I haven't told a lot of people this, but…"

Doctor Jan had worked with him over their last few sessions to help Symon open up about the accident and be honest with the people in his life about needing help. It had been a lot easier with Charli and Gran, but deep down, he knew Brody was a good friend, too. He wouldn't judge him.

He swallowed down the last bit of fear and gave Brody a brief version of the story.

"So you haven't been airborne since?" The other man nodded, considering what he'd been told. He looked over the hill, down toward the practice jumps and then back to Symon. "Okay," he said after a moment. "So, we get you in the air. No problem."

"No problem?"

"Sy, it's what I do. I've been the coach of this team for almost eight years now. I take kids who've never jumped and have them doing one eighties by the end of the season. If I can do it with ten-year-olds, I can do it with you. But first, let's go for a rip. For old time's sake."

Symon couldn't disagree with that.

Next to skiing with Charli, racing Brody down the hill, through the moguls and trees, in knee-deep powder, had been the most fun skiing he'd had in years. By the time they got to the bottom, he was out of breath, feeling the burn in his quads and smiling from ear to ear.

"Damn, Sy." Brody joined him seconds later, a matching grin on his face. "For an old man with a bum knee, you're pretty damn hardcore."

All his time in the gym *had* paid off. Symon truly was in better shape than he'd ever been, and it showed.

"Now, let's go see what we can do about getting you back on top."

⸻

They worked for hours, with Brody coaching him just the way he did the kids, taking it step by painful step until Symon began to feel the familiar pull in his gut. His body tensed and readied itself. And most importantly, his brain could visualize every moment.

"I'm ready," he told Brody before the coach could run him through another drill.

"You're ready?"

"I'm ready. Let's go."

His friend eyed him carefully before finally nodding once. "Okay, but just a jump. Nothing fancy. No D-Spin or Lincoln Loop or even a daffy. Just a simple jump. Up in the air and down. Easy."

"Easy," Symon agreed.

"I mean it, Sy."

Symon knew how the coaching worked. It was important to work the kids up to the tricks slowly. He also knew it was important for him in this situation to work up to it slowly. He'd come a long way, but he still had a long way to go, and he wasn't going to fuck it up by pushing too hard too soon.

"Let's go."

Brody did it with him, setting the pace as they skied side by side and made the easy turns. By the time they hit the jump, Symon was ready. Everything fell into place and muscle memory took over. He bent just a little into the jump and then his skis were up and in the air. He soared through the air and, true to his word, forced his body not to do any tricks at all, keeping it as simple as he could.

When he landed seconds later, both skis hit the snow and his body easily absorbed the impact.

Perfect.

He'd done it.

It took a moment for his brain to register the success, but when he did, he threw his arms into the air and let out a shout. "Fuck yeah!"

Brody joined him as they both skied to a stop. He pulled him into a hug and clapped him hard on the back. "I can see the gleam of gold already, Sy. You've got this."

With the lease signed, there was only one more thing to do. She'd been putting it off long enough, but Charli needed to order the flowers right away if they were going to arrive in time.. But first, she needed to run the numbers. Again.

The way they did every time she looked at them, the numbers swam on the page in front of her. She'd done her best to keep track of her expenses and her income, the way Steven had instructed her to. Chase had even sent her a short video that was supposed to make bookkeeping look easy, but all it had really done was make her sick to her stomach.

She couldn't help it. Numbers, spreadsheets, and equations of any kind made her break out in a cold sweat, want to throw up and mostly curl up in a corner with a blanket over her head.

They always had. And she'd tried, too. She really had. In high school, her teachers were all exceptionally patient with her, going over and over the concepts with her after school until she thought she had a grasp on them. But then she'd go home and attempt the homework, only to struggle for hours. Her dad got her a tutor, and for a while, she was sure she'd gotten over the hump and was finally understanding everything. But that only lasted until the next exam and the resulting grade that, once again, fell just short.

Fifteen years later, Charli should be long over those feelings of complete and total inadequacy. But she wasn't.

She did her best to fumble through the columns. Adding and subtracting and scratching out new numbers with pencil until finally, she was certain of the dollar amount she had left to invest in fresh flowers. Or, at least, certain enough.

"Ready or not." She pushed the notebook away, pulled her laptop over, and opened up the online shop she'd found in her internet searches earlier in the week. The flowers weren't going to be as fresh as she would have liked and they definitely weren't the quality that she'd come to expect with her own flowers that she grew from seed all winter long in her greenhouse, but they'd have to do.

She worked quickly, tapping in her order, using her best guess for how many arrangements and Valentine's bouquets she could sell on pre-orders. It was a guess, she knew that, and she would have vastly preferred to secure all the pre-orders as well as some healthy deposits that would help her with the cost of the flowers, but there wasn't enough time.

Charli dug the credit card she was using for business expenses out of her wallet and entered the number. She hesitated for just a moment before hitting the submit button that would confirm the order.

"Sorry, Dad." She shook her head, knowing that everything

she was doing probably went against every bit of business advice her father would have given her if he'd been there.

But he wasn't there.

That was the whole point.

"I'm just doing what you asked."

Lilly, disturbed from her nap on Charli's lap, mewled in protest, stood, and stretched.

She scratched the cat's ears. "It doesn't matter how it gets done, does it, Lilly? Only that it does."

Charli clicked her mouse on the "complete order" button and it was done.

She squeezed her eyes shut and tipped her head back. "Okay, Dad. Here we go. All in."

Her siblings were counting on her. And Charli hoped like hell she wasn't about to let everyone down.

Chapter Twenty

IT HAD BEEN LESS than a week since Symon made his first jump with Brody. He'd worked hard and very quickly graduated to twists, rotations, and even a simple flip with Brody's coaching. Each time he completed a skill, his confidence grew.

Symon wasn't the only one who was pleased with his quick progress, either. His head coach, Alan, whom he'd kept updated, was thrilled. He'd even worked with Brody on a training program to help Symon get back up to speed as quickly as possible.

"Sounds like you're on track, Sy," Alan said when Symon called to check in. "Brody's been great at sending me video and progress reports. If I'd known you had someone local to help coach you back to full power, I would have been all over that from the start."

"Brody is pretty great," Symon agreed. "I had no idea until I got here that he was the coach of the local junior team."

"Well, they better watch it, or we might steal him away for Team Canada."

Symon laughed, because as good as Brody was, he knew his friend wasn't about to go anywhere.

"Speaking of the team," Alan segued easily. "Do you feel ready to rejoin us on the circuit?"

"Now?" The laughter died on his lips, the smile falling away. Rejoining the team had always been the goal, but for some reason, Symon didn't think it would be so soon. On one hand, his entire body yearned to race again. Even his brain was finally on board with competition again. But rejoining the team would mean leaving Trickle Creek, and his heart wasn't fully buying into that idea. Not yet.

"Soon," Alan continued. "It needs to be soon, Sy."

"The team's strong this year," Symon said. "I've been watching. We should have a good chance at putting guys on the podium."

"We *should*." Symon heard the hesitancy in his coach's voice. "But Derek's hip has been giving him some trouble. He's doing intense PT right now, but depending on how this next race goes, he might have to take some time off. And if that happens…"

Symon didn't need Alan to tell him that he'd be needed for the next race. On Valentine's Day. He knew what it meant.

"Let's cross that bridge when we come to it, shall we?" Symon glanced at the clock on his dashboard. He was going to be late for the Carlson family dinner if he didn't get moving. "I still need to pull off a D-Spin in practice before I can even think about racing again. Give me a few more sessions, okay?"

"Okay," the coach agreed. "But I want you back, Symon. Soon."

He ended the call with the coach and scrubbed his face in his hands before starting the truck and making the drive down the mountain, through town and up to the big house, where Charli was waiting for him.

Almost everyone was already there when he arrived. They were still waiting for Craig and Meredith, not that Symon could tell. With so many people already in the house, the noise level was deafening with everyone talking at once, but he didn't mind. After growing up on his own, Symon enjoyed the energy of the big Carlson clan, and he knew how it made Charli happy. Especially now that her eldest brother was back in town. She reveled in the weekly dinners.

Just as he knew he would, Symon found Charli in the kitchen, helping to prepare the meal. "Hey there, gorgeous." He'd planned to greet her with a chaste, family-appropriate kiss, but the moment his lips touched hers, he got greedy and deepened it until she moaned.

"Okay, okay." A kitchen towel hit Symon's back. "That's enough. There are children present."

Reluctantly, Symon pulled away to see Kat grinning at him, Asher frowning, and no children in sight.

"Grady just fled in terror," Chase said as way of explanation. "But seriously, we don't need to see that."

"Really," Asher agreed. "We don't."

"As much as I like it when you two agree on something," Kat lifted her glass of wine, "I for one think it's great to see these two together *finally*."

"That doesn't mean we need to see it firsthand."

They all laughed, but Symon didn't miss the way Charli's smile didn't quite reach her eyes. She was under a lot of stress with the countdown to the pop-up imminent He tried to help as much as he could, but there was only so much he could do. His main role was to be supportive, and he thought he'd been doing a good job with that. "Hey." He leaned close to her ear so the others wouldn't hear. "You doing okay?"

She nodded. "I got some more orders today."

"That's great." He rubbed her shoulders to ease some of the tension she was holding there. "Are you on track to meet your goal for pre-orders?"

She shook her head a little. "Not yet."

"But she will be soon." Annie jumped into the conversation. "Wait until you see the new flyer and order forms I helped her put together." She put a sample on the table in front of them, and Symon moved to pick it up.

He scanned the form with the catchy graphics and glossy pictures. "This is great. Do you need some help handing them out? I bet you'll have more orders than you can even handle."

"Oh." Charli dropped her head in her hand. "Don't say that. The last thing I need is something else to worry about."

He kissed her forehead. "You're going to be amazing. And it's all going to work out perfectly. I just know it."

"Of course it is," Asher said from the other side of the kitchen. "It's in your blood, Charli. It's going to be a smashing success. In fact, I'll be surprised if you even come back to work at Carlson Corp."

Symon looked from Charli to her brother. "Are you considering—"

"No." She stopped him before he could finish the question. "The only thing I'm considering is my sanity." She forced a smile. "The break from Carlson Corp has only been so I can get this done. But I don't want to talk about it anymore. Tell me how it went today. Does Brody have you flying through the air yet?"

Symon glanced around the room. Although they hadn't told everyone specifically what his problem had been in training, the Carlson siblings all knew he was working hard to get back into racing shape.

"It went really well. In fact, I…" He hesitated, unsure whether he should say anything about his call with the coach. Of course, Charli wanted to know how it was going, and they'd talked about how his goal was to rejoin the team, but always in kind of a vague way. It had always felt so far off and now, with things starting to feel a little more *real*, and the potential for him to be recalled for the Valentine's Day race, well...he wasn't about to add any more stress to her right now. "I actually think I'll take a rest day tomorrow."

"Really?" Charli turned in her chair. "Is your knee bothering you again?"

Worry was all over her face, and Symon instantly felt guilty because his knee had never felt stronger. But at least if she was concerned about his leg, she wouldn't have to worry about him leaving to rejoin the team. There really was no need to concern her with that until something was decided.

He shook his leg a little. "It's just a little tight is all."

"I have just the person to help you with that."

Everyone turned at Craig's voice as he arrived in the kitchen, and he wasn't alone. "Hey everyone. Sorry, I'm late." Craig walked into the kitchen. "But look who showed up unannounced."

"Andy!" Charli jumped up from her chair to hug Craig's friend. Everyone else greeted the new arrival with enthusiasm. Symon waited until Kat was done saying hello. It was a much longer hug than Charli had greeted him with, but no one else seemed to notice, so he didn't say anything.

"Hey there." Symon extended a hand. He vaguely recognized Andy from years earlier but wasn't sure they'd ever officially met. "I'm sure we met years ago."

"We did," Andy said. "But I don't think that counts anymore. It was a long time ago." He smiled easily. "I have heard a lot about you lately, though. How's that leg holding up?"

"Andy, I'm glad you're here." Charli appeared at his side. "Symon's here working on building his strength back, but right before you walked in, he was just saying that his leg is acting up. Maybe you could take a look?"

Symon looked between them, confused.

"Andy's a physical therapist."

"Is that right?"

"Well, not technically." Andy shook his head. "Not yet. But I will be very soon. I'm just finishing up my practicums. But I'm happy to take a look at your knee if it's giving you a hard time."

He didn't want to mislead anyone, but one glance at the anxious look on Charli's face, and Symon bit his lip. "It's a little tight." He patted his knee. "I've been pushing it lately."

"Well, I'll take a look whenever you like."

"It'll have to wait." Chase brushed past them with a tray of roast beef. "It's time to eat."

Even at night, the greenhouse was warm and inviting. Charli let herself in and flipped the lights on. Family dinners were usually one of her favorite parts of the week. Her family grounded her and generally helped to clear her mind, but driving away from the big house earlier, she hadn't felt the sense of peace and comfort that her family usually gave her, which was why she'd decided to stop in her greenhouse instead of going directly into the house. Symon, who'd taken to spending the nights with her most of the time, had gone ahead to feed Lilly, who'd also grown used to having him around.

She moved slowly down the rows of her seedlings, stopping in front of a tray that had sprouted up over the last few weeks. If Charli closed her eyes, she could visualize exactly how they'd look in a few months. Blooms of purple and white would be perfect in her bouquets. But that wouldn't be for a few months yet. With a sigh, she turned away. It had been a niggling thought in the back of her mind from the moment she'd placed the order for the flowers.

They weren't *her* flowers. Charli had only ever arranged her own bouquets from blooms that she'd grown and nurtured and tended. She'd never before worked with commercially grown flowers, nor had she had training of any kind. *What if it was different? What if she didn't know how to work her magic with flowers that weren't hers? What if it* felt *different?*

That was the craziest thought, but she still couldn't shake it. Especially now as she stood in her greenhouse, surrounded by her own seedlings. It felt almost as though she were cheating on them with cheap replacements.

But it was a means to an end.

Hopefully.

It was a feeling that continued to grow inside her, but there was no way she could actually say it out loud. It would sound ridiculous. They were just flowers.

She walked deeper into the greenhouse, inhaling the earthy scent that never failed to ground her.

Except for now.

She dropped her head to her chest and breathed out slowly.

"Hey."

Charli jumped a little, but Symon wrapped his arms around her from behind and pulled her close.

"I don't mean to interrupt." He spoke into her ear. "But I thought you might like some company."

Charli leaned back into his embrace and let herself melt into him. He felt so good. So safe. "Thank you." Her head dropped back against his chest.

"For what?"

Symon's lips brushed the sensitive skin under her ear. She could feel his lips curl up into a smile.

"For being you." She closed her eyes. "And for being here for me."

Without releasing her, Symon rubbed her arms and pulled her in tighter. "Charli, I'll always be here for you. I hope you know that." He spun her in his arms and looked down into her eyes. He held her chin with his thumb and forefinger. "I'm here for you." His lips were soft on hers in an easy kiss.

When he pulled away, there were tears in her eyes. She swiped at them and laughed. "I don't know why I'm crying." She shook her head and more tears fell until finally, she was sobbing.

"Hey." Symon pulled her close again and squeezed her tight. "I've got you, Charli. It's okay, and it's going to be okay."

Was it, though? Was anything going to be okay?

She just didn't know, and that was the hardest part. She'd put everything on the line and if it didn't work out…well, she couldn't let herself think about what exactly it would mean if it didn't work out.

She let the tears flow, and Symon didn't rush her. He rubbed her back and held her until finally, her tears began to slow down.

"Better?"

Charli didn't dare answer. She felt like she was walking a very thin line and if she started to cry again, she might not ever stop.

"What if it's not?" Her voice was small, almost as if she didn't ask the question at all. But she had, and now it was out there. She'd said it out loud. *What if it wasn't okay? What then?*

Symon pulled back so he could look into her eyes, but he didn't release his hold on her. A fact she was thankful for. "What's going on, Charli? You're not usually so pessimistic." She shook her head and tried to look away, but he stopped her. "Charli. Talk to me. I know this is a lot and you're worried and that makes sense. But there's something else going on. What is it?"

She took a deep breath and led him to the bench at the back of the greenhouse. Once they were seated, she took his hand and twined her fingers through his. "Why do you think my dad gave me this task?" Before Symon could answer her rhetorical question, she continued. "Chase had to stay in town and get involved with the community. Obviously, Dad was trying to show him that he belonged in Trickle Creek and that he always had."

Symon nodded. "That makes sense."

"But a business? For me? It doesn't make any sense. Especially because my dad was the only one who knows that I…"

"That you what?" He squeezed her hand.

It was reassuring and deep down, Charli knew that he wasn't going to think any differently of her if he knew the truth. It was years ago, and it didn't matter anymore. Not really, except for demonstrating exactly why her father never should have given her this task.

She took a deep breath and blew it out her nose before looking up. "My father was the only one who knew I didn't graduate from high school."

There. It was out. Her shameful secret. She'd spent so long trying to hide it. She'd even lied on job applications when she was younger. It was why she'd never even considered going to college like the rest of her siblings, and her father had never pushed the issue and had instead given her a job at Carlson Corp. It was her dirty little secret that, no matter how hard she'd studied and how many after-school tutors she had, she just hadn't been smart enough or good enough to do the one thing that had been expected of her.

For a minute, Symon didn't say anything at all. She waited

and watched until finally, Symon scrubbed a hand over his face.

"But you walked the stage with me. We were at the ceremony together. Afterward, we were…we went to Fairy Creek Falls together. We did it together."

"No." She shook her head. "We didn't. *You* did. I tried." She wouldn't cry again. She'd shed enough tears over her secret over the years and although it didn't hold the same hurt it used to, she couldn't deny the impact it had made on her entire life.

"Wait."

He sat back and looked at her with such a confused expression on his face that for a minute she regretted telling him the truth. Maybe it would have been better to keep it a secret after all.

"Let me get this straight. You didn't graduate?"

She shook her head.

"But…how? Why?"

"I failed my math final exam, and I was three percent away from a passing grade. I don't think I would have even found out if I hadn't overheard my dad talking to the principal on the phone, offering him a healthy donation if he let me participate in the ceremony with everyone."

"Seriously?" Symon scrubbed a hand over his face.

Charli could see how hard he was working to piece together his memories from all those years ago with what Charli was telling him now.

"Seriously."

"But why didn't you tell me? Why didn't you say anything?"

"I only found out that morning, and at first, I didn't want to ruin our celebrations."

He blinked slowly then, no doubt thinking about how his actions had taken care of that anyway.

"I was actually going to tell you at the falls but then…well, you remember what happened." She shrugged. "After that, it didn't seem important. For a while, I thought I might try and take math again so I could pass and put it behind me, but ultimately, I just stopped caring."

"But that's not true."

He was right. It wasn't true at all. She'd always cared. The fact that she didn't have her high school diploma had always bothered her and made her feel *less than*. Never more so than recently.

"Damn, Charli." He moved so he was closer to her. "I wish you would have told me. I'm so sorry. I…this explains a few things."

She nodded and tried not to laugh, because nothing about her being an idiot was funny.

"This is why you're so worried that you can't do this business, isn't it?"

Charli nodded again.

"Just because of some stupid piece of paper from a million years ago that doesn't matter."

"But it does matter."

"No. Charli, this doesn't make you any less capable." Symon took both her hands in his and pulled them together. "It doesn't mean anything. You're smart and strong and talented and so incredibly creative, and your dad knew that, too."

She wanted to believe that he was right. Charli wanted more than anything to trust that her father believed it, too. Still, the doubt persisted.

"You've had so much more life since then. You've accomplished so much. And, Char," Symon shook her hands a little, pulling her back into the moment, "remember, you're not doing this alone. I'm right here with you for whatever you need."

It was the only thing that was going to get her through the next few days. With her siblings trying to respect the rules of the challenge by not getting too involved, Charli didn't know if she could do this without Symon's support.

"Just having you here with me is exactly what I need."

He kissed her lightly, and the way she always did when Symon was around, Charli began to feel better. She knew she'd find a way to get through the next few days and pull it off; she had to. But having Symon to cheer her on, and hold her up when she thought she might fall down, was a bigger help than he knew. Charli couldn't even begin to imagine what it would have been like to do all of this without him. Thankfully, she didn't have to.

In a way, they were both going through the same thing in a different way. She believed in his success; was it all that crazy that he believed in hers? There wasn't any reason why they both couldn't be successful. When Charli closed her eyes, she could see Symon standing on the top of a podium, getting that gold medal put over his head. Maybe if she squeezed her eyes a little tighter, she'd be able to see her win, too. After all, life had a funny way of working out just the way it was supposed to.

Chapter Twenty-One

THE NEXT MORNING, Charli was up before Symon's alarm had even gone off. He rolled over to pull her into a snuggle the way he did every morning, but her side of the bed was cold. Not the way he'd been hoping to start their day, but Symon wasn't surprised either. Charli's flower delivery was expected to come in that afternoon, which meant that she'd not only have to process all the flowers, but then also put together her pre-orders. Never mind all the arrangements she was hoping to sell to walk-ins. With Valentine's Day only a few days away, it was crunch time.

It was going to be a hectic few days to get everything done. Symon had never seen her so stressed, but also, so determined. His heart swelled with love and pride for her, and he'd meant it when he told her that he believed in her. She was beyond capable of pulling this off; the revelation about the lack of her high school diploma meant nothing. Not to him. But he could see how much it had impacted her. So much so that she'd kept it a secret all these years. It must have eaten away at her confidence. But all that would change in the next forty-eight hours.

There wasn't a doubt in his mind that she'd handle everything beautifully.

And it would be his job to make sure she knew that, too.

After a quick shower, Symon found Charli in the kitchen, going through her ever-present notebook. "Good morning." He gave her a kiss on the forehead before pouring himself a cup of coffee and topping up hers. "Please tell me you got some sleep."

"Some."

She offered him a small smile, and he knew there was no point pushing it. It's not as if he was going to be able to get her back into bed now.

Charli's eyes took in his appearance. He wore his wool shirt and already had his ski pants on. "You're going to the hill? I thought your knee was bothering you."

Symon shook his leg. "It's all better today, and I had Andy give it a quick look last night. He said it's strong and it was just a little inflammation that I shouldn't be concerned about." That wasn't entirely true, and he hated lying to her. Andy told him his knee was perfect. His muscles were strong and there was no inflammation at all. In fact, when they were in the living room at the big house after dinner so Andy could do a quick assessment, he told Symon he couldn't see any reason at all why his knee should be giving him trouble.

"Still, maybe you should take a few days off? Just to be safe."

Her face was lined with concern, and he hated it. The last thing Charli needed to be worrying about was him. She had enough on her mind. His job was to make her life easier, not more stressful. Not in any way.

Symon bent to kiss her on the forehead. "Don't worry about me. I promise I won't push it. And I'll have plenty of time to help you dominate the flower business."

She groaned, but he saw the flicker of a smile before she turned away. "Just promise me you won't push yourself too hard. I know how much you want to rejoin the team."

And there it was. The opening he had to let her know that he'd been talking to the coach, and he thought Symon was ready.

He opened his mouth to tell her the news but closed it again when she ran a hand through her ponytail.

"I'm not going to lie, Sy. I'm excited for you, I am. But I'm so glad we don't have to think about that for a few more weeks. I just don't think I have the mental capacity to process everything all at once."

He closed his mouth tight and twisted it up into a grin, because that was exactly why he wasn't going to say anything. There was no point putting more on her plate right now. Symon finished his coffee without even sitting at the table and rinsed his cup.

"Well, it's a good thing we don't have to. I'm just going to do a few easy runs," he said. "And I'll meet you at the shop to do all your heavy lifting."

"You're amazing. Thank you."

Symon kissed her lightly. "It's all going to work out, Char. I promise."

———

"Yes!"

Symon skied to a stop and turned to see Brody with one arm in the air in a cheer and the other holding his phone, where he knew his coach had been watching via a live video stream.

"You nailed it!"

Symon squeezed his eyes and sent up a silent prayer to the

ski gods. He *had* nailed it. The D-Spin that he'd been worried about had been flawless. It was as if there hadn't been an injury at all. He was in top shape, and he knew it. And now his coach knew it, too.

Alan had insisted on the video call this morning. He said there'd been a development but hadn't pushed the issue. Not that it mattered because, after that performance, there would be no doubt that Symon would be rejoining the team right away.

"You killed it." Brody skied to a stop next to him, his phone still in one hand. He handed it to Symon, who turned it to look at his beaming coach.

"Damn, Sy. That's the strongest I've seen you look in years. I dare say that your injury turned out to be a good thing. Shook you up a little."

"I don't know if I'd go that far, Coach. But I'm feeling good. Strong. Really strong."

"And that D-Spin. That's a point earner, for sure." Alan didn't bother hiding his excitement. "I want you back with the team as soon as possible. We have a few weaker skiers who are struggling with some nagging injuries. They may need to—"

"I can be there next week." Symon quickly added up the days in his head. He'd still have time to travel to Whistler after helping Charli with the store. It would be tight, but as long as there were no weather delays or freak snowstorms, he'd make it.

"Next week?"

"It has to be next week, Coach. I can't—"

He caught Brody, wide-eyed, shaking his head as if he couldn't believe Symon was telling his coach no, which he probably couldn't. But Brody didn't understand everything else that was at risk. If he was careful, he could have it all. It wouldn't be a big deal.

"What you can't do is let your team down." Alan interrupted him. "I need you back now, Symon. You know I went out on a limb letting you have the mental health break of going back to Trickle Creek. The race is in Whistler and—"

"I know where it is, Coach." Symon was very well acquainted with the race schedule. He also knew it was on Valentine's Day, and Charli would need his help with the shop. "I'll be there next week, Coach. I promise. I just don't think I can get there before then."

"Listen," Alan said after a moment. "I'm not going to lie to you, Symon. From what I've seen on that video and what Brody's told me, you're skiing better than you have in years. We need you. Your teammates look up to you and as far as points go, we could use your contribution. But…"

Symon held his breath. If Coach decided to pull rank and order him back today for the Valentine's Day race, he didn't know how he'd break the news to Charli. It would be hard enough saying goodbye in a few weeks after the stress of the store was behind them. But right in the middle of things? The timing couldn't be worse.

"I know it's been hard for you to come back from your injury," Alan continued. "I don't want to rush you into something you're not ready for, Sy. So, I'm going to leave the decision up to you. I need you to consider that you're part of a team and that team needs you. But only you know if you're truly ready to compete now or in a few weeks."

Symon took a deep breath and exhaled slowly.

Skiing was a solo sport, but it was also very much a team sport, and he *was* part of a team. He'd been watching the televised races. He knew they could use him, and if he raced well in the February races, it would improve Team Canada's standings overall. Without those points, they'd fall out of the top ten and they wouldn't be able to get it back.

"Think long and hard."

Symon agreed and ended the call.

He handed the phone back to Brody, who watched him with disbelief on his face.

"I don't know why this is a question, Sy." He tucked his phone into his parka. "You're ready. You *know* you're ready. And don't even try to tell me you're not, because we both know you'd be lying. What's the issue? Why are you hesitating?"

Symon inhaled and looked out over the ski hill to the town below, where Charli would be hard at work in the shop, trying to get things set up. He'd already been at the hill longer than he'd planned because the training was going so well and then Brody wanted to get Coach on the phone and…he should have been there for her already. But staying on the hill to train was important, too.

"Have you ever felt that no matter what you do, you're making the wrong choice?"

"The only wrong choice is not making one." Brody shook his head. "If it helps, I find that when I'm faced with a hard decision, going for a good hard ski to clear my head helps."

"Fuck it." Symon pulled his goggles down over his eyes. "It sure can't hurt." He'd already kept Charli waiting; what was a few more hours? Especially if it meant he'd have something to tell her when he saw her. Because the one thing he knew he didn't want to do again was let history repeat itself.

Three days.

She had three days to make her pop-up shop work.

It seemed like both an eternity and a blink.

But she had a plan. As long as everything went according to plan, it would be fine. *She* would be fine. Charli stood in the middle of the plaza under the gazebo where she always felt closer to her father and looked toward the empty shop that, for the next few days, would be hers.

Three days.

All the insecurities she'd been fighting, all the doubts and reasons why she had no business attempting such a thing flooded in, threatening to overwhelm her. But she shook them off. The one thing she didn't have was time. She couldn't afford to let any of those negative feelings in because if she did, they would paralyze her. She pulled her father's note from her pocket. She'd brought it with her to keep close to her for the next few days.

You can do anything you put your mind to.
I believe in you.

"At least that makes one of us, Dad."

Charli exhaled long and slow, tucked the note back into the back pocket of her jeans, and stepped out of the gazebo and over to the store for the first time.

Marta had left behind all the shelving and tables that she'd used for her pottery when she'd closed out, which was perfect because Charli didn't have the time—or budget—to get anything else.

In the back room, she'd already moved over the evergreen arrangements she'd made up at the house. She'd be adding red and white carnations to many of them for Valentine's Day displays. But others meant to be outdoor window arrangements or shop displays and were all ready. She lugged a few of them to her own storefront. Hopefully, they'd attract some walk-in business. And she put the rest close to the front to make the shop look fuller.

She spent the next few hours organizing her lists of the pre-orders she'd taken and double-checking her inventory list of what she'd ordered. She prioritized the arrangements she'd have to make right away after her big delivery arrived. To try to ease some of the burden of a busy Valentine's Day, Charli offered a discount for any orders that requested an early delivery date of the day before. It was still going to be busy, but she was hoping that strategy would give her a bit more breathing room when it came to the big day.

"Are you open for business yet?"

Charli lifted her head to see Annie and Kat walk in the front door.

"It looks great in here already." Kat shook her head in wonder as she took in the full shelves. Even the ones that were missing their fresh flowers looked great, and Charli had to admit that the store was starting to look more and more like a flower shop. She glanced at the clock on her phone again, eager for the flower delivery to arrive. That's when things would really start taking shape.

"There's still so much to do." Charli shook her head, but she couldn't stop the smile that crossed her face, and Annie noticed.

"It's exciting, isn't it?"

Charli nodded and then laughed. "It's mostly terrifying. But yes, it is kind of exciting. I just hope it—"

"No hoping." Kat held up a finger. "Knowing." She waited for Charli to meet her eyes before she continued. "This is going to be amazing, Charli."

Annie nodded. "But you know what you're missing?"

The two women grew serious, and Charli had a flash of panic in her gut. "Oh no. What did I forget?"

"It's pretty important." Kat gave Annie a look, and her friend nodded in agreement.

"Really, I can't believe you didn't think of it already, Charli."

"You guys are scaring me. What is it?"

Annie broke first. She extended her arm, which Charli noticed for the first time had been hiding behind her back. "Here."

"We thought you could use this."

With shaking hands, Charli took the item, a roll of vinyl, from Annie's hand and started to unroll it. "Oh!" Her hand flew to her mouth, and Kat rushed forward to grab the vinyl before it fell to the floor. She finished unrolling it completely so Charli could see the full display.

Alpenglow Flowers

"You had a sign made?" Tears flooded her eyes. She'd always called her little table at the farmers' market Alpenglow because the pink and purple glow on the mountains when the sun set was one of the most beautiful things Charli had ever seen, next only to her flowers. She hadn't even considered giving her pop-up shop a formal name and had registered her temporary business license under her name only. But now that she saw the sign, and the beautiful logo that had been created to go along with it, Charli knew it was perfect.

"This is amazing." She blinked back the tears. As touched as she was, there was still no time to let emotion creep into her day. "I can't believe you did this, ladies. It's absolutely perfect."

Kat put the sign aside and she, along with Annie, pulled Charli into a tight hug.

"It will look amazing hung over the door," Annie said. "And then everyone who hasn't heard yet will know that *this* is the place for flowers."

"Speaking of flowers…" Kat looked around. "They're not here yet?"

Charli had been trying not to worry, but she'd expected the delivery almost an hour ago. "Any minute. I'm sure the truck was just delayed in the mountains. The weather is…" She trailed away because the sun was shining on a beautiful, blue-sky day. There was no snow or severe weather in sight.

"I'm sure it will be here soon." Annie nodded. "Do you want us to hang this up for you before we get going?"

"I have clients in ten minutes," Kat said. "But on delivery day, I'm all yours."

Charli felt a surge of warmth for her sister and all her siblings who'd volunteered to be her delivery drivers on Valentine's Day. It was the only way she was going to be able to get everything done, and Steven had approved of their help considering they weren't offering anything but general labor.

"Don't worry, ladies. I know you both have to run." She took the sign from Kat and rolled it up again. "Symon will be here soon, and he's agreed to be my go-to guy and take care of all the things."

"I bet he did." Annie wiggled her eyebrows.

Kat laughed. "He'll be taking care of *all* the things, won't he, Charli?"

"You guys are ridiculous." Charli rolled her eyes, but she didn't bother to hide her smile and then, unable to help herself, she added, "But he certainly does take care of *all* the things."

They all dissolved into giggles for a minute and the release of it left Charli far more relaxed than she had been before the girls had shown up.

"Seriously," Annie said when they'd regained control of themselves. "It's incredible to see the two of you together."

"It really is." Kat nodded. "We tease, but it's true. You and

Symon were always meant to be together, and I think it's all about timing. And finally, the timing is perfect."

"Agreed. It's like it's all coming together, just the way it was supposed to. With his injury and coming back to town just when you were embarking on this new journey."

Charli chuckled. "I wouldn't call it a new journey."

"Well, whatever you're calling it, it's awesome."

"And it's so great that he's skiing well."

Charli looked at Kat. "Have you been up on the hill?" She herself hadn't been skiing with him for the last week or so, she'd been so busy. And once he'd started training with Brody, Symon had a pretty full schedule himself. "I mean, he's always skied well, but I haven't seen him myself in a bit."

Kat waved her hand. "I haven't seen him either, but Lauren mentioned how she'd run into Brody earlier and he told her about how he thought Symon was ready to race this week."

"This week?" Charli's stomach flipped. Symon hadn't said anything about a race this week. He'd mentioned the March race, but that was still weeks away. "He can't be considering it if he didn't mention it," she told the girls. "He's probably not ready yet."

"That's not what Brody said." Kat shrugged. "But I'm sure you'd know more than I would. Either way, I love the two of you together."

"Me too." Annie beamed. "Trickle Creek's new power couple."

Charli burst out laughing. "I hardly think that I'm any part of a *power* couple."

Annie gave her a look. "You two are perfect. Every part of your relationship is amazing. Let's just leave it at that."

Annie was so sure, but Charli couldn't let herself totally agree because although she'd confided in her friends about how she felt about Symon, she'd only told them how excited she was when she was with him, and how good it felt and how connected they were and how totally happy she was. All of that was true. But what she hadn't told her friends was that she was also terrified.

Falling in love with your best friend was amazing and thrilling, and because a part of her had been in love with him since they were kids, it also felt very natural. But the flip side of that was so scary that sometimes it caught her off guard and she found it hard to breathe.

She knew it was ridiculous to hold onto old childish feelings, but there was still a part of her that felt that pang of rejection when he'd run from her to pursue his amazing dream the day after she'd experienced her biggest failure. He was going to be a star, and she…well, she just wasn't good enough.

And here she was again. Feeling completely out of her depth with this pop-up shop and this massive goal hanging over her head and… *What if she still wasn't good enough for him? And what was this about a race coming up this week?* He hadn't mentioned it at all. *Why?*

"Char?" Kat stepped forward and grabbed her arm. "What's wrong? You look…"

"Pale," Annie finished for her. "I don't have to go to work. Do you need me to stay?"

Charli shook her head. She was being silly, and she knew it. She had enough problems that the last thing she needed to be doing was inventing any. They were grown-ups now. It wasn't the same as when they were kids. Symon knew the truth about her education, and he didn't care. They loved each other. It wasn't about any of the other stuff.

"I'm fine. Honestly." She managed the most reassuring smile she could. "I just got lost in my thoughts again for a second. Go to work." When her friend and sister didn't move, she pushed them gently toward the door. "I mean it. Get out of here so you can help me out later. I'm going to need it when the bouquets and arrangements are all done. Never mind with all the walk-in sales that I hope we get."

"That you *will* get," Kat corrected her.

She needed those sales to make up the difference and finish the task. *If the flowers ever arrived.*

Charli didn't need to check the clock to know they were almost two hours late by now.

"At any rate, go. Go." Charli continued to push them toward the door. "The delivery will be here soon and then I won't have time to even breathe, let alone worry about anything."

Chapter Twenty-Two

CHARLI CHECKED OUT HER PHONE. Again.

It had a full charge. Full service. And no missed calls. Or texts.

Not only was the flower delivery late, so was Symon. And he wasn't answering his phone. Or any of her texts.

Just in case she missed it, Charli checked again. She'd sent her last message over thirty minutes ago.

Where are you? Is everything okay? Flowers still aren't here.

He hadn't replied.

She paced the shop again, adjusting the arrangements on the shelves. While she'd been waiting, a handful of people had walked in, curious about the new shop, and despite her total lack of inventory, she'd presold ten bouquets for pick up the next day and five evergreen centerpieces. Charli should be elated at the positive start despite the *hiccup.* That's what Chase had called it when she phoned him to tell him about the flowers and ask for advice on how to handle the problem.

"This type of thing happens all the time in business, Charli. It's just a little hiccup."

"A hiccup? It feels more like a vomit. Or maybe that's just what I feel like I'm going to do if the flowers don't show up soon. How am I going to sell flowers if I don't have any?"

"You'll have them."

He was so calm, it was annoying. How could her older brother be so calm when their entire future as a family was left in her completely incapable hands? *What if she'd screwed this up beyond fixing? What if the flowers didn't show up? What if she couldn't fulfill her orders and had to return the deposits? What if—*

"Stop running *what-ifs* in your head."

"What?" Charli froze in place and glanced around. "I'm not running—"

"You are." He chuckled. "Stop it. It'll be fine. You need to keep busy. Maybe just use your time while you're waiting to think about the next time. Start making lists of what you'll do differently and—"

"Next time?" She almost choked on the words. "There will be no *next time*, Chase. I don't think I could survive the stress of it."

She didn't bother saying how she didn't think she'd survive the stress of *this* one time. Never mind how she still thought it would be some sort of miracle if she was actually able to pull it off at all.

"Why don't you just wait and see how you feel, Char. I think you might surprise yourself."

"I think you're crazy."

She'd ended the call without feeling much better than she had before. However, Chase had given her the idea to keep busy. Not that she planned to make any lists for the *next* time.

Charli had hoped that Symon could help her with the sign, but considering he still hadn't shown up to help her—a detail she was trying not to be pissed at—she might as well do it herself.

She found a ladder in the back storage room and lugged it through the shop to the front door. Inside, she took a hammer and nails from the *just-in-case* toolbox she'd brought over, snatched up the sign, and headed out into the cold.

The sun was starting to set, which also meant that the ski hill would have closed at least an hour ago. But she tried not to think of Symon, or his absence, as she climbed up the ladder with two nails pinched between her teeth and the sign and hammer tucked under one arm.

Charli hadn't centered the ladder properly and had to reach over to one side to get the nail into the wood properly. She leaned over as much as she dared before starting to fumble with the sign and the nail. With it mostly in place, she tapped the nail head and missed, hitting her finger instead.

"Ouch!" She caught herself before saying a bad word out loud. After all, there were children shopping in the plaza with their parents, and she didn't need to be responsible for offending anyone outside of her brand-new business.

She tried again and this time, not only did she miss the nail, but the sign fell to the ground below. She swore under her breath, less worried about anyone overhearing her this time as she made her way down the ladder. A quick adjustment and she went back up. This time, Charli successfully hit the nail and secured one side of the sign. She repeated the process on the other side and was about to descend to the ground to admire her work when she heard a honk at the back of the shop, indicating her flower shipment had arrived.

She quickly scrambled down the ladder and with her hammer in one hand, tried to collapse the ladder quickly so she could receive her order and get started.

"It's crooked."

The voice caught her by surprise, and she swung around, almost hitting Symon with the ladder as she did so. "What?"

It's not that she needed him to repeat himself because she hadn't heard him. She had. She just couldn't believe what she'd heard. He was hours later than he said he'd be, with no phone call or text, and the first thing out of his mouth on what he knew was going to be a hard day was criticism. Charli couldn't quite believe she'd heard what she thought she had.

"It's crooked." He held his chin in his hand as he evaluated her sign. "Here." He reached for the ladder she was still awkwardly holding. "I can straighten it for you."

Maybe it was justified, maybe it wasn't. Either way, all the stress, annoyance, frustration, questioning, doubt, sadness, and every single other emotion Charli had experienced in the last few days, and especially the last few hours, erupted.

"You know what *you* can do?" Without waiting for an answer, she thrust the ladder in his direction. Symon looked at her with shock and something that looked dangerously like it might be the start of a grin, until she added, "You can go to hell."

She regretted the sharp words the moment they came out of her mouth, but there wasn't time to take them back. A second honk that came from the back of the shop sounded. "I don't have time for this." She turned on her heel and went to receive her order.

Symon didn't bother trying to stop her. He'd heard the honk of the delivery truck. And even if he hadn't, he didn't blame her for being pissed. He should have called. He should have texted. Hell, he should have *been* there.

He'd told her he'd be there for her. He'd promised her.

And then he hadn't.

But did that promise mean giving up on his dreams? Did it mean that he should tell Coach no and stay in Trickle Creek, missing the race? Did that promise mean that he should give up on skiing and the promise of gold?

It wasn't a fair question. He was acting like a petulant child, and he knew it.

He'd known it when he'd turned his phone to silent and insisted on continuing the training with Brody long after he'd planned to leave to help out at the shop. And even longer, after Brody had left. And he'd known it when, after the hill closed for the day, he'd sat in the pub and nursed a beer while he weighed the options in his head. And he knew it now.

With a sigh, he bent and picked up the ladder. He set it up and centered it in the doorway before picking up the hammer Charli had dropped as well.

It only took him a few minutes to straighten the sign over the door. When he was finished, he stepped back and admired it.

Alpenglow Flowers

It was perfect, and along with the displays Charli had put outside, and in the window, it really made the store look official. It was all coming together for her. She'd worked so hard and had accomplished so much in such a short time. And she'd done it almost entirely on her own.

See? She doesn't need you.

The voice in the back of his head that he'd successfully ignored for most of the day piped up, but he shut it down before he could let himself go down that spiral again.

Even if it were true, and Charli didn't need him, that wasn't a justification for doing what he knew in his heart he wanted to do.

Join the team for the race in Whistler.

Symon looked into the well-lit store but couldn't see Charli anywhere. She was likely still receiving her order. She had a lot to unload and unpack. And he had some apologizing to do. A decision about skiing was going to have to wait.

He found her just where he'd expected to: in the back, surrounded by boxes. The cold air from the back door blasted into the warm storage room as the delivery driver brought in more boxes.

Charli looked up from an open box, saw him, and looked down again. She compared whatever was in the box to what was written in her notebook, but Symon didn't miss the lines of worry on her face as she flipped through the pages and looked back at the box again.

"Char, I'm sorry I—"

"This is wrong."

She looked up again. This time, the worry on her face had turned into full-blown panic.

Symon put the ladder against the wall and moved through the piles toward her and peeked into the box she'd been staring into.

"Roses." He pushed the plastic aside and lifted one. "I thought roses were a Valentine's flower. What's wrong with—"

"They're yellow."

"Yellow?" He held up the flower. It was, in fact, yellow.

"Yes." She grabbed it from his hand and held it up as if that would change the color. "It's yellow. I didn't order yellow."

"What's wrong with yellow?" He was trying to get up to speed, but there was a lot he didn't know. And judging by the look on her face, he really didn't know anything about the proper color of roses.

"Yellow roses signify friendship." She stared at him as

though he were stupid. She may not have been too far off. "Valentine's Day is about love."

"Right." He nodded slowly and took the rose from her hand, putting it back in the box.

"I ordered red and pink and some white to accent them. But not yellow." Again, she flipped through her notebook, as if there were something written there that would tell her why yellow roses had dared infiltrate her space.

"I'm sure the flowers you ordered are here." Symon moved through the boxes that had already been brought in, examining the labels as he moved. "Here." Triumphantly, he patted the top of the box the driver was currently carrying before taking it from him and taking it to where Charli looked like she was about to have a full-on panic attack. "The label on this one says red."

She exhaled slowly and lifted the tape seal. Charli pulled the paper back to reveal bunches of flowers—red ones—wrapped in plastic.

"See?" Satisfied that he'd help avert a crisis, he turned to face the growing pile of supplies to find another box that would make her happy. "Nothing to worry—"

"They've been frozen."

"What?" Symon spun around to see Charli holding up what was a red rose. He didn't know whether it had been frozen or not, but even from where he stood, he could see that it didn't look good.

"It's been frozen or something." Charli's voice began to rise. She dropped the offending flower to the side and dug into the box again, pulling out more damaged flowers. "They're unusable. Ruined. I can't use these."

Symon started to say something reassuring, but she ignored him.

"Excuse me." Charli pushed past him and went straight to

the delivery driver. "I can't use these flowers. I'll need to check all the boxes, but those roses are damaged. They're unusable."

The driver shrugged. "You'll have to contact the sender."

"No." Charli's voice wavered. "You don't understand." She grabbed him by the shoulders. "I need more flowers. I can't use these."

"Sorry, lady." He shook free of her grip. "Not my problem. I'm only the driver."

"Not your problem? Not *your* problem? Well, whose problem is it—"

"Whoa." Symon slipped himself between them. He gave Charli what he hoped was a reassuring look and turned to face the driver. "Are there any more boxes on the truck?"

The man shook his head. "I need someone to sign for these before I can go."

"I understand." He took the clipboard from the man but didn't dare turn around. He could feel Charli vibrating with anger behind him. At least for the moment, that anger wasn't directed at him. "We'll have to check the order against what you brought in, of course."

Symon didn't have the first clue as to what he was supposed to do with an order like this. Especially one that was damaged. But checking the order would be the first step. And maybe with any luck, it would give Charli a chance to calm down. After all, it was only one box. It wasn't the end of the world.

———

"It's four boxes!" She'd gone completely numb and couldn't feel her fingers. Or her feet. The very fact that she was still standing upright was a friggin' miracle. Her stomach churned so violently, it was a good thing there hadn't been time to eat lunch, or she would have thrown up from the stress of it all.

"Four, Symon! Four. And the yellow roses? What am I supposed to do with those?"

He nodded, but she could tell by the look on his face that he had no fucking idea how critical the situation was. And really, what did he care? Obviously, he didn't. He'd been…well, she had no idea where he'd been all day. But he hadn't been helping her the way he said he would and now, he stood there, surrounded by flowers she wouldn't be able to use, acting like it was no big deal.

And it was a big deal. It was a very, *very* big deal.

"It's only four, Charli." He held up four fingers on one hand and his other palm up, like he was trying to make peace. "It's not that bad. I'm sure we can—"

"Can what?" She tossed her notebook down on the pile of boxes. "I can't call the wholesale company. They're closed. And even if I could get through to someone, it's not like they're going to be able to send more flowers out by tomorrow. This order took almost a week." *And I paid extra to rush it.* She hadn't told anyone the part where she'd been so scared to finally order the flowers that she'd waited too long. The only way to get them to her in time for Valentine's Day was to pay almost triple the usual shipping rate, which was already high because of their location in the mountains. She'd already miscalculated the cost of the vases she'd bought and with the shipping, she was completely over budget. She had nothing left.

Which was why Symon's next suggestion almost put her over the edge.

"I'll drive to the city," he said. "Right now. I'll go to every flower shop there is and buy all the roses and…whatever those white things are that you needed. And…well, whatever you need, I'll get them."

"No." She shook her head. "No. You can't do that."

"I can." He stopped what he was doing and moved for his coat. "I'll go right now and first thing in the morning—"

"No, Symon." When he didn't stop moving, she yelled, "No! Stop."

He did stop then. Right in front of her. She knew he was only trying to help and more than anything she wanted to lean into it and let him. She wanted to fall into his arms and let him hold her and tell her it was all going to be okay. But she couldn't.

She took a deep breath in an effort to slow her racing heart and bring herself back under control.

"Where were you today?"

"Where? What? Char, we don't need to talk about this right now. I—"

"But we do." She already knew the answer, but it suddenly seemed so important to know the truth. To know just how unworthy of him she was. "Were you skiing?"

He nodded. "I know I said I was only going to do a few runs. But then—"

"It's what you do. You're a skier."

"No. I mean, yes. I am. But—" Symon reached for her hand, but she pulled away. "Charli. Coach wants me to rejoin the circuit and I...well, I'm not going to...I just needed to think...and look, it doesn't matter. I'm here now."

He *was* there, but Charli heard what he'd said even if he hadn't. What was more, she could see it in his eyes. He wanted to be on the hill. He wanted to be skiing, and so did his coach. Symon was a world-class skier. That hadn't changed. She didn't have to ask him what it was he'd needed to think about all afternoon. Because as far as she was concerned, there was nothing to think about. And the girls had already told her about the race that was coming up. He needed to be in that race, and she wasn't going to be the one to hold him back. *For what? A stupid failed pop-up flower shop?*

He was still too good for her. He was going to be a star. He was going to win gold at the Olympics, and she…well, she couldn't even manage to put flowers together.

"Charli." Again, Symon reached for her, but she turned her back to him. "Talk to me, Char."

She shook her head and tried to process everything. He was conflicted because of her, and that was ridiculous. He was only there now because of some sort of sense of duty, but it wasn't where he needed to be. He needed to be with his team, getting ready to win. Charli wasn't stupid. He was ready. And there was only one reason he hadn't told her about it.

She swallowed hard and looked around at the boxes of damaged flowers she still needed to sort through and process. There was no way she was going to let him throw away his future for…whatever it was she was trying—and failing—to do here. There was no point in both of them losing everything.

Charli cleared her throat but couldn't dislodge the lump that had formed there. Tears burned in her eyes, but she refused to cry. She couldn't. "You need to leave, Symon."

"Excuse me?"

She cleared her throat and worked to take the emotion out of what she was about to say. "Leave. I don't want you here." Saying the words hurt her on a physical level, but she couldn't let him see that. She couldn't let him think that there was any way they could fix things or that she was lying through her teeth and what she wanted more than anything was to be with him. If she let it show, even a little bit, he'd stay, and she couldn't let him do that. Not for her. "You let me down," she continued, forcing coldness into her voice. "I needed you today, and you weren't here."

"I screwed up, Charli. I'm sorry. I am."

She could hear the desperation and confusion in his voice, but he didn't reach for her again. She took a step back to put even more distance between them.

"Right now, we need to—"

"*We* don't need to do anything." Even to her own ears, her words were harsh. Cold. She didn't sound like herself, but she couldn't stop. She needed him to leave before she changed her mind and fell into his arms. "This isn't your problem," she continued. "It never was."

"Charli, you don't—"

"Go." She squeezed her eyes shut for a moment and took a breath. "This was never going to work."

"You don't mean that."

She didn't. She didn't mean any of it. But she couldn't take it back. She needed to be strong. Because she loved him too much to ask him to stay.

With a strength she didn't know she was capable of, Charli opened her eyes and looked straight into Symon's. "I do." And then she said the one thing she knew would make him leave. "I don't love you." The words were acidic on her tongue, burning with every syllable. "I don't think I ever really did."

He opened his mouth but closed it again with a shake of his head. Finally, Symon took a deep breath, exhaled slowly, and without another word, turned and left.

Charli didn't move until long after she heard the front door close behind him. She stood motionless until finally her legs gave out, and she crumpled to the ground and allowed herself to cry.

Chapter Twenty-Three

IT WAS past midnight by the time Charli had finished processing her flower delivery. At least, what she could salvage from it.

Unboxing a flower shipment involved a lot more than simply unwrapping each bloom. She had to trim the stems and any damaged foliage before putting each one in a bucket with the right ratio of flower food to water. It would have gone a lot faster if she had help, but the work ended up being cathartic and allowed her the perfect distraction from her aching heart.

She worked methodically, flower by flower, until finally they were all done. There was a larger-than-expected pile of damaged flowers that she wouldn't be able to use, but she'd managed to save a few of the red roses and most of the pink ones.

After taking a quick break to stretch and fill her coffee cup with the thermos she'd brought with her, Charli started the process of cataloging what flowers she did have and cross-referencing that list to the list of orders she had. She could barely keep her eyes open when she was finished, and considering her track record lately, she wasn't sure she trusted her calculations completely, but if she was right—and she hoped like hell she was—there would be just enough fresh flowers to complete the orders. Especially if she shorted a few of the arrangements by a flower or two. Beyond that...well, she didn't want to think about it yet.

Charli locked up the shop behind her and made the short drive home to catch a few hours of sleep. She'd have to get an early start if she was going to get all the orders arranged and prepped the next day. After that, well...she'd have to figure out how to break the news to her family that she wasn't going to meet her goal and that all her hard work was for nothing because even if she fulfilled all of her pre-orders, the reality was that she hadn't left herself any room for error and she just didn't have enough product. With no actual bouquets to sell on Valentine's Day to walk-ins, or for the last-minute orders she expected, she wouldn't hit her goal.

She'd failed.

Fortunately, Charli was so drained from the hard work of the day that she fell easily into a deep sleep that even her worries and her heartbreak couldn't wake her from until her alarm went off a few hours later.

Symon was still trying to wrap his head around how things had gone so wrong, hours later as he pulled his truck into the parking lot of the residence where his bed was waiting for him, along with the rest of his team. It was almost three in the morning, but he could still catch a few hours of shut-eye before the team started their morning training routine.

After Charli had sent him away, he knew there was only one place to go. To his team. If she didn't want him, they would.

He'd stopped just long enough at Gran's to grab a few things and give her a hug.

"I'll be back soon," he told her, unsure whether it was a lie or not.

She squeezed him extra hard and kissed his cheek. "Why so sudden, hon? Why are you leaving like this? What's—"

"I can't talk about it." That much wasn't a lie. He didn't know how to talk about what had just happened with Charli, because he didn't understand it himself. Yes, he'd screwed up by leaving her waiting when she needed him. That was a dick move, and he knew it. But he'd come to tell her that he chose her. He'd rejoin the team in March because there was no way he could leave her with the shop and everything. He'd promised her she wouldn't have to do it alone, and he'd meant it. He loved her and he wouldn't leave her.

But she'd told him to go. Hell, she'd all but kicked him out of there.

He couldn't close his eyes because every time he did, he could see the hurt in her eyes when she'd told him to go.

"Symon." Gran pulled away and held him at arm's length. Despite the fact that she was at least a foot shorter than him, she had a formidable presence. And just like she'd always been able to do, she saw right through him. "Talk to me, Symon. What happened? Where's Charli? You—"

"She told me to go, Gran. She doesn't want to be with me." He shook his head. "It's not going to work out between us."

"I don't believe that."

"Well, you should." His words were harsher than he'd meant them to be. "Because it's over. I thought it…it doesn't matter. She doesn't love me."

"Symon. She does."

"No." He shook his head, completely unwilling to rehash what had been the worst conversation of his entire life with his

232

grandmother. "I need to meet up with my team. There's a race. They need me."

"She needs you, too."

Her words sank into his heart. He wanted to believe that Charli needed him just as much as he needed her. But that look on her face. The words she'd said.

"I don't think she does, Gran." Symon exhaled and shook his head slowly. "I need to get going if I'm going to get there before dawn."

"You won't stay the night? Sleep on it and see how things look in the morning. A fresh day always brings a fresh perspective. I think you—"

"I appreciate that you want to fix this, Gran." He interrupted her softly. "But I don't think this can be fixed."

"Nonsense." She stepped back, giving him the space to leave. "I know you can't see it right now, Symon, but you will." He started to shake his head, but her voice stopped him. "I also understand that you have other commitments and that's important, too." She crossed her arms over her chest, pulling her robe tight around her. "Your dreams have always been important, don't ever forget that. But the other thing you need to remember is that Charli's love got you to where you are right now. And often, the only way to actually achieve your dreams is to realize that not only do you not have to do it on your own, but you shouldn't. There are many kinds of teams, Symon."

Gran's words played on repeat in his brain for his entire drive through the mountains. It was only when he finally fell into his bunk in the athlete's residence and closed his eyes that her voice faded away. Replaced instead with Charli's face and the pain in her eyes when she'd told him to leave.

Working with flowers never failed to make her happy. At least they usually did.

Charli had already spent three hours working on bouquets and vase arrangements, and despite the less-than-ideal shipment of flowers, they looked great. When she stepped back to look at the table full of her finished product, she should have felt pride and happiness. But the only emotions she could muster was disappointment and a deep sadness.

The bells over the door chimed and before Charli could turn to see who it was, Chase stood at her side.

"Those look fabulous," he proclaimed. "Wow. Charli, they look great. You should get some of those vases in the window display with a sign about last-minute ordering. I can get Annie to do up a—"

"Don't bother." She lifted a hand and let it fall to her side before walking away from her work. There were still more arrangements to put together, and then she had to start on the delivery tags.

"What?" Chase followed her into the back room. "You don't think a sign would help bring in those last-minute orders that will push you over the top?"

"No," she said. "I think that's exactly what it would do."

"I don't understand. Maybe I misheard, but I thought you said you needed those orders to meet your numbers. In fact, you said you needed a big percentage of walk-in and same-day orders to meet your goal."

Charli knew very well what she'd said. A part of her wished she'd just kept quiet about it and not told them how close to the edge she was. That way she could put off disappointing them until after it was all said and done. Then again, there was no point in waiting. It might be easier to rip off the Band-Aid and let her brothers and sister know how badly she'd screwed up their future for them.

"I did say that." She reached for a carnation and some baby's breath to start another bouquet. "My pre-sales alone won't be enough. I'm going to fall short."

"Before the same-day orders…"

"There won't be any more orders, Chase. It's over. I failed." She dropped the arrangement she was working on and stared up at him. She was too tired to cry and probably still too numb from the shock of the realization, so she simply looked at her brother until he shook his head and demanded that she explain what was going on.

For the next few minutes, Charli filled him in on the damaged flowers, the poor accounting and the miscalculations, and the reality that she couldn't pull flowers out of thin air. With nothing to sell, there was nothing else that could be done. "I failed, Chase. I'm sorry." She dropped her chin to her chest. "I was hoping to wait until after the deliveries were done to tell the others. If you wouldn't mind, I think it would be best if it came from me."

"No." Chase stood abruptly from the stool where he'd been sitting and listening.

"No? You don't think I should wait to tell them?"

"No, I don't think you should tell them at all, Charli. Because you're not going to fail."

"I already did."

"No." He slammed his fist down on the worktable so hard it bounced some of the blooms. "You have not and will not fail, Charli, because that's not what this is about. That's not why Dad set this up for you. And the fact that you still haven't realized that yet blows my mind. You're smarter than this."

"I'm not." She shook her head, tears finally pricking at her eyes. There was no point in keeping her secret any longer. Not only was her entire family about to find out what a loser she was, but the whole town was also, so what did it matter if they all learned that she'd always been a loser? "I'm not smart, Chase. I never have been. Maybe that's why Dad set me up to fail. So that I'd stop keeping secrets and finally tell you all that I never graduated from high school because I'm too stupid."

A tear slipped down her cheek. "He covered for me all those years ago and made a donation to the high school so that I could walk across the stage with everyone else. But my diploma was fake because I didn't earn it like everyone else. Now you know and everyone else is going to know, too. I'm the family moron. Too stupid to do anything with her life except play in the dirt with flowers. And even then, I couldn't turn that into anything." She dropped her head into her hands and let her tears fall onto the table below.

It was silent for a few minutes except for the soft sound of Charli's sobbing filling the room, along with the occasional sniffle. She wasn't sure how much time had gone by when, finally, Chase cleared his throat. "You done?"

Whatever response she'd been expecting from her big brother, that wasn't it. Charli lifted her head and swiped at her eyes.

"You done?" he asked again, his lips curling into a wry smile. "Because from where I'm sitting, you still have a lot of work to do."

Charli sniffed hard. "Didn't you hear anything I just said?"

"I heard it all."

"And?"

"And what? I already knew you didn't graduate from high school, Char. Do you think I care? Do you think any of us care? It's just a piece of paper. You've done amazing work at Carlson Corp. Asher's been going on and on about how much they need you over there now that you've had this time off. It's getting more than a little annoying, to be honest."

"Wait." She shook her head. "You knew?"

Chase nodded. "I knew. And it doesn't matter, Charli. Not unless it matters to you. But as far as I'm concerned and Asher, and…well, I'm pretty sure as far as Dad was concerned, it doesn't matter. Some people don't thrive in the traditional educational system, but it doesn't mean they're stupid. And you are not stupid. Far from it." He chuckled a little. "I can't even believe I have to tell you this, Char, but you are one of the most creative, brightest people I know. And I'm not the only one who thought so."

"What does that mean?"

Her brother's smile was soft. He tipped his head a little. "Did you get a letter from Dad yet?"

Charli knew that Steven, their father's assistant and best friend, had given Chase a letter from their father right when Chase needed it most and had been about to leave town. It had been this perfect gift to encourage him and tell him all the things that he should have said to Chase before he died, but never had a chance to right when he needed it most. She had definitely not received such a letter.

She reached for her notebook and pulled out the folded note. "I only got this with the start-up check." She held up the paper and dropped her head again. "I just don't get it, Chase. The test Dad gave me…he knew I couldn't do it. Why would he do this?"

"What's the note say?"

"What's the note say?"

She handed it to her brother.

"Charli," Chase started reading out loud the words she'd already memorized. *"You can do anything you put your mind to. I believe in you. Love, Dad."*

Hearing her brother read their father's words squeezed her heart. She sucked in a breath as Chase carefully folded the note and handed it back to her.

"How many times have you read this? Because I think this note says everything pretty damn clearly."

She unfolded it and traced the words with her finger as she read them again. And again.

"Dad believed in you," Chase said softly.

She finally met his eyes, the note still clutched in her hand.

"The real question now, Charli, is do *you* believe in yourself?"

Chapter Twenty-Four

SYMON HAD NEVER SKIED BETTER.

Trickle Creek was his home hill, but Whistler was the hill he trained on and raced on. The moment he skied off the chairlift onto the familiar terrain, he was at home.

Alan hadn't been as surprised to see him as Symon thought he'd be. Although he did chastise him for driving through the night when he needed his rest, the coach was happy he'd be at the race the next day.

Together, the team worked on some easy warm-up runs before hitting the practice jumps. Symon used the relaxation and focus tools that Doctor Jan had given him in their sessions before each jump. He visualized each and every one from start to finish, and every single skill was executed perfectly.

Alan was thrilled. As were his teammates.

"It's good to have you back, Sy."

"We missed you."

"With jumps like that, we've got this cinched."

"You're going all the way to gold."

Symon accepted all the well wishes and compliments as

graciously as he could, but Gran's words continued to echo in his head.

The only way to actually achieve your dreams is to realize that not only do you not have to do it on your own, but you shouldn't.

Symon looked around at the guys on his team. He *wasn't* doing it on his own. He had them. But he also knew that's not what Gran meant. And he knew exactly who he wanted *and needed* on his team. And it had nothing to do with skiing.

"Hey." His coach, bundled in a parka against the blowing snow, appeared at his side. "You're skiing well out there."

"Thanks, Coach."

"But you look distracted. Did something happen while you were home, Sy? Because I need your head in the race tomorrow. We can't have you distracted. I won't risk another injury."

"There won't be another injury, Coach. I got this."

"You good then?"

No. I'm not. But I'll be good to race.

Alan bit his bottom lip and sucked in a breath. "A woman?"

"Why would you say that?"

Alan laughed. "Because when a man looks the way you look right now, despite having just skied better than he ever has, it's gotta be a woman. Am I right?"

He wasn't wrong. Symon shrugged, because it was so much more than *just* a woman he couldn't stop thinking about. It was Charli. *His* Charli. And nothing about what had happened the day before between them felt okay.

Had he made a mistake leaving? Should he have stayed and forced her to let him help her? What about the race?

There were too many questions that he didn't have answers to, and it was too late now. Tomorrow was Valentine's Day. The race was first thing in the morning. His teammates and coach were all counting on him.

Besides, Charli had enough on her plate without him barging in at the eleventh hour to add more stress. More than that, she didn't want him to.

I don't love you. I don't think I ever really did.

Fuck. The words still stung, as if he'd just heard them.

But also, the more he thought about that moment, the more he pictured her face and remembered the way she looked while she'd delivered her death blow to his heart, the more he knew something was off.

Very off.

She hadn't meant what she said, and he knew it.

He needed to talk to her. Face-to-face. He needed to look into her eyes. A phone call wouldn't be enough. Not even close. And a text message? That was completely out of the question.

He needed to see her. But it would have to wait.

At least for a little bit longer.

———

At Chase's insistence, Charli left him in charge of the shop with the promise that he would take care of moving the flower displays into the window and onto the shelves while she was gone. They kept the shop cool enough that the flowers weren't going to need to be in a cooler overnight. Especially considering they would all be delivered the next day. She couldn't let herself think about all the other pieces she should be currently creating with the nonexistent product. And her impending failure.

The real question now, Charli, is do you believe in yourself?

Did she?

She wanted to.

More than anything, she wanted to.

When Chase kicked her out of her shop with the strong suggestion that she get some food and fresh air before returning, there was only one place Charli could think to go. She grabbed a burger from the Shed, the permanent food truck by the river—because once Chase mentioned food, her stomach started to rumble—but then she got in her car and made the short drive to the trailhead, eating while she went.

Fairy Creek Falls.

She'd meant to revisit them with Symon, where maybe they could make a proper wish together. But she'd sent him away.

Charli faced the frozen waterfall and sucked in a deep breath. She'd been so busy and so preoccupied with the rest of her life crashing around her that she hadn't been able to think about what that really meant.

She'd felt his loss when she'd woken up to an empty bed. It had only been a few weeks, but already she'd grown used to falling asleep in his arms, and waking up with him wrapped around her, holding her close. She didn't even want to think about how hard that would be in a few days when all of this was over for good.

Charli crouched down and scooped up a handful of snow. Now that she had given herself a minute to think about him, she wished she hadn't. Her chest ached and she couldn't get the look on his face out of her memory. It hurt. More than anything else she'd ever experienced. When her father died, she thought the pain of his loss might kill her, but this was different. It was a death of a different kind when she sent him away. But there hadn't been another choice. Symon left her once to follow his dream. The difference between then and now was that this time it was on her terms. And she couldn't let him stay. Not with her, when it meant giving up his dream. There wasn't a doubt in her mind that he loved her. And that's why she'd had to make him go.

With her mittened hands, she shaped the snow into a ball and tossed it from hand to hand.

That's not the only reason you sent him away.

Charli threw the snowball into the frozen waterfall and watched it blow apart.

No. It wasn't the only reason she'd sent him away.

Her mind raced with everything she'd always believed about herself and her life and her worthiness.

Do you believe in yourself?

Ever since the second will reading, Charli hadn't been able to understand why her dad had set up a test that would put her inability on display in such a way. She'd doubted herself every step of the way. But Symon hadn't. Even after he knew the truth. Chase hadn't either. None of her siblings had. And her father hadn't. He'd written it in black and white, right there for her to read.

You can do anything you put your mind to.
I believe in you.

It was only her who had the problem believing.

Charli scooped up another handful of snow and made a ball. She threw this one immediately into the ice.

And then she did it again.

With every snowball she threw, everything became clearer.

In only a few short weeks, she'd pulled together a business. Even in the off-season. With no product of her own. With only her imagination, her creativity and sheer will, she'd brought Alpenglow Flowers to life. Sure, she'd stumbled along the way, but she'd come so far.

She threw another snowball.

And there was no reason she couldn't go all the way.

"Yes. I *do* believe in myself." She threw her head back and laughed into the silent winter air. "I am worthy. Of Symon. Of success. Of all of it." She nodded as an idea formulated in her head. So far, she hadn't used any of her own products in Alpenglow Flowers because of the season. All her seedlings were still growing. But what about the flowers that she'd grown last year? What about the reams of dried flowers and herbs that she'd carefully tied and hung in the back of her shed?

Would there be enough? Could she pull it off?

There was only one way to find out.

Chapter Twenty-Five

INSTEAD OF DRIVING BACK to the shop in the plaza, she headed straight for her shed, calling Chase on her way. As clearly as she could, she managed to explain her idea.

"Everlasting love." The name was perfect. "I'll make wreaths mostly and some small arrangements," she told him. "Instead of flowers that die in a few days, you can give your sweetheart an everlasting love display that will last months. Years even."

"I like it."

She could hear the smile in her brother's voice.

"I need you to stay at the shop. I know it's a big ask, but—"

"No problem. Whatever you need."

"I'm glad you said that." She laughed. "Because I was hoping you could make up some signs. For the window. And maybe Annie can make up some more flyers. These ones should talk about the very exclusive everlasting love flowers that will only be for sale on Valentine's Day in very limited quantities."

She giggled with excitement at the idea. It was perfect. There wasn't much time, but if they could create a little urgency for limited edition products, maybe she'd be able to sell enough to make up the difference and it wouldn't be a failure after all.

"I'll text her right now," Chase said. "And Grady will be more than happy to distribute the flyers to as many people as he can in exchange for the promise of an ice cream."

"Perfect. Thank you. I'll be as quick as I can, but I might be here all night, depending on how many I can make."

"Don't worry, Char. We got you."

Warmth filled her, and she felt something else instead of the panic and worry that had been her constant state of being since the will reading. There was something else. Excitement. Hope. And belief—in herself.

She was just about to hang up when Chase spoke again. "Hey, Charli?"

"Yeah?"

"You've got this. We all believe in you. Dad, too."

She had to swallow hard against the lump in her throat. There was no time to cry. "I know, Chase. Thank you. And you know what else?" She didn't wait for him to answer before she added, "I believe in myself, too."

Symon rode up the chairlift alone. Usually, on race day, he liked to be immersed in the energy of the other skiers. He liked the friendly banter and ribbing all the other racers participated in. At least until he got to the top of the mountain.

But not today.

It was Valentine's Day, and the wind and snow that had been whipping across the mountain the day before had given way to a bright blue sky, and crisp February weather.

The snow would be perfect.

He'd had a good sleep, even if it was filled with dreams of Charli and their time together in Trickle Creek. They'd been so real that he felt as if he were back there again. In the plaza, hand in hand, kissing on the ski hill, cooking in her kitchen, making love in her bed. He'd been dreaming so deeply that when he woke it took him a minute to realize he was in the single bunk with Davidson still snoring above him. In Whistler, hours away from the woman he loved.

And he knew she loved him too. He felt it. There was no way you could have a dream like that and not know it in your bones. No way. She was his, and he was hers. Just the way it had always been. That hadn't changed, and he was going to tell her exactly that.

Just as soon as he won this race.

Symon skied off the chairlift and into the pre-race area, where the officials checked his number and had him sign in. Alan moved over to talk to him, give him last-minute advice and talk to him about the snow conditions, but Symon wasn't listening. He'd already done the work. He'd spent his time before breakfast meditating, and he'd already visualized the entire race, from the starting gates to every single turn he'd take, to the way his skis would slide over the jump, and he'd lift in the air. He'd practiced in his mind how his body would twist, and his legs would move in perfect formation as he nailed the tricks perfectly. And finally, he'd pictured skiing across the finish line to see the clock and his time before looking to the judge's score and the fast time that would put him in first place. In his mind, Symon had already taken first place.

He had this.

"You've got this, Sy." Alan clamped a hand over his shoulder.

"I know." He nodded once and pulled his goggles down over his face before skiing to the starting gate to win the race.

Chapter Twenty-Six

"CHARLI! ARE YOU SERIOUS WITH THIS?"

Kat yelled across the store, to where Charli was processing an order from a walk-in customer on her tablet with the point-of-sale app Craig had helped her download. She looked up long enough to make eye contact with her sister before returning to the customer who was paying for one of her ever-lasting love dried flower wreaths.

"Thank you so much," Charli said to the woman. "I really hope the person you bought it for enjoys it for months."

"Are you kidding?" The woman grinned and pulled the wreath close to her chest. "This is for me. Everlasting love for myself. It's gorgeous, and I'll be hanging it on my front door as soon as I get home."

Charli laughed as the woman left. But she appreciated the sentiment and was thrilled she could make someone so happy. In fact, she'd been making people happy all day.

The dried flower arrangements were a hit, but not like the wreaths. She'd managed through some sort of miracle to make ten the night before, finishing right before dawn. She was exhausted.

But it had been worth it to see the reaction of the customers who were thrilled, not only with the last-minute gifts for their loved ones but also with the idea that they wouldn't die in a few days.

It turned out that more people than Charli expected didn't want to spend a bunch of money on flowers that were only going to be thrown out a week later. They were such a big hit that there were only two wreaths and three little flower arrangements left. If they sold them all, she would achieve her goal.

Even the friendship bouquets she'd put together with the yellow roses that had been sent by mistake had all sold out.

She was so close; the anticipation was making her even more nervous than she'd been when they opened their doors that morning.

"Charli!"

She blinked, remembering her little sister who still stood at the front of the store, her arms outstretched wide. "Please stop yelling." She joined her little sister and rubbed her head. "I didn't get much sleep last night." *Or any at all.* "I can't deal with the yelling." She dropped her hand. "What are you yelling about anyway?"

"Look at this." Kat waved her arms around the store.

Charli followed her gaze and then looked back at her, confused. "What am I looking at?"

"Empty shelves!"

"Again, with the yelling." Charli protested, but she was grinning broadly. "But it's pretty great, isn't it?"

"It's fucking incredible, Char. These wreaths are killer. And everyone we delivered to was thrilled with their flowers. They're already asking about Mother's Day."

"Mother's Day?"

Kat nodded. "I wrote down all the names and numbers of

everyone who was interested." She handed Charli the list. There must have been at least twenty names on it.

"You told them this was a one-time thing, didn't you?"

"I certainly did not." Kat stared at her, clearly appalled. "There is no way this is a one-time thing. It's a massive success."

"I don't know about massive." Huge understatement. She was so close to not making it, it would be funny if it weren't so damned scary. Only Chase had any idea how close to the line she really was. "Never mind the…well, no. After today, I'm done. I'm not cut out for the business world."

"I beg to differ." Chase walked in, Annie and Grady with him. "We just finished our deliveries, and I've got to say, Charli, people loved them. And what they don't know is how much more they're going to love the arrangements you make with your own home-grown flowers in the spring. You're killing it here."

"You really are," Annie chimed in. "And these wreaths… they're absolutely gorgeous. They're going to be gone in no time and then it's time to celebrate."

"With ice cream?" Grady looked hopeful.

"I don't see why not." Charli laughed. "That's how we celebrate—"

"Excuse me."

A little voice grabbed her attention. Charli turned toward the customer to see a little girl who couldn't have been much older than six or seven holding the smallest of the everlasting love arrangements that were left on the shelf.

"How much is this one?"

Charli bent down to be closer to the little girl who held the flowers and looked at the tag. "That one is twenty dollars."

"Oh. I don't have enough." The little girl's face fell, and she looked at her feet as she held the flowers out to Charli. "I wanted to get my mom something because I love her so much and she's..." The girl's lip trembled, and something in Charli's chest tugged.

Charli took the flowers and set them on the shelf. "I bet your mom is a great mom." She put her hand on the girl's shoulder and squeezed gently until she looked up at Charli.

"She's the best." The girl wiped her nose with her sleeve. "But she's sick, and I want her to know that I love her."

"I'm sure she knows." Charli swallowed hard and looked up to keep tears from spilling from her eyes. "How much do you have to spend?"

"I got five dollars from saving my allowance."

"Five dollars, huh?" Charli stood and walked over to the shelf where the largest arrangement sat. It was priced at fifty dollars. She pulled the tag off and stuck it in her pocket. "This one is five dollars."

She held it out to the little girl, whose head snapped up hopefully. "Really?"

"Sure is."

Charli pulled a tissue from her pocket and blew her nose loudly after the little girl left with her flowers. She fingered the paper tag in her pocket and tried not to think about how razor-sharp her margin of error was to hit her goal.

Her fingers closed around the tag, scrunching it into a little ball. It didn't matter. Some things were more important than money.

———

It was almost six o'clock. All the flowers had been delivered and most of the everlasting love arrangements had been sold. Charli didn't know whether she'd hit her goal or not. She hadn't had time to look. And if it weren't for the whole family legacy thing, she wouldn't even care, because when Charli looked around at the near-empty shop, full of her family and friends who'd come together to help her, who all believed in her and encouraged her to go for it, she felt nothing but pride.

She was beyond proud of herself, not only for what she'd pulled off but also for finally getting over her own bullshit and really going for it. She believed in herself and that was the biggest accomplishment. For the first time in her life, she'd really believed in herself, and it felt really fucking good.

There was just one thing missing. Or more specifically, one *person* missing.

She'd tried not to think of Symon all day because she knew if she let herself, she wouldn't be able to focus on what needed to be done. But now that it *was* over, he was the one person in the world she wished she was sharing the moment with. And the only reason she wasn't was because she'd sent him away.

She'd been so cruel. So harsh. But it had been the only way.

Without even watching the race, she knew he'd won. She could feel it. Not that there'd ever been a doubt.

"So, I think that's probably it." Craig walked through the door, holding a pail of ice cream and a stack of bowls. Meredith was behind him with a cup full of spoons. "The plaza is pretty dead," he said. "I doubt they'll be many more walk-ins. Besides," he looked around with a grin, "I'd say you did pretty awesome, sis. You killed it."

"She did." Steven walked through the door next. The old family friend had been in and out all day, checking on the progress of her sales, offering some friendly advice and lots of encouragement. Charli knew the man had a hard job. He'd been tasked with overseeing their father's final wishes, but he was also like an uncle to them all. It was more than likely diffi-cult for him, too.

He gave her a hug, and she let herself sink into it, pretending for a moment that Steven was her father.

"You did good, Charli. He would be very proud of you."

"I don't know if it was enough," she said when he released her. In her pocket, her fingers wrapped around the paper price tag from the arrangement she'd sold the little girl. Logically, Charli knew a difference of only forty-five dollars wasn't going to be enough to make or break her business. But the fact was, it represented how close she was to crossing the goal line. "I still need to run the—"

"We'll double-check them later." Steven silenced her. "Right now, I think it's just as important to celebrate your successes with those who love you."

She nodded in agreement and turned to look at the people who'd gathered for her. Again, Symon's absence was a knife to her heart, and for the first time all day, she realized that not one of her friends or family members had asked about him or where he was.

"Hey, Asher?" She joined him at the table, where her brother was digging into a bowl of ice cream. She knew that out of all of her siblings, he would be the most honest when it came to Symon. It's not that Asher was cold, but he'd never had a romantic relationship that any of them knew about, and he definitely lacked some of the sensitivity that the others had when it came to matters of the heart. "How come none of you have asked where Symon is?"

Her brother put another bite of ice cream in his mouth and took his time savoring it before finally answering. "Because we know."

She tilted her head in question.

"He's at the race, right?"

She nodded, despite the fact that she couldn't be one hundred percent sure.

"That's good. He didn't belong here. He belongs on that team. Always has." Asher took another bite, completely oblivious to the pain she was going through.

But that's why she'd asked him. She and Kat liked to joke sometimes about how their brother was a little *dead inside*, but she appreciated his bluntness.

"You're not wrong." She nodded and turned to walk away. "Thanks."

"Hey, Char." Asher stopped her with a hand. "For what it's worth, I think he belongs with *you*, too."

That was unexpected. "Thanks, Asher."

"And whatever went down with the two of you…" He shrugged awkwardly, clearly uncomfortable with the show of any emotion. "Well, I hope you guys can sort it out because the two of—"

"Hey!" The door flew open, and all eyes turned to Brody and Lauren, who stood together in the door of the shop. "Sorry to interrupt." Brody lifted his laptop high in the air. "But I know you were a little busy today, and I didn't think you would have had a chance to see this yet."

Charli walked through the crowd toward him. "See what?"

"The race." It was Lauren who spoke up. "Symon's race."

Charli gave her friend a look and glanced to Brody. There were questions there that she would ask, later. "I didn't see it," she said to Brody. "Why?"

"I think you should."

Without waiting for a response, Brody walked toward the table and set up his laptop. "This was recorded earlier this morning, obviously."

"Obviously."

Everyone crowded around the small screen as Brody clicked the buttons. A moment later, Symon was on the screen.

Even in his full ski gear, helmet, and goggles, he made Charli's heart flip.

They all watched as Symon was announced. Then the countdown and the lift of the gate. He was off, skiing better than she'd ever seen him ski. He bounced through the moguls effortlessly; his knees looked as if they were hitting his chin, but he was totally in control. Charli held her breath as he flew over the first jump. The 360 trick was executed perfectly. He landed, his knees absorbing the impact, and then he was off again, racing through the moguls toward the second jump. He flew off the jump, getting more air than the first time. Charli held her breath as he executed the trick she knew was called the D-Spin. A backward summersault followed by a full twist. The one he'd crashed on last time he'd attempted it.

A collective cheer went up among the group when Symon landed it perfectly and finished the moguls with ease. He sailed over the finish line in only twenty-five seconds. Symon's arms went up in the air, his poles over his head as he celebrated what was an amazing time. The rest of the scoring would be determined by the judges based on his turning technique and the skill he demonstrated in his tricks, but Charli knew. He'd won. It had been a perfect run.

A few minutes later, the final score was announced on the screen, followed by another cheer around her. He'd done it.

Tears blurred her eyes, and she tried to turn away, but Lauren stopped her. "There's something else," she said kindly. "You need to see it."

Charli let herself be guided back to the table and into a chair that had appeared. Brody reached forward and clicked a few buttons on the computer to advance the broadcast.

Her breath caught in her throat when Symon appeared on the screen again. This time, his helmet was off, and she could see his eyes. They were sparkling with excitement as the interviewer shoved a microphone in his face.

"Symon Scott," the interviewer said. "That was quite a run. How does it feel to win first place in your first race back after such an injury?"

"It feels damn good, Dan. Really damn good."

Charli smiled. Symon deserved this celebration so much. He'd worked so hard. She'd made the right choice sending him away and to the race. Even if it felt in her heart like the wrong thing. He was exactly where he should be.

The interviewer continued with a few more questions until he finally asked one that caught Charli's ear. "What do you attribute your comeback to, Symon?"

Charli watched as his toothy grin turned serious as he addressed the reporter. "I can't lie to you, Dan. It wasn't easy and there were times when I wasn't sure I would even ski again."

"Is that right?" Dan seemed genuinely shocked. "What changed for you? Because you did not look like a man who didn't think he'd ever ski again when you were out there."

Symon nodded seriously as Dan chuckled. "It took a team I didn't expect, Dan. Obviously, my coach and Team Canada teammates are and always have been instrumental in my success. I don't know if you know this, but I went home to Trickle Creek for part of my recovery, and that's where I had a different kind of team."

Symon went on to list Brody and Gran and even Doctor Jan. She squeezed her eyes shut.

"But it was someone very special who made the biggest difference."

Charli's breath caught in her throat.

"She taught me how to not take myself so seriously and have fun again."

"Fun?"

"That's right, Dan. Fun. It's the most important thing. I mean, what's the point of skiing if we're not having fun, am I right?"

There was a cheer in the crowd around them and a few chuckles from those gathered in the shop, but Charli was focused on the screen.

"She also helped me believe in myself again, and she believed in me when I didn't." Symon turned now to face the camera, as if he were looking directly at her. "Charli Carlson, you are the most amazing woman I've ever known and the only one I've ever loved. I couldn't have done this without you, and I never want to do it without you again."

"Wow." The announcer attempted to take back control of the interview. "She sounds like a pretty special lady."

"She is." Still, Symon looked straight into the camera. "And it's because of her that I was able to be at the race today."

The interview ended, but Charli didn't notice. Tears streamed down her cheeks. Someone put a tissue in her hand and someone else rubbed her back.

It was too much. The lack of sleep, the stress of the past few days, the heartache. She needed to get out of there. Charli pushed back her chair and turned blindly, hoping she could somehow get to the back of the shop to find her purse and go home. But before she could get there, someone stopped her.

"I hope you're not leaving yet."

Chapter Twenty-Seven

SHE FROZE under his touch and slowly lifted her head to look at him. "Symon?"

He flashed her the biggest, brightest smile he could. "You didn't really think you could get rid of me that easily, did you?"

"But…how…" She looked back to where Brody was gathering up his laptop.

He owed his old friend in so many ways, but the timing of him showing Charli the video was outstanding.

"You were just…aren't you in Whistler?"

"I was in Whistler," he corrected her. "This morning. That was filmed hours ago."

She shook her head, still confused. "But Whistler is like—"

"Eight hours away." He couldn't not touch her for a moment longer. His hand reached out and stroked a strand of hair off her cheek. "I got lucky. There was a film crew doing a Hallmark movie on the hill, and I convinced them to let me hitch a ride back to Calgary. I rented a car when I got there and…"

"You're here."

He nodded. "I should have been here all—"

"No." She stopped him. "You shouldn't have been here. You needed to be at that race. And...congratulations, by the way."

He shrugged. "I couldn't have done it without you."

Tears streamed down her face, but he didn't try to wipe them away. "No." She shook her head. "That was all you, Symon. You're strong and you trained and—"

"You said the words that made me go."

She blinked and looked at him with wide eyes. "About that..."

"It took me awhile to figure it out," he said. "Longer than I'd like to admit, honestly." He chuckled a little at his own ignorance. "But I know why you pushed me away, Charli. You wanted me to go race."

"I'm not going to hold you back."

"I know. You never could."

She looked down at her feet, but Symon needed to know she heard him when he said what he needed to say. "Charli. It's always been you. I meant it when I said I love you. I've always loved you, and I don't care what you say...I know you love me, too."

He didn't need her to say it; he knew it. It would take a lot more than one emotional outburst at the height of her most stressful moment to push him away. He just wished he'd realized all of that sooner.

"We're a team, Char. And that means we need each other to succeed." Guilt flashed through him. "I can't apologize enough for leaving you the way I did when you needed me most. I told you I was going to be there, and I should have been, no matter how hard you pushed. There's no excuse for leaving you right when—"

"No." She pressed a finger to his lips to silence him. "I needed you to leave and not just for you, but that was important, too. But I think on some level I knew if you stayed, I'd lean on you, and I needed to do this on my own, Sy. I don't even think I realized how important it was for me to do it on my own until just now. But you know what…for the first time in my life, I stood on my own. When it would have been easier to quit and every single part of me wanted to do just that, I didn't. I believed in myself enough to see it through."

Symon had never been prouder in his whole life. Not just of his win; that was really such a small part. But mostly of the woman he loved. "Damn, Charli. You amaze me more and more every day." He cupped her cheek in his hand. "I'm incredibly proud that you're—" He stopped himself. "Tell me you're still mine. Tell me you love me. Tell me you—"

"I was a fool to say the things I said to you." She held his face in her hands, too, so they stared into each other's eyes, completely oblivious to the world around them. "I didn't mean them."

"I know."

"I love you, Symon. I've always loved you. It's always been you."

He kissed her then, his lips crashing to hers in the kiss he'd been craving all day.

Someone cleared their throat and someone else laughed nervously, but they didn't care. Symon deepened the kiss. He could taste the salty tears that were still streaming down her cheeks. He kissed her until the tears stopped and only then did he pull away gently, still keeping her wrapped in his arms.

"I want to hear everything," he said. "The shop looks…" He looked around for the first time. Besides all the people who were milling about, trying and failing not to look at them, there wasn't much in it. "It looks empty," he finished. "Does that mean you sold out?"

"Is there anything left?" The bells over the door, along with the voice, announced another visitor. A voice Symon recognized. The crowd parted to reveal Jim, Gran's next-door neighbor. "I need something for my sweetheart, and I've been busy all day." His eyes swept around the store. "Someone at the grocer mentioned the beautiful arrangement his daughter had bought for her mother, and I knew I needed to come see." Jim's eyes landed on Symon.

Symon smiled brightly, and Charli stepped forward. "I think I have a wreath left and maybe a small everlasting love arrangement, if that will do?"

Everlasting love? That's what he had with Charli.

"I'll take them both." Jim handed over his credit card, and he turned to Symon with a wink. "You think your gran will approve?"

Symon shook his head. "She better. You're a good man, Jim."

The older man finished paying for his goods, and when he was gone, Chase moved to lock the door behind him. "That's official then," he said. "Charli, you sold out. You did it."

She should be ecstatic. She should be celebrating and cheering with the rest of them.

But she couldn't because all she could think about was the numbers in her notebook not adding up. The overspending on the flowers that were all damaged. The discount she'd given the little girl. The calculations that she must have missed somewhere along the line.

"Char. What's wrong?" Symon wrapped an arm around her and spoke into her ear.

Damn, his touch felt so good. But she couldn't let herself enjoy it the way she wanted to. Not yet.

She shook her head. "I don't know if I...I don't think I did it, Sy. I mean, I think I came close, but—"

"Charli?"

Steven stood behind Symon, his black leather portfolio in his hands. "Can I speak to you alone for a moment?"

Her stomach sank. This was it. This was Steven telling her she'd failed. She hadn't fulfilled the requirements of her father's request, and their family was going to lose everything. All because of her.

She swallowed down the lump in her throat and grabbed Symon's hand as she nodded. "Symon can come, too."

"Are you sure?" Symon asked her. "You just finished telling me that you needed to do this on your own."

"And I did. Now I need you. Didn't you just say something about a team? You're part of mine."

He squeezed her hand. "Always."

Steven led them away from the others and into the back room, where they sat on the stools around the workbench. The older man put his portfolio on the wood between them, and she couldn't help but stare at it as if it held the fate of her future. Which it likely did.

"I need to tell you, Charli," Steven began. "You've done a remarkable job here and in such a short time. I know when your father and I spoke about this particular caveat to his will, neither of us expected you to go after the project with such... shall we say, urgency."

There was an urgency, all right. An urgency to get it done and out of her life.

"But there was one thing both of us expected from you," Steven continued. "And you proved us to be absolutely right in that regard."

"What's that?"

Steven's smile was kind. "We knew that whatever you

decided to do, you'd do it with passion, Charli. The way only you could do it."

Warmth filled her to hear that, and she was reminded of something Tony had said to her in his antique store weeks ago.

"I hope you know by now that your father never doubted you for a minute when he requested this of you."

She did know that. It took awhile to come to that realization, but now, Charli could feel it deep inside. Her father had always believed in her; she was just so clouded in her own self-doubt that she couldn't see it. Until now.

But there was still one very important detail that needed to be discussed. "Steven, the numbers…I don't know if I was able to meet the objective," she confessed. "I think I fell short. There were the damaged flowers and—"

"You met the objective, Charli."

"But you haven't looked at my books yet."

"I don't need to."

Charli sat back, thankful for Symon's hand on her thigh, grounding her. "I don't understand. You said that I needed to double the investment and—"

"The real objective wasn't about the money or the profit you made or lost," Steven explained. "It never was. It's always been about believing in yourself, Charli. It's all your father ever wanted for you. He wanted you to see for yourself what we've always seen in you. Just how amazing and creative and uniquely talented you are."

She sat stunned, trying to process what he'd just told her. After a moment, Steven pulled his black portfolio to him and without ever having opened it, he stood. "I'm proud of you, too, Charli." Unshed tears swam in his own eyes. "And for what it's worth, I don't think this should be the end of Alpenglow Flowers. You're on to something here. It would be a shame for it to be a one-time thing. If you want to pursue this seriously, we should talk. I'd be happy to help you."

"Thank you, Steven." She stood from the stool and hugged him tightly. "Thank you," she said again. "I'll…well, I need to sleep before I make any decisions."

"Sleep is a good idea." He laughed and looked over her shoulder to Symon. "Maybe you should take this one home?"

"You don't have to tell me twice."

Charli took a step back and was instantly wrapped in Symon's protective arms. It was only then that she let herself lean fully into his embrace and relax into his touch. Not only was everything going to be okay, but it was also going to be amazing.

Just as soon as she got some sleep.

Epilogue

"TELL ME THIS ISN'T A DREAM." Charli traced her fingers down Symon's chest, causing a reaction in his groin that was definitely not dreamlike.

They'd spent the last two days holed up in Charli's farmhouse, making up for their missed Valentine's Day and their time apart. It had been an absolutely perfect few days of catching up on sleep, making love, and just being together.

He captured her hand in his and slid it down his body. "If it is, I do not want to wake up."

She chuckled and wrapped her hand around his hard shaft, eliciting a deep groan from him.

His hand traced lazy circles on her back while she gently stroked him, her head still settled on his chest. As far as he was concerned, it was the perfect morning, and he happily would have stayed that way all day if it weren't for the loud rumble that emanated from his stomach, causing Charli to jump up.

"Was that your stomach?" She looked down at Symon, who only laughed.

"Hey." He shrugged. "It's not my fault I'm always hungry

these days. Coach and Brody's training schedule has my metabolism fired up, but even their intense schedule has nothing on sexy times with you." He reached for her, wanting her naked body pressed to his again. He kissed her deeply. "Mmm. See?" Symon pulled away. "There's no workout quite like the one you put me through."

She giggled as he rolled her over. But as much as he'd like to postpone breakfast for even longer, something else weighed on him. Something they hadn't discussed yet.

He stopped himself from climbing on top of her because he knew once he started kissing her again, he would never stop. "There's something I need to talk to you about."

Her face transformed instantly, and he regretted his abrupt choice of words. "When are you leaving?"

He knew she was worried about his travel, and they'd discussed the importance of his training and racing for the rest of the season. Symon wasn't worried about her support. He knew she supported and valued his career, and it meant the world to have her by his side. But just because they'd cleared up all their misunderstandings didn't mean it was going to be any easier to say goodbye when it was time.

There was no point in putting off the discussion any longer. With a sigh, Symon sat up against the headboard and scrubbed a hand over his face. "Soon," he told her honestly. "Friday, actually."

"Friday?"

He nodded and despite his best attempt to look serious, he was fighting a losing battle when it came to leaving the teasing tone out of his voice. "But the season is almost over and then we get a break before summer training and…"

She tilted her head and narrowed her eyes suspiciously. "And, what?"

"I was going to wait until it was official to tell you, but I think it's safe to let you know that Coach and I have been talking." She pulled herself up and the bed sheet she had wrapped around her slipped a little, distracting him. He forced himself to look away so he could focus on what he needed to say. "Our usual summer training facility is in bad shape, and we were looking for a new place that had all the amenities and also was a bit of a destination. The team needs downtime, too."

"So…"

"So, I proposed Trickle Creek as an alternate location. We have Stoney Lake just outside of town that's the perfect depth to practice jumps, a brand-new weight room in the condo building at the ski hill thanks to Carlson Corp, and enough condos to rent them out for the whole team. It's a win-win."

In so many more ways than one.

Her face transformed again as she took in everything he was saying. "You organized all that?"

"It's not official yet."

But he was pretty sure it would be a go. He'd put together a quick proposal that even his coach and team managers had been impressed with.

"But yes. Of course, I did." He ran a finger along the sheet that was wrapped around her chest, wanting very much to pull it off completely. "I don't want to be apart from you if I can help it, Char. And I know that you support my dreams. It's one of the many reasons I love you so much. But I want to be as close to you as I possibly can. And selfishly, I'm hoping if I can get the summer training moved here, I might be able to get the winter training moved to the hill, too. Because I've decided next year will be my last season racing."

"What?"

He nodded. It was the other thing he'd been waiting to tell

her. But there didn't seem to be a better time. "After the Olympics. I've decided it's time. Besides, I want to transition into a new role."

"What's that?"

"Your husband."

The sheet she'd been holding up slipped down, presenting Symon with the most gorgeous view of the woman he loved, flushed, half-naked, and smiling. "What are you saying?"

"I'm saying that I plan on being your husband, Charli Carlson. If you'll have me."

She nodded and covered her hand with her mouth.

"I've loved you my entire life, and I refuse to waste any more time without the whole world knowing you're mine." He quickly flipped himself over and grabbed the ring box he'd stashed in his nightstand the day before. He'd slipped away under the ruse of needing more groceries, and made a quick stop to see Chase, who'd honored him with their mother's ring for Symon to present to Charli.

When he turned around again, the box was open to display the diamond solitaire ring that had been her mother's. "Charli, will you please do me the honor of making my wish come true forever and being my wife?"

"Symon." She smiled through the happy tears that streamed down her face. "You know I will."

"Thank you for meeting me, Charli."

She would have rather spent her last day with Symon before he had to rejoin the team cuddled up in bed, but when Cathy texted that she needed to talk to her at the shop in the plaza, Charli had reluctantly agreed, worried that she hadn't locked up properly or maybe had some last-minute paperwork that she'd forgotten to sign with the Realtor.

She hadn't been back to the shop at all since Valentine's Day. Chase and Annie had grabbed her few personal possessions that she'd left here and locked up for her. Charli had been so sure that she'd never want to see the store again after all the angst of trying to get her business up and running, but the moment she walked up to the front door with Symon's hand in hers and saw her sign still hanging, there was a flash of something in her gut that she couldn't quite recognize.

Was it pride she was feeling for pulling it off? Or regret that it was over?

The last thing she'd ever expected to feel was disappointment that it was all over. Underneath all the stress and the chaos, once the smoke cleared, she'd actually had fun with it. As crazy as it was, it was a twinge of sadness that she felt now that it was behind her.

Next to her, Symon wrapped his arm around her as if he understood what she might be feeling.

"Of course," Charli said to Cathy, forcing herself to focus. "I hope I didn't forget anything. The new tenants are probably eager to take over and get set—"

"That's what I wanted to talk to you about, actually. There's been a change of plans."

"In what way?"

"Why don't we go inside and talk?" Cathy used her key to unlock the door and they followed her in.

The shop still smelled of flowers and foliage. Charli inhaled deeply and closed her eyes, committing the moment to her memory.

"What is it that's changed?" Symon asked the Realtor. "Was there a problem with the pop-up?"

"Oh no." Cathy clutched a folder to her chest. "It's nothing you did at all, Charli. In fact, from what I saw and heard all around town, Alpenglow Flowers was a massive success. Congratulations."

Her instinct was to brush off the compliment, but she caught herself. "Thank you," she said simply. "I'm really proud of what we did."

"Of what *you* did." Symon pulled her in for a side squeeze. "It was amazing."

"And how would you feel about doing it again?"

"Excuse me?" Charli shook her head and stared at the other woman. "Another pop-up shop? Do you have a location that needs to—"

"Oh no." She shook her head. "Sorry, I'm not being very clear. Let me start over."

Even the briefest mention of doing it again had set flames alight in her belly. *Was that excitement? Did she want to do it again?* Charli swallowed hard. She was getting ahead of herself.

"The tenant that was lined up to take over the space has backed out for financial reasons," Cathy said. "It's actually a bit of a mess, really, and the owner is eager to fill the space quickly. So eager, in fact, that he's willing to waive the first month's rent and damage deposit in lieu of what you paid already for the pop-up."

"Wait. What?"

"He's willing to waive the—"

"I heard that. It's just…" Charli's mind raced to keep up. "He wants to lease the space. To me?"

Cathy nodded. "And just between you and me, I think he realized the price he'd given you for the pop-up was gouging in this market and feels bad. It's a great deal. As your friend and Realtor, I must advise you to take it."

"Take it?" She shook her head and looked at Symon, who grinned. "But I wasn't going to…"

Wasn't she? Didn't she want to?

"I think you should take it, Char."

"You do?"

Symon nodded. "You were in your element, babe. Surrounded by flowers and doing what you love. No, it wasn't the best of circumstances, but you pulled it off." With her hand still in his, he led her to the far side of the shop. "Picture this place with *your* flowers in it. Imagine working at that table, creating arrangements all year round. Everlasting love *and* fresh. With your flowers. It could be incredible."

She took in everything he said and slowly looked around at the empty shelves and tables. There was space along the back wall for a cooler to keep the blooms fresh. She could imagine locally made handicrafts, like Marta's mugs on display, mixed in with her flowers. As she turned slowly in a circle, the picture became crystal-clear, and she could visualize it perfectly in her mind.

"No," she said to Symon. "It *will* be incredible."

"Absolutely it will."

Charli walked back to where Cathy was waiting. "I'll take it."

There were a lot of details still to discuss and Charli's first call was going to be to Steven and then Chase and Asher to get all the advice she could, but she knew it would all work out.

She felt it. And more than that, she believed it.

Peak in on Symon and Charli a few months later at their engagement party with an exclusive bonus scene. Click here to grab that scene!

Next up is Craig's Story in Always Be Mine coming fall 2023!

And if you want even more romance…click HERE for an exclusive FREE novella that isn't available anywhere else!

About the Author

Elena Aitken is a USA Today Bestselling Author of more than fifty romance and women's fiction novels. The mother of 'grown up' twins, Elena now lives with her very own mountain man in the heart of the very mountains she writes about. She can often be found with her toes in the lake and a glass of wine in her hand, dreaming up her next book and working on her own happily ever after.

To learn more about Elena:
www.elenaaitken.com
elena@elenaaitken.com